MURDER IN SHADES OF WOOD AND STONE

RIPLEY HAYES

NOTE TO READERS

UK academic titles are different to those in the US. People teaching in UK universities are known as 'tutors' or 'lecturers'. The title 'Dr' is reserved for those with a PhD. Most tutors or lecturers will have a PhD, but not all. The title 'Professor' should only be conferred on people of the highest academic standing. All the UK universities I know are very informal. Staff and students will generally use first names, except to the most senior staff. The ultimate management of a university is usually a Board of Governors.

Llanfair College of Art (which is entirely made up) is the academic equivalent of a university.

1

RUDE AWAKENING: SUNDAY

ocial media post

OP: *What's happened to Inigo Vitruvious? My favourite social activist and painter has been conspicuously absent from social media since his alleged sacking from Llanfair College of Art. I say alleged because that's what I heard. There are lots of rumours, but no facts. Does anyone know? I keep checking his page and there's been nothing for months. I know there was a student died at the art college. But I don't see what that's got to do with Vitruvious. Is he in jail?*

NP: Hi, OP. No, V isn't in jail! He's been suspended, but some of us are organising to get him back at work. If you're a college student, send me a private message for the deets.

ANN HATHERSAGE, secretary to the college principal, thought this was something Tom Pennant, her boss and friend, probably ought to see. He wasn't going to like it, but he should know what people were saying. She picked up her laptop and went into the principal's office, with its glorious view of the college courtyard and the hills beyond the town.

Ann showed Tom the thread. "Not to make you paranoid, just so you aren't in the dark."

"Thanks, I think," Tom said.

~

IT WASN'T the 3am phone call of doom, but it might as well have been. DS Charlie Rees and Tom Pennant were both deeply asleep in Tom's big soft bed spooned together, Tom's arm around Charlie's waist, bearded face nestling into the back of Charlie's head. Outside, the rain hammered against the windows but neither man heard it. It had been raining for days and the river had burst its banks; spreading out over the low-lying fields as it did two or three times every year. It would recede—an inconvenience rather than a danger.

The evening had begun with dinner, made by both of them together in Tom's kitchen, laughing and teasing and kissing as they boiled pasta, grated cheese and chopped veg. The level in the wine bottle dropped enough to stimulate desire, but not enough to frustrate it. They'd talked over dinner and then after-wards they'd stretched out on the couch and talked some more. They were finding out about each other's lives through conver-sation, and about each other's desires though their bodies. So far, so good, and getting better. It was new, and Charlie still didn't trust that it wasn't all about to go pear-shaped, but Tom kept asking him on dates and he kept saying yes. More often than not, the dates ended up in Tom's bed. Charlie was getting used to waking up with Tom wrapped around him and the light coming through the curtains across the big bay window. He was getting used to morning cuddles and a shared breakfast before a walk through the slowly wakening town to the police station.

His boss, DCI Freya Ravensbourne, had made good on her promise to refurbish the tatty police station, so his workplace now smelled of paint and new carpet rather than mould. There were still only four of them, but they were coping. They were an odd bunch, but they were becoming a team: DC Eddy Edwards and the two uniformed constables, Patsy Hargreaves and Mags Jellicoe. The police station now opened to the public for a few hours every weekday. The telephone was answered. Lost dogs were found, and burglaries investigated. Recently, a lot of burglaries, but that was police work. There were fashions in crime, as in every other part of life. The fallout from the murder of Rico Pepperdine still polluted the art college, and no one in the town would forget the series of assaults on women students anytime soon. Kaylan Sully was in prison awaiting trial; Inigo Vitruvious had been suspended from his job as senior painting tutor along with college finance director David Yarrow. Tom was doing his best to keep the college functioning. But things were beginning to feel calm. Calm enough for Charlie to plan a weekend off. Not an entirely stress-free weekend. He was going to meet Tom's daughters for the first time, and he was dreading it. Twice in the last year, he had faced down armed men with less trepidation than he felt at the forthcoming lunch with two thirteen-year-olds.

The girls' pictures filled Tom's house. They were both dark-haired, and tall, like Tom; obviously identical twins, but rarely dressed in the same clothes. Charlie expected to get them mixed up, though Tom insisted he wouldn't. He hadn't shared his fears about meeting the twins with Tom, or not all of them. The two girls had a college principal and renowned printmaker for a dad and their mothers were highly educated, well-read and comfortable in the world of art and culture. Charlie felt like an ignorant oaf in comparison. Tom had let it slip that the girls were desperate to meet Charlie *because Dad never lets us meet his boyfriends.* So, the die was cast. Sunday lunch at the Red Dragon Arms, a foodie pub a few miles outside Llanfair.

· · ·

WITH FIVE HOURS TO GO, the phone rang, and lunch was off.

THE RAIN HAD STOPPED. That was the first thing Charlie noticed after the call ended. The second thing he noticed was how good Tom looked sitting up in bed, dark hair tousled, ink tracing intricate patterns across his arms and shoulders.

"I have to go," Charlie threw his phone onto the bed. "That was Mags. She's on phone duty this weekend. It looks like someone has drowned in the river near the Castle Hotel. A kid —a teenage boy, Mags said."

Charlie started looking round for his clothes, thanking his past self for folding them over a chair rather than dropping them on the floor.

"I'll make some coffee to take with you," Tom said, getting out of bed and padding to the bathroom naked and barefoot.

"I'm really sorry about lunch," Charlie said to Tom's back. "Even if it's straightforward, I'm bound to be tied up all day."

"The girls will be disappointed, but I'll explain. They'll understand." Tom replied, sounding as if he meant it and not as if he were storing up the row until later.

I need to get my bloody mother's endless disapproval out of my head. This is Tom. Tom isn't like that.

Charlie dressed in yesterday's clothes, wishing he had the confidence to bring a change of underwear and socks with him when he came round to Tom's house. Tom had presented him with a toothbrush the first night Charlie had stayed, and it lived in the bathroom, next to Tom's own, but anything more felt presumptuous.

He turned his mind to the task ahead. Mags had made the first calls, but they were going to be busy. He didn't have time to worry about anything else.

Less than fifteen minutes later he was standing next to PC Mags Jellicoe and a middle-aged male paramedic, looking down at the figure of a teenage boy dressed in soaking black sweatpants and grey sweatshirt, battered Vans trainers on his feet. The boy lay on his back, eyes open, staring up at the sky. His hair had been buzzed short and acne marred his skin. He looked very young, and very dead.

THE CASTLE HOTEL described itself variously as a 'country house hotel', a 'resort' and a 'venue'. Charlie had seen signposts pointing down a narrow lane on the outskirts of Llanfair, but he'd never seen the hotel itself until now. From the front it was a fantasy castle: an asymmetrical honey-coloured building with three round turrets, a square tower, battlements, Gothic arched windows, and every other romantic embellishment the Victorian designers could think of adding. Wales had a lot of castles. More than any other country, Charlie had been told. But this wasn't one of them. This building had never been intended to defend a river crossing or an important pass, or to provide a garrison for soldiers guarding the border with England. It was a rich man's folly, and obviously so. Why it had been built here, on the edge of a small town, Charlie didn't know, but judging from the neat lawns and well-kept flowerbeds filled with late-blooming roses, it was doing well as a hotel. Bees buzzed around the flowers and the scent of the roses flavoured the autumn air. The front door—another Gothic arch—stood open, but he ignored it and followed the signs around the building to the car park at the back. He parked his Golf next to the police patrol car and looked round.

The back of the building was as neat as the front, though nowhere near as ornate. The hotel itself stood on a slight rise, with a wooded hill to the left and gardens to the right. Behind the hotel, the car park sloped down towards the river so the rooms at the back would have views across the valley. From the front, the views would be of the grounds and of wooded hillsides.

Charlie saw that the service entrances were all facing the car park, and that efforts had been made to keep them tidy. No smokers' detritus marred the space, though he could smell cooking bacon through what must be the kitchen door, and it made his stomach rumble. A wall surrounded a neatly sign-posted bin store, and another set of signposts directed guests to the front entrance.

THE BODY LAY next to the expanse of grey water covering most of the hotel car park. A woman in chef's whites and two men in black trousers and white shirts were standing next to the hotel, arms wrapped round themselves against the chill, looking at the activity with worried curiosity. A few cars had their wheels in the water, but most were parked on wet, if unflooded, tarmac. Beyond the car park, the water extended into the distance. The grey of the water matched the sky. Clouds lay low on the horizon. Mags nodded towards it. "Flood plain," she said, and then looking down at the body. "One of the hotel staff called us and the ambulance. We arrived at the same time." She looked at the paramedic, whose marked car was parked a few yards away.

"We turned him over. He was lying on his side, half in the water. But he might have been alive. I mean, I knew he wasn't, but he might have been." Mags gave an uncertain smile. "I'm just glad I wasn't on my own. I didn't know if it was too late to try CPR."

Charlie understood. Never assume anything. Mags had done the right thing. He turned to the paramedic, who nodded.

"I did what I could, but we were too late. Poor bugger."

The three of them contemplated the boy's body for another

moment, then Charlie took a deep breath and remembered that he was supposed to be in charge.

"Could you make an educated guess about when he died?" Charlie asked the paramedic.

"Not my area of expertise, mate, but not long. No more than an hour or two."

"COULD you get some details from the person who found him?" Charlie asked Mags. "I'll start making calls."

"I'll be off then," the paramedic closed his bags. "I'll get a blanket to cover him."

Charlie stood still, gazing out over the flooded fields, and rehearsed his to-do list, while he waited for the paramedic to return with a blanket. When the boy was decently shrouded, he would start his calls, bringing the whole panoply of investigation into this place until they knew what had happened, when and how. None of it would bring the boy back. Charlie sighed.

He heard footsteps and turned, expecting to see the paramedic. Instead, he was faced by a man of about forty thrusting a bright red face towards Charlie.

"Who the hell are you? And what the hell's going on? Who's that?" He pointed at the body.

Charlie produced his warrant card. "DS Rees. There has been a fatality. Please step away." He put his hand very gently on the man's arm and tried to steer him back towards the hotel. The man threw him off, angrily.

"Don't tell me where to go in my own hotel car park," he said in an expensive private school accent.

Charlie's heart sank. The job of the police was to serve the public, but sometimes the public made it difficult.

"Sir, please move away. Could you tell me your name?"

Thankfully, the paramedic appeared with a well-washed

waffle blanket and covered the boy. The action seemed to bring the red-faced man to his senses.

"He's dead?"

"Yes, sir," Charlie said, and this time the man allowed himself to be led towards the group of people standing next to the hotel. As he approached, they all melted back inside, leaving Charlie and the red-faced man by themselves.

"You said this was your hotel, sir," Charlie began.

"Rupert Bosworth, General Manager," the man said, and Charlie saw that he had a small lapel badge with those words on his suit jacket. A decent black suit, with a well-pressed white shirt and a plain purple silk tie. Charlie dropped his eyes for a quick look at the man's shoes. In his mind, shoes told him a lot. Bosworth's shoes were pointed, black and polished. Charlie approved the polish, but the long, pointed toes reminded him of brash mobile phone salesmen, so were an odd choice for the manager of an upmarket hotel. Perhaps Rupert Bosworth was not from the patrician background his name and accent proclaimed. Or perhaps he just liked pointed shoes.

"As you saw, Mr Bosworth, the body of a young man has been discovered in your car park. Until we know who he is, and what happened to him, we are going to need to treat this entire area as a crime scene."

Bosworth's face went a deeper red, and this time when he spoke, spittle flew. "That's not possible. The hotel is full. We have a wedding. It's been booked for over a year. We can't have you here." He flapped his arms, as if waving would free the hotel from police, paramedics and bodies alike.

Charlie resisted the temptation to yell back. He spoke as slowly and calmly as he was able. "I'm very sorry, Mr Bosworth, but we need to treat the area as a crime scene, and our work takes priority over everything else." He took a breath, and spoke again, hoping to prevent another outburst. "I wonder, could the young man be one of your guests?"

This time, the colour drained from Bosworth's face. Charlie could see the wheels turning in the man's mind, and then the colour flooded back.

"Let me see his face," Bosworth demanded.

The body had already been moved, and if Bosworth could provide an identity, it was worth letting him look. They walked slowly back to the blanket covered figure, and Charlie lifted enough fabric to show Bosworth the boy's face, then dropped it gently back into place.

"He wasn't one of our guests," Bosworth said, with absolute certainty. "I've never seen him before in my life, but I bet I know who he was."

2

TEMPTING TOWERS: SUNDAY

From: Bryson Carroll, Chair of the Governors, Llanfair College of Art

To: Professor Tom Pennant, Principal

Hi Tom

We need to do something about the Vitruvious situation. I'm getting emails from both staff and students demanding his return to work. I haven't heard anything from the man himself, or from his union rep. (which I think is telling). How are we getting on with finding out what happened to the cash he solicited from international students? Any movement on the police investigation?

Don't get me wrong, I don't want him back any more than you do, and the governors are 100% in agreement about that. We just need to cover our backs. I'm concerned that having it all unresolved will affect student recruitment. Any idea about numbers for the coming year?

Bryson

TOM SIGHED. Then he asked Ann where to find the student recruitment figures. She showed him. He sighed again.

CHARLIE WAITED for Bosworth to speak.

"Do you know what parkour is?" Bosworth said in the end. "Some people call it free running."

Charlie nodded. "The most direct way from point A to point B, regardless of obstructions," he said.

"That's who that boy will be. One of them. It's the towers. They can't resist the towers."

"Climbing them?"

"Climbing them and putting funny flags up or hanging stupid signs over the battlements. They're a menace. It was only a matter of time before one of them fell off. There you are: case closed."

Bosworth folded his arms and turned his head slightly to the side, as if to indicate that the discussion was over. Charlie wondered if the man thought someone could fall from one of the towers at the front of the building and somehow end up in the car park at the rear. Or if he had considered how a body would look if it had fallen from the top of one of the towers.

"I'm not sure it's quite that simple," he said. "Either I or one of my colleagues will need to look at the towers and the roof of the hotel at some stage, but for now, we will need to restrict access to the car park, and I must make some calls. Excuse me."

Bosworth began to go redder again, so Charlie turned away and called Freya Ravensbourne. When she answered, he walked away from Bosworth altogether, hoping the manager would get the hint and go back inside.

He quickly outlined the situation to Ravensbourne, who promised to get there as soon as she could. She said she would organise the pathologist and the scenes of crime teams.

"Secure the scene and start interviewing, Charlie," she said. "You know what to do."

He did.

Charlie began by calling Eddy and Patsy. It was Sunday, but police work didn't care about weekends. Eddy was actually pleased to hear from him.

"Mum's been going on about laying a patio, and I'm running out of excuses," Eddy sounded cheerful. By contrast, Patsy sounded half-asleep, and Charlie heard someone say "Who's that?" in the background.

HE REMEMBERED the flask of coffee Tom had handed him as he left the house and went to collect it from his car. They might be next to a hotel full of food and drink, but somehow, he wasn't expecting Bosworth to provide any of it to them, especially once Charlie demanded access to all the guests with rooms overlooking the back of the hotel.

The coffee was good, and it reminded him of Tom, which made him feel as warm as the coffee. Thinking of Tom brought guilt at the relief at the escape from lunch with Tom's daughters. *There's nothing I can do.* He swigged the rest of his coffee, screwed the lid back onto the flask, and went to find the rest of his team.

PATSY AND EDDY arrived together in Eddy's souped-up Golf. It might look like Charlie's car, but it was a different beast under the bonnet. The two of them got out, bickering as usual.

"Morning, sarge," Patsy visibly shuddered, "remind me never to ask Eddy for a lift ever again."

"I'm a highly trained police driver. She's just mad because I interrupted her love-fest." Eddy drew himself up to his full six foot five and folded his arms.

"Technically, the sarge interrupted us," Patsy said to Eddy's predictable groan.

"Um, dead body?" Charlie interrupted, leading the way

towards the flooded area. He lifted the blanket in case either of them recognised the boy. Neither did.

MAGS APPEARED from the hotel kitchen door. She looked visibly pregnant now, walking with less ease, though the baby wouldn't be born for another three months. Charlie felt protective, despite the frequency with which Mags said she was pregnant, not ill. He still wasn't going to take her up to the towers though, because there would be stairs, and possibly ladders.

"I spoke to the waiter who found the body. Landon Emery," Mags said. "He's obviously upset, but he's more worried about Bosworth—that's the manager—finding out he'd sneaked off for a smoke in the middle of the breakfast service."

Charlie nodded. "I've met Bosworth. Fair to say, he doesn't want us here."

"Wait till the rest of the circus turns up," Eddy said, and then with a big grin, "and the boss."

DCI Freya Ravensbourne gave new meaning to the word 'unkempt', but she was as sharp as a scalpel blade. Charlie thought she would make mincemeat of Bosworth and of him, if he didn't get organised.

"We need all this car park taped off, and the tent to cover the body," he said, "then we need to get the names of anyone who could have seen anything, which means the staff, and all the guests on this side of the building. At the moment, we've got a tentative time of death of a couple of hours before the waiter found him. Let's say 5am onwards. I'll go and get the names from the manager and ask for somewhere we can talk to them. I also want to go and have a look on the roof."

The others looked at him with curiosity.

"Bosworth said our body was a parkour practitioner. Someone who liked to climb the towers, and who fell off."

Patsy spluttered. "That would be quite a fall," she said. "What with the towers being at the front of the hotel."

"I know. But if he did climb onto the roof, there might be evidence we should see."

"It's a Thing," Mags said. "In Llanfair at the moment. Parkour, I mean. Last year, someone climbed up the clock tower and changed the time on the clock, and someone put a gay pride flag on the post office roof. There were lots of huffing and puffing about vandalism, but most people think it's funny. It took months to get the clock put right. They needed scaffolding."

"The council should just have asked the people who changed it to put it back," said Patsy. "Parkour is cool."

"It's a crime," Eddy said.

"I don't think so," Patsy replied. "Or if it is, maybe trespass at the worst. Assuming that they don't do any damage, and they have rules about that stuff." Patsy blushed.

"You're a practitioner?" Charlie asked.

"A *traceur*." Patsy said. "That's what they're called. No. I've played about with it a bit, but I don't have the time or self-discipline to do it properly."

Charlie made a mental note to find out more. In the meantime, he had work to do.

"You can come and look at the roof with me," he told Patsy. "Once we've got everything else set up."

Patsy grinned.

"Up the stairs. On the inside," Charlie said firmly, "and we're going to see Bosworth first."

CHARLIE AND PATSY found Bosworth in the front hall of the hotel, next to a round table holding a leather-bound book and a vase of Chrysanthemums, explaining to a small group of well-dressed people that the police would be gone soon, and there was nothing to be alarmed about. "Just an accident, that's all."

I don't think so.

"A word, please, Mr Bosworth," he said. "We're going to need to talk to some of your guests." Looks of alarm spread over the faces of the well-dressed group like a Mexican wave. Charlie smiled disarmingly. "It'll only take a few minutes."

Probably. Patsy shuffled her feet behind him, and he heard her almost silent snort of laughter.

The hall they stood in must function as a reception area for the hotel, though it was unlike any hotel reception he'd ever seen. The floor was dark polished wood, showing the attractive patterns of the grain in the planks. Dark wood panelling extended up the walls to ceiling height, which should have made for a gloomy space. But a wide curving staircase with an ornate brass banister led up to a galleried landing, and above it, a huge Gothic arched window allowed light to flood in. A similarly huge window over the open front door admitted even more. The window and door surrounds were dressed honey-coloured stone, complementing the polished wood.

A chandelier with dozens of candle-shaped light bulbs hung down from the high ceiling. Paintings from the school of Romantic country house painting adorned the walls—stags at bay, dramatic waterfalls, towering cliffs. A round table with several antique-looking chairs stood to one side of the front door and judging from the sleek laptop sitting on it, probably functioned as a desk. There were several wooden settles around the walls, decorated with traditional Welsh fabric cushions. Various doors led off the hall, each labelled in discreet gold lettering: Bar, Dining Room, Library, and Staff Only.

The castle was a Victorian fake, but it was hard not to like the polished wood, smelling faintly of lavender, or the vast leaded windows. However red-faced and impatient Bosworth might be, he seemed to be on top of the job of running the hotel. Everything was spotlessly clean, every cushion perfectly plump, and no finger marks marred the surface of the table or banister rail.

"My daughter is getting married this afternoon," said one of the group, a tanned, muscular man wearing beige trousers and a navy sweatshirt. Casual clothes before getting dressed up. The man's comment was directed to the space between Charlie and Bosworth, and Bosworth jumped in first, putting his hand on the man's arm, as if to pacify him.

"Nothing will disturb her special day," he said. "I'll make sure of that."

"Make sure you do," the man said, and Charlie wondered if he had imagined the underlying tone of menace.

Charlie said nothing. There had been a suspicious death, and it was going to be investigated, wedding or no wedding. Any decision to cancel it would be taken by DCI Ravensbourne, and he was content to let things lie until she arrived. In the meantime...

"Mr Bosworth, we do need to talk to you," he said.

"Oh, very well," Bosworth snapped. Then he turned to his guests. "Enjoy your breakfasts," he said, gesturing towards the dining room door. When they left, he turned back to Charlie. "This way," he said.

The Staff Only door led to a corridor painted in an institutional pale green, with a vinyl floor to match. Charlie could hear a busy kitchen coming from the far end: shouts between the staff, the ping of a microwave, the clatter of pans and cutlery. Bosworth opened the first door they came to and ushered Charlie into a pleasant modern office. Bosworth sat behind the desk but didn't invite Charlie or Patsy to sit. Charlie pulled up a chair and sat anyway. Patsy did the same and took out a notebook. It was time to get real.

"There is a dead teenager in your car park," he began. "We don't know how he died, or who he is. My boss and other colleagues are on their way from Wrexham. Like it or not, this investigation is going to happen, and it will take priority over anything else. If we don't need to disturb the hotel, we won't, but if we need to, we will." He shrugged to indicate that it was all out of his hands. What would happen, would happen. "For now, I need the names of everyone staying or working here, with an indication of whose rooms look out over the car park. I'd also like to look on the roof. We are taking your idea about people climbing the towers seriously, sir." The last was a concession, and it worked. Bosworth's face softened slightly, if not to friendliness, to slightly less annoyed. It didn't last. Not after Charlie asked again for a complete list of staff members and all the current guests, with contact details. Bosworth's face reddened once more.

"Most of the staff are self-employed," Bosworth said, as if it mattered.

Charlie raised his eyebrows. "I'm not concerned about their employment status right now," he said, "I need to know who is here today."

Bosworth reddened again. "We open for events," he said. "Weddings, parties, special dinners, that kind of thing. We're busy, but if there's no event, we close. The staff tend to come and go. That's all I meant."

"I would like the information about the people in the hotel this morning," Charlie said. "At this point, I don't know what else we might need."

"So, you're just trawling for personal details regardless of the impact it has on an important local business?"

Not for the first time, Charlie wished it didn't take so long to drive from Wrexham to Llanfair.

"Let's just start with the rooms overlooking the car park," he said, and face still red, Bosworth turned his computer on.

There was a knock at the door.

"Yes," Bosworth shouted, and the door opened. A young

woman in a neat black suit put her head around the door. She saw Charlie and relief showed on her face.

"There's a man to see you," she said. "Doctor Powell?"

Charlie smiled his thanks to the young woman, who closed the door again.

"Dr Powell is the pathologist," he told Bosworth. "I need to talk to him. But I'll still need that list. PC Hargreaves, will wait here for it."

HECTOR POWELL WAS WAITING for Charlie outside the blue and white police tape surrounding the car park. The shrouded figure of the teenage boy was hidden behind the parked cars.

"I should thank you, Charlie," Hector said. "You've saved me from a morning at the DIY store. Apparently pink is no longer acceptable for teenage girls' bedrooms. Though I could wish to escape choosing paint colours for a better reason." He lifted the tape. "Shall we?"

Charlie threaded his way between the cars and down to the edge of the flood, where the body waited inside the small white tent put up by Mags and Eddy. He could see them on opposite sides of the car park, noting car registrations and checking the shrubbery for anything potentially interesting.

"He was lying in the water when he was found," Charlie said. "But my colleague and a paramedic moved him."

Hector nodded. "Of course." Then he lifted the blanket and looked down at the dead boy. As he did, Charlie heard heavy raindrops land on the tent and begin to splash on the ground. He ducked out of the tent and jogged over to Eddy.

"You and Mags get inside. See if you can find Patsy. She should have a list of staff and guests. Ask Bosworth for a place we can use to interview them all."

"Shouldn't we wait for DCI Ravensbourne?" Mags asked.

"No," Charlie said, and then wondered if he should.

3

NOT IDEAL: SUNDAY

From: J Hartford, solicitor
To: Prof Pennant
I'm writing about my client, Dr Inigo Vitruvious. I understand that he has been suspended from the college and that an investigation is taking place about his role in the death of an international painting student. I further understand that his name has been linked to the solicitation and payment of irregular monies supposedly for the benefit of the College.

As I am sure you are aware, my client denies any involvement in the death of his student, and with the payment of any money to the College. That being so, I can see no reason for his continued suspension from work. Were this suspension to continue, my client would have a strong case for Constructive Dismissal and would be entitled to bring a case to an industrial tribunal. Damages in these cases can be punitive.

I look forward to your timely response,
J Hartford

. . .

TOM'S FINGER hovered over the trash icon. It was tempting, but he forwarded the email to their legal adviser. He looked down at the sketchbook on his desk, where there was a pencil drawing of a lean, fair-haired man, lying in bed with his head propped up on one elbow, laughing. Tom ran his finger over his drawing and wondered (not for the first time) why on earth he'd agreed to take the principal's job. Then he closed the sketchbook and clicked on the next email.

CHARLIE LOOKED up at the sky. The clouds were on top of them, grey and heavy with rain. There was room in the tent for the body, Hector, and at a squeeze, one other. Charlie didn't want it to be him, but he was the man on the spot. He stood in the doorway even though it meant half of his body was in the rain. He watched as Hector removed the blanket altogether and began to run his fingers over the boy, peering into his eyes and mouth, manipulating his limbs. Charlie looked away when Hector produced his thermometer, and he didn't look back into the tent. Hector was respectful of the dead, not given to making macabre jokes or commenting on clothing or body shape, but Charlie didn't want to see the boy prodded and poked. It was as if death was the most important thing about this boy, which was all kinds of wrong. He had parents, perhaps siblings, and friends. He might have been there to climb up the towers, or to ask for a job, to meet a friend, or to steal a car. Over the next few days and weeks, they would find out as much as they could about this boy. They would probably know more about him than anyone should know about one of their fellow humans. But for now, all they knew about him was that he was dead.

"WHAT TIME WAS HE FOUND?" Hector asked.

"Call logged at seven forty-eight," Charlie replied.

"And it's just before nine now." Hector stared into space for a moment. "He's been dead for between two and four hours, probably closer to two."

"So, not long before his body was found?"

"Exactly."

"You think he stumbled into the water in the dark and drowned?" Charlie asked.

"Oh no. He didn't drown. Look."

Charlie squashed himself into the tent, crouching down beside Hector.

"He was stabbed," Hector said, lifting up the boy's sweatshirt to show a small cut in the skin of his chest.

"That?" Charlie said, wondering how such a little wound could end a life.

Hector nodded, sitting back on his heels. "I won't know for sure until the post mortem, but that looks to me like a stab wound made by a straight-bladed knife. It's in precisely the right place to slip between the ribs and into the heart. The water washed the blood away, so it doesn't look like a big deal. But I'm pretty sure that's what killed him."

Charlie stared at the wound, no more than a darkish slit an inch wide. The boy's chest had a few strands of pale hair, and his body was lean and youthful without any fat around his stomach. "Did whoever did this know what they were doing? Where to stab him?"

Hector shrugged, as much as he was able to in the tight space. "I can't say. I don't see any other wounds, which doesn't mean there aren't any. It could be someone who knew what they were doing, or it could be someone got lucky, if that's the right word."

"Is there anything to help us identify him?" Charlie asked.

Hector shook his head. "I felt in his pockets, but they were empty. No phone, no keys, no wallet."

"He would have a phone," Charlie said, because every teenager in the western world depended on their phone as a lifeline. "He must have dropped it in the water. Dammit."

The rain started to hit the tent roof harder. When Charlie looked through the doorway, the air was a blur of falling water, bouncing off the ground and the cars between them and the hotel. If it carried on, more of the car park would flood, and they would have no chance of finding any of the dead boy's possessions. More than that, the water would flood where they were crouched in the tiny tent. Charlie could see it beginning to creep under the flaps.

"I think we're going to have to move the body," Charlie said. "I wanted the DCI to see him, but with this rain...photographs will have to do." He stood up, feeling creaky and under-caffeinated.

"The body has been moved, so this exact spot isn't the crime scene," Hector said. "The mortuary van will be here soon, but we can wait for the DCI if the flood holds off."

Charlie stepped out of the tent and was instantly soaked. His hair flattened against his head and dripped water onto his neck. Small streams ran under his clothes. His jeans turned black from rain. He ducked back into the tent and looked outside from its shelter. The rain agitated the floodwaters, every drop bouncing off the surface in a frenzy of silver and black. There was every chance that the boy's phone, and his wallet if he had one, were under the water, but was there any realistic chance of finding them? He knew the river was close by, though it was indistinguishable from the rest of the flood, and anything washed that far would be gone forever. It wouldn't be safe to wade into the floods. The crime scene was being swept away as he watched and there was nothing he could do.

"Let's move him as soon as we can," he said to Hector. Hector nodded and rearranged the boy's clothing to cover his chest with its tiny wound. Both of them edged around the space, taking as many pictures as they could, Charlie trying not to drip on either Hector or the dead boy As they worked, the water continued to creep under the walls of the tent.

"Poor bugger." Hector echoed the paramedic.

THE MORTUARY VAN arrived at the same time as Ravensbourne, who arrived in an unmarked police car driven by a uniformed officer. The DCI had acquired a huge rainbow golf umbrella, so she arrived at the tent relatively dry. Charlie thought she looked tidier than usual, hair brushed, and a new—or at least undamaged—black padded jacket. The black trousers were a little frayed at the bottom, but clean. She looked at his soaked self and raised her eyebrows.

"You should get an umbrella," she said, and delivered one of her knock-out punches to his arm. Did she not know her friendly blows left bruises?

Ravensbourne handed Charlie the umbrella and stepped into the tent. Hector showed her the wound and told her about the time of death.

"Thanks. I can see you need to get this lot moved before it floats away. I'll get the rest from Charlie." Despite the confined space, Hector ducked away from her attempt to pat him on the shoulder.

The two mortuary men (struggling awkwardly with their own umbrellas) brought a trolley and a body bag, and five minutes later, they were gone, leaving Hector, an empty tent and a crumpled blanket. Ravensbourne went back into the tent, giving the umbrella to Charlie. He suspected her aim was to light a cigarette, and he was right. She stood in the tent doorway, just out of the rain, drew the smoke into her lungs, and then carefully blew it away from Charlie and Hector when she exhaled. Not that it made any difference; the wind swirled around them, carrying droplets of water as well as the smell of smoke.

"I'll call you," Hector said to Ravensbourne.

"Call Charlie," she said. Hector raised his eyebrows and then nodded, before stepping out into the rain and running for his car.

"Tell me all about it," Ravensbourne asked Charlie. There was little enough to tell, but he told her what there was: the absence of identification on the boy's body, Bosworth's assertion that the boy had come to climb the tower, the waiter's discovery of the body, and the wedding supposedly taking place later that day. "What should we do about the wedding, boss?" Charlie asked. In typical Ravensbourne fashion, she turned the question back to him.

"What do you want to do about it?"

"See if we can talk to all the staff and guests before it's supposed to start, get all their contact details and let it go ahead. Assuming nothing sets off alarm bells. We don't know if our victim was killed near where we found him and anyway, it's all underwater. We might want forensics people, but not right here, right now."

He got a sharp nod in return. "What about the murder weapon?"

"It could be anywhere, boss," Charlie said, looking round the tent to the lake of floodwater. "My guess would be the killer dropped it in the water. A bloodstained knife isn't something you want in your wedding party luggage."

"You're ruling out searching the hotel? What about the kitchens?"

Charlie didn't answer immediately. Years of police experience told him to look for the simplest explanation. The simplest explanation was that whatever had brought the boy to the hotel had led to his death. A waiter found the body. The body was less than a hundred yards from the kitchen door; a kitchen containing any number of suitable knives. If the boy had come to the hotel to meet someone, that someone could as easily have been a guest as a staff member. Then he looked back at the floodwaters. If the knife was in there, no amount of searching the hotel would find it.

"It would take a big team to search the entire hotel," Charlie said. "But I want to have a look on the roof, and, after that, I just don't know. If one of the guests did this, we should be going through their things with a fine-toothed comb. But if it was a guest from the wedding party, they could still have dropped the knife in the water."

"I agree. No search," Ravensbourne said.

"We need to identify the victim," Charlie said, because that was the first thread they needed to pull. "Once we know who he was, we might have some chance of working out why he was here. Sorry, that's obvious. I'm thinking aloud." Charlie would have blushed, but his wet clothes were getting cold and stiff on his body. He shivered.

"I told you," Ravensbourne said, "you need an umbrella. Given that you haven't got one, maybe a change of clothes before you start interviewing all the hotel staff and guests?"

That was typical Ravensbourne, he thought. Jokes and sympathy with one breath and a mammoth task with the next.

Ravensbourne held her hand out for the umbrella and set off back across the car park to her car. The rain began to ease and as she was driven away, it stopped altogether. It was too late for Charlie. He was already soaked.

CHARLIE WALKED AROUND to the front of the hotel in search of his colleagues. Patsy was waiting for him by the door.

"You're dripping, Sarge," she said.

"I won't dissolve. Not straight away. Are we ready to go with interviews?"

Patsy nodded. "Come and see."

She led him through the door marked Library, into a room lined with bookcases and groups of comfortable chairs which they passed through to another, bigger, emptier, and colder room. The walls were plain white, and the carpet an elderly royal blue. Old-fashioned wall lights with candle bulbs seemed to be the only available lighting. Eddy and Mags were putting the finishing touches to four sets of tables and chairs as widely spaced as possible. Each table had a pad of blank paper and a couple of sheets of paper stapled together—presumably the lists of staff and guests. He was pleased to see a tray with empty mugs, a teapot, sugar bowl and milk jug on a spare table by the door. It looked as if Bosworth had relented enough to give them a drink.

"It's a ballroom," Patsy said. "But they don't use because it needs work. Apparently weddings and so on are held in the dining room and the reception hall." She pointed to the arched window, which had a few broken panes, and an alarming damp patch spreading from the window to the ceiling. Charlie went to look out. They were on the side of the castle, at the very end of the building. Trees and shrubs pressed up against the outside wall.

"Bosworth is prepared to let his guests see this place?" Charlie wondered aloud.

"I don't think he thought it through," Patsy said. "He didn't want *us* anywhere nice, so here we are, and here the guests will see us. How are we going to do this?"

"Thoroughly," Charlie said.

Eddy came over to them. "Where's the boss?" he asked.

"Gone, taking her umbrella with her," Charlie replied, and he didn't think he'd imagined the look of disappointment on Eddy's face. "Sorry, mate, it's just us."

4

A SET OF KEYS: SUNDAY

From: Tom Pennant
To: Bryson Carroll

Thank you for your support at the meeting last night. As I said, there is nothing 'alleged' about V's involvement in Rico Pepperdine's death. I saw the drawings and they are damning.

You also asked about the financial irregularities. David Yarrow from Finance was suspended at the same time as V, but we are making some progress on that side of things. It's something I'd rather not report to the full governors just yet, but it appears that David must have been involved in collecting the 'donations' from international students. What happened to the money after the College received it is what we need to find out. Our legal adviser has been talking to David's solicitor, and although things move very slowly, there is some hope that David will spill the beans in exchange for immunity from prosecution. That's the good news. The bad news is that we probably won't get all the money back. The even worse news is that I've already had a couple of letters from people who paid 'donations' demanding the return of their money.

It's such a shame that no one on the Governors noticed all this going on under their noses for YEARS.

Tom

"CAN I TRUST BRYSON CARROLL?" Tom asked his secretary.

Ann didn't answer for a moment.

"I'm trying to decide between 'no' and 'fuck, no'," she said finally.

"WE'LL LET them come to us," Charlie said. "Patsy can do staff; Mags can do guests with windows overlooking the car park and Eddy can do everyone else."

Eddy raised his eyebrows.

"I'm going to find Bosworth and, I dunno, the father of the bride or someone else who knows all the wedding guests and say that we need to see them all as soon as we can. Then I'll triage. If I sit down in here, I'll freeze to death. We need verifiable contact details. We need to know where they were between say, six and eight this morning and if they saw anything suspicious. Find out if they're parked in the car park where we found the body. Ask them if they saw a teenage boy, about five foot ten, grey eyes, buzzed hair, grey sweatshirt, black trackies and Vans on his feet. Bosworth insists the victim wasn't a guest but ask anyway. If anything seems off, well, you know, write it down."

Patsy scribbled on her pad, and Eddy put the description into his phone.

"What did Dr Powell say?" Mags asked, and Charlie realised he hadn't told them.

"He said our victim was probably stabbed with a straight-bladed knife, and that's what killed him. And that he died not long before he was found. But ask about a longer time frame than that, because this time of death stuff is an art as well as a science. I'd put money on Hector Powell being right, but even he can't know for sure."

"Any identification?" Mags asked.

"Nothing in his pockets, no sign of a phone or a wallet."

"It's murder, and the DCI has left? Shouldn't she be organising a proper Major Incident Team?" Eddy demanded.

Charlie spoke carefully. "We are the Major Incident Team, or as near as we're likely to get. Ravensbourne is at the end of the phone if we need her."

She trusts me, and it's time you did, too.

BOSWORTH WASN'T PLEASED to see Charlie again, despite the news that the police were likely to allow the wedding to proceed as planned. He didn't want to ask his guests or his staff to agree to what he called a *police interrogation.* Charlie simply repeated himself until the man gave in.

"If you could arrange for the staff to come to the ballroom," Charlie said, "then I can ask the father of the bride to tell his guests."

Bosworth's face reddened, as Charlie expected.

"His name is Mr Stefan Crane, and *I* will talk to him."

Charlie bobbed his head, as if in gratitude. "Thank you," he said. "I'm sure you want to start as soon as possible, so that we can all get on with our jobs."

AS HE MADE his way back to the ballroom, Charlie's phone rang.

"Dr Powell, what can I do for you?"

"We found some identification on your boy. I can't do the PM yet, but he lost one of his shoes as we moved him, and it's got a name written inside. They both have. Big black letters on the insole and small black letters on the back of the tongue.

Both say *Lewis*. That's all, no idea whether it's first name or surname, but it might help."

"He looked about fourteen, so he'd still be at school and I could ask there," Charlie said, not really expecting an answer.

"Fourteen would be a good guess," Hector said.

"School it is, then," said Charlie, hoping one of his team would know who to contact on a Sunday.

Mags did know, and Charlie headed home to get changed into dry clothes. Home was still Dilys's guesthouse. He kept meaning to move out, but that meant having somewhere to move into, and so far the only option had been a damp house close to the river, and an equally damp flat with great views... and a leaky roof. So, he stayed where he was, in his cosy room, with Dilys's bacon sandwiches for breakfast.

Half an hour after leaving the hotel he parked outside the school entrance. The rain had stopped, although the air was damp and chilly.

Like many others in rural Wales, the school shared its site with the town's leisure centre and swimming pool. The car park was divided into sections. The leisure centre and pool didn't look busy, and there was only one other car in the school car park, an elderly people-carrier. As Charlie turned his engine off, the door opened and an overweight, unpleasant-looking man in golfing clothes got out. He was in his forties and beginning to go bald. He stepped forward and held out his hand. "Dr Ellis?" Charlie asked. The man nodded, still frowning. His voice was friendly enough.

"Come on in, and let's see if I can help."

Charlie decided the headteacher had spent so long trying to keep teenagers in order, that frowning had become the default.

Dr Ellis opened the school front door with one of those complicated keys that can only be bought through the original locksmiths and are impossible to forge. But Charlie noted that several of the windows on the ground floor of the school didn't quite close, and some of the fire exit doors were very flimsy. He imagined money for school maintenance was in as short supply as money for upgrading police stations. The school had obviously been cleaned recently. There was a smell of floor polish overlaying the odour of teenage sweat. The school slogan was *Be part of a learning community* which Charlie thought was no worse than any other. He didn't understand why there had to be a slogan, but there always was, and they all seemed to include the same few words in a variety of combinations.

The office Charlie was led into had a desk with a computer and a table covered in paper. Organised paper: exercise books, cardboard files, and piles of photocopied forms—some crumpled and others neatly stacked. Ellis sat behind the computer and turned it on. "Who are we looking for?" he asked.

"A boy called Lewis," Charlie said. "Or rather a boy who had the name Lewis written in his shoes." He described their victim to the headteacher.

"Lewis Evans," Ellis said slowly, and carefully. "It sounds like Lewis Evans. Just a minute." He clicked around on the computer and then turned the monitor to face Charlie. Ellis had blown the picture up as far as he could, but it would have been clear without it. Grey eyes looked out from their victim's face with its few spots, and very short hair.

"He's got two younger brothers," Dr Ellis said. "They're all much of a size, and apparently have put on the wrong shoes without realising, so they write their names inside. My secretary was telling me about it last week because something from one of the brothers turned up in the lost property. Oh, this is dreadful. Dreadful. His poor mother." Ellis shook his head slowly. "What happens now?"

What happened now was that Charlie would get Lewis Evans's address, call Ravensbourne for a Family Liaison Officer, and go round there to devastate an entire family.

"I'd like to make a very quick call," Charlie said. "And then, if you don't mind, I'd like to find out everything you know about Lewis Evans."

"Of course," the headteacher said. Charlie thought that the head of a reasonably large secondary school seemed very familiar with their victim. He phoned Ravensbourne and asked for an FLO. She promised to get back to him.

He also rang Mags, to tell the team back at the hotel that they had a name. "Have you got anything?" he asked her.

"Bad temper from the guests and the staff are all rushed off their feet and don't want to talk to us. Eddy's right. There should be a proper team here."

"We are the proper team. The DCI trusts us to know what we're doing, and so do I."

"Dr Ellis, you obviously know Lewis Evans...?" Charlie let the question hang open for Ellis to answer.

Ellis lifted his face from the contemplation of his computer and looked directly at Charlie. The frown was still in place. *It's just what he looks like.*

"Lewis Evans was bullied. Please tell me he didn't kill himself?" The terror in Ellis's voice was palpable. Charlie heard it in the raised pitch, and the pleading tone.

"We don't know how he died," Charlie said, "and we won't until the post mortem has been done, but suicide isn't the obvious cause of death." It was always possible that Lewis Evans—if it was him—had taken an overdose before being stabbed. "All I can say is that the death is suspicious. Could you tell me about the bullying?"

"I think I'd like a cup of coffee, DS Rees. Would you join me?"

"I'd love one, thanks."

Ellis seemed to need a moment or two to collect his

thoughts. Charlie hoped that was it, and not that Ellis was looking for a way of backing off from the bullying revelation.

Ellis had a kettle in the corner of his room, plus some mugs and instant coffee. Charlie noticed that the headteacher's hands weren't quite steady as he poured. But then, learning that one of your students was dead wasn't going to be good news, however he died. When Ellis had given them both a mug of black coffee, which smelled and looked much too strong, he pointed at the screen of his computer, and the image of Lewis Evans.

"He never fitted in," Ellis said. "The family came here about two years ago from Hereford. Mother, step-dad and three boys. Lewis wasn't an outstanding student, or a particularly poor one. Neither sporty, nor a slob. Both his brothers have groups of friends, but Lewis never did. I think maybe he tried too hard." Ellis shook his head, as if trying to clear it. "Teenagers can be ruthless. They see weakness and they're on it like flies. Lewis was vulnerable, though he shouldn't have been, not with two brothers in the school, but it's as if he got bullied for being the new boy, and it stuck, even though he wasn't the new boy any more. We moved him to a different class this year, but the same boys carried on picking on him anyway, just outside of class. I've suspended two of them already. Just last week in fact."

"What kind of bullying?" Charlie asked.

"Name-calling, pushing and shoving, grabbing his bag or his coat and hiding it. Ripping his books. Lewis wasn't the only boy getting targeted. Bullying is a problem here. It's a problem everywhere, and don't let anyone tell you otherwise. We're trying to deal with it, but it's an uphill struggle. If we don't see things happening, we can't take action—students almost never talk about it to their teachers or even their parents."

Ellis looked like a man trying to deal with an intractable problem. The frowns made sense. So did the strong coffee. It was like trying to drink coffee-flavoured mud.

"Do you know if Lewis Evans was involved in parkour?" Charlie asked.

Ellis groaned and ran his hands over his face, rubbing his skin as if applying cream.

"He may have *wanted* to be," Ellis said. "But the parkour crowd are very tightly knit. All natives of the town and friends since they were in nappies. Did you hear about the clock tower?" Charlie nodded. "No one involved in those kinds of stunts wants to take anyone new along for something like that. I'm sure I know who did it, but they wouldn't admit it under torture. Lewis wasn't in the inner circle."

"Is there anything I should know about the family?"

"Nothing to set alarm bells ringing," Ellis said. "But you would get a better idea by talking to Lewis's form teacher. I know about the bullying, because that's my responsibility and my priority, and like I say, we suspended two boys last week."

Charlie asked for the names of the boys who'd been suspended, and for the second time, saw fear on the head-teacher's face. "You don't think..."

"I don't think anything yet," Charlie said. His phone rang. It was Ravensbourne to say he should break the news to Lewis Evans's family, and that the Family Liaison Officer would get there as soon as he could. "I'm sending PC Brian Telford. He's good." Now all Charlie needed was the address, and courage to tell a mother that her son was dead.

5

A LOCAL LAD? SUNDAY

From: Bryson Carroll, Chair of the Governors
To: Professor Tom Pennant, Principal
How much money are we talking about?

From: **Professor Tom Pennant, Principal**
To: **Chair of the Governors**
It depends...this year's painting cohort had eight international students, and they paid $40-50,000 each. That money has disappeared. Kaylan Sully (the painting student with the gun) turns out to be a computer hacker with a history of making money disappear. What we don't know is how many previous students paid extra. I do know (I asked) that international painting students from the last couple of years aren't up to the standard we expect. So potentially they could all have paid extra, and there are between six and eight every year. Worst case scenario, we could be looking at finding upwards of a million. And that's before the reputational damage.

Do you have any contacts with the Welsh Government who could be discreetly canvassed for help?
Tom

O<small>R WILL</small> you leak it to the first journalist who offers you a drink?

L<small>EWIS</small> E<small>VANS HAD LIVED</small> in a house not far from Tom's. Charlie sat outside in his car, thinking of the reasons he needed to be elsewhere. He should check up on the rest of the team back at the hotel. He should contact Hector Powell to see if he'd found anything new. He should hang on for the Family Liaison Officer to arrive. The truth was that all those things could wait.

It was a gable-fronted detached house, painted white, with a bay window on the ground floor. There was an attractive front garden with a small lawn and several coloured dogwoods and an acer with a few almost purple leaves still clinging to its branches. A short driveway led to a garage, and in front of it, some kind of large SUV was being washed by two boys who looked uncannily like the dead boy. They had a garden hose with a fixture to pressurise the water and had obviously used it to soak each other as well as the car. They must be freezing, Charlie thought, remembering the feel of his wet things. Peeling off his jeans back at Dilys's had been unpleasant. But he was simply making excuses.

Charlie unclipped his seatbelt, took the keys from the ignition and forced himself out of the car.

"Hi," he said to the two boys. "Is your mother at home?"

"Sure, just knock," said one of the boys. He looked to be the oldest of the two and slightly taller than his brother. He politely turned the hosepipe away from Charlie, so that he could walk up the brick path to the front door un-splashed.

He knocked and got his warrant card out from his pocket ready to identify himself. The door was answered by a slender woman in jeans and a red fleecy top. She had the same brown hair and grey eyes as her sons, though her hair was long and streaked with silver. She waited for Charlie to speak.

He held out his warrant card, shielding it from the two boys with his body. "Mrs Evans?" The woman nodded. "Detective Sergeant Charlie Rees. Could we go inside?"

She flicked her eyes to the car-washers and led him to a kitchen at the back of the house. A bald man, also in jeans and a fleece, was unloading a dishwasher.

"Nev," the woman said, "there's a policeman."

This was it. Charlie took a deep breath.

"I'm very sorry to have to tell you that this morning a member of the public found the body of a young person who we believe to be your son Lewis."

The woman's mouth opened as if she was screaming silently. Charlie thought she had forgotten to breathe. He pulled a chair out from the kitchen table and pushed it towards her. The man stood up from the dishwasher and helped her sit down.

She drew in a ragged breath. "No. That can't be right. Lewis is here."

Charlie had a moment of doubt, and then the man said, "No, he isn't, Gina. He went out this morning. I heard him."

"I never heard him go out. He's lazing about in bed." The woman—Gina Evans—stood up and pushed her husband away, to run out of the kitchen door. Charlie heard footsteps pounding up the stairs, a door slam open and a scream.

"Could you wait here please?" the man asked.

"I'll make some tea," Charlie said.

A few minutes later, the two came back. Gina's husband had his arm around his wife, and he helped her back to her chair. He pulled another out from under the table and sat next to her. Charlie had boiled the kettle, found mugs, tea bags, milk and sugar. He made two strong cups and added lots of sugar.

"It helps," he said, but neither of them did more than wrap their fingers around the warm mugs.

"Why do you think it's Lewis?" the man asked.

"It can't be him," Gina said.

"I've seen his photograph," Charlie said, "and the person we found looks like both you, Mrs Evans, and the two boys outside washing the car. I'm assuming they are Lewis's brothers." The man nodded.

"I want to see him!" Gina cried. Her husband put his arm around her shoulder and muttered "There, love."

"We will need a formal identification," Charlie said. "That'll be in Wrexham, and we'll arrange it."

"Can you tell us what happened?" the man asked.

"I can tell you that he was found near the Castle Hotel. Do you know any reason he might have gone there first thing this morning?"

"He had no reason to go there. It can't be him." Gina was still fighting the knowledge she didn't want.

Her husband merely shook his head. "How did he die? You're a detective, right?"

"I'm sorry, but all I can say at the moment is that there are suspicious circumstances. We're arranging for a liaison officer to come here and keep you informed."

"Suspicious circumstances? What does that even mean?" Gina was well on the way to hysteria, and Charlie didn't blame her. Her husband stroked her hair and kept murmuring reassurance.

"It means that although we don't know how he died, we are sure that it wasn't an accident, or natural causes. There will be a post mortem examination, and then we'll know more."

"This is all wrong," Gina sobbed, and Charlie agreed with her, though he said nothing.

"I know it's a difficult time for you, but may I please ask a few questions?" Charlie said.

The man nodded and switched his attention to Charlie, away from Gina. He seemed detached; interested, but not intimately involved.

"You're Neville Evans, Lewis's stepfather?"

The man nodded. "I'm his legal father. I adopted all the boys."

"And you've been here for the last three years? Where were you before that?"

"Hereford. I was a soldier. Now I work at the art college. Head of Campus Services."

"And you can't think of any reason Lewis would be at the Castle Hotel? Did he have friends working there?"

"He didn't have friends, just his brothers. We should tell them." Charlie noted that Lewis's lack of friends had been noticed at home as well as at school. He also wondered at the two other boys washing the car, while Gina assumed Lewis was still in bed.

"Do you have a recent picture of Lewis we could have?" he asked. Neville got his phone out and started scrolling. He stopped and showed Charlie a picture of Lewis in shorts and a T-shirt, obviously taken in the summer. Lewis was smiling for the camera, but the Charlie's eyes, there was something uncertain about Lewis's expression. He wanted to ask more, but now wasn't the time. Lewis's mother was staring into the middle distance, once more looking as if she had forgotten to breathe. Neville sent him the picture, and Charlie explained that the Family Liaison Officer would be arriving soon.

"I'll see you out," Neville said. "And get the boys."

Charlie offered his help and was politely rebuffed.

"We'll be fine, won't we, love?" Neville said to his wife.

Charlie doubted Gina would ever be fine again.

· · ·

BACK IN HIS CAR, Charlie sent the photograph of Lewis to Mags and the others back at the hotel, as well as to Ravensbourne. He considered waiting for the Family Liaison Officer, but he felt the need to find out if the hotel interviews had produced any information. He also wanted to check in with Tom, if only to apologise again for missing the lunch with his daughters. But he was honest enough to admit to himself that he also wanted Tom's impression of Neville Evans. Something about the calm way Neville had taken the news struck Charlie as odd. Maybe it was because he had been a soldier, maybe because Lewis had been an adopted child. Charlie didn't know why he found it odd, he just did. He knew people responded to news of a death in different ways, but he would have liked to be a fly on the wall when the other two boys learned about Lewis.

Tom answered his phone on the first ring.

"Hi there," Tom said, and Charlie had a powerful image of a naked Tom making him coffee and quietly accepting the loss of their weekend without fuss or drama. As if Charlie was a professional, who had an important job to do. An adult. Tom treated him as an adult. He wanted to tell Tom how he felt, but he didn't have the words.

"I'm sorry, but there's no chance of me getting back in time for lunch. I'll be lucky if I get home before midnight. To Dilys's, I mean."

"You can come here. Doesn't matter if it's late." Tom said.

In the background, Charlie heard high-pitched voices. "Dad! Let's go."

"Wait," Tom said, though whether to Charlie or to his daughters, Charlie couldn't tell.

"It's OK. I need to get back," he said.

"Please ring me later. Charlie?"

"Sure," Charlie said, and ended the call, feeling miserable, but unable to do anything about it. Tom wanted him to meet the two girls, but Charlie wasn't convinced the two girls wanted to meet him.

He realised he'd forgotten to ask Tom about Neville Evans. It would have to wait. Tom deserved lunch out with his daughters.

Charlie drove back to the hotel. The roads were starting to dry out, and the worst of the puddles had receded, leaving the level of the flood marked with lines of dead leaves and twigs. He parked round the back of the hotel and walked down to where the tent still stood. The water had retreated a few yards back towards the river, leaving a thin film of mud in its wake, and a smell of wet, decaying vegetation. Charlie saw a silver glint between the tent and the water and went to investigate. It was a set of car keys with an electronic fob and a metal key. He picked them up, intending to take them into the hotel. Even though new key fobs were supposed to be waterproof, he couldn't believe it would have survived the deluge, but the key itself should be OK. He let his eyes roam across the newly exposed section of car park, wondering whether anything of Lewis's had dropped to the ground. He walked towards a couple of muddy lumps and turned them over with his toe. Nothing but bits of stone, probably dragged from the car park itself. He could hope, but even if Lewis's phone appeared, it would have been damaged by immersion. They might get the data, and he made a mental note to get onto the phone companies for call records.

Charlie walked back round to the front of the hotel and into the reception hall. He could hear people talking behind the Staff Only door. Bosworth's voice was louder than the others, saying something about a two o'clock deadline. This was not the time to present the hotel with a set of muddy car keys, so he slipped them into an evidence bag and into his back pocket and went to look for his team.

Eddy, Patsy and Mags were sitting round one of the tables in the library, near to the (closed) door to the ballroom. All of them were looking down at their phones. Patsy at least, was playing a game. A pile of paper sat on the middle of the table.

Eddy looked up first.

"Sarge. Thank God."

"You've finished? Why didn't you ring me?"

"I wish. Half of them maybe."

Mags nodded. "The guests were better than the staff, but we are still missing about eight of them. We've got their names from the hotel records, but we haven't seen them in person. Some of the staff came, but most haven't. We should have seen about twenty—housekeepers, bar staff, kitchen staff and waiters. We've seen six."

"Shit," Charlie said. "Right. I'm off to put a rocket under Bosworth."

Bosworth began by demanding to talk to Charlie's superiors. He hadn't been hard to find, fussing about in the dining room.

"It's up to you, sir," Charlie said. "I'll give you their phone numbers. In the meantime, I don't need your co-operation to interview your guests or your staff, so that's what I plan to do." He produced the list of staff. "Christina Wood. Head Chef. I'll start with her. Kitchen this way?" Charlie went towards the Staff Only door.

Bosworth let out a yelp and grabbed for Charlie's arm. "You can't go in there!"

"I think you'll find that I can," Charlie said.

6

SCHOOLBOY STORIES: SUNDAY

S ocial media post
OP: *Students at Llanfair College of Art are organising a lobby of the next Governors' meeting to demand the return of our senior painting tutor, Dr Inigo Vitruvious. The Governors are the people who have the final say about what happens in the college. They can tell principal Tom Pennant to bring Vitruvious back. Lots of us wanted to come here because of Vitruvious, and now he's gone, with no explanation. We're also down one painting tutor, and it shows in cancelled tutorials and a lack of guidance in the studio.*

NP: *is the Student Union backing the lobby?*

OP: *No! They are being totally pathetic. Completely in bed with college management. Arseholes.*

THE PRINTOUT of the email was on Tom's desk. Scribbled across the bottom was:

"The next full Governors' meeting isn't until next term. It'll all be sorted by then. Also, I think there are about five students, total, who care. Ann x"

IDENTITY CHECKING the remaining guests and staff at the hotel proceeded apace. Charlie had only mentioned the phrase *obstruction of the police in the course of their duties* once for Bosworth to decide this wasn't the hill he wanted to die on. There were some raised voices from within the kitchen, and then a steady stream of hotel workers made their way to the ballroom. The remaining guests did the same. By one o'clock they were done. Everyone in the hotel when Lewis had been killed had been spoken to, and their whereabouts at the crucial time established. The four of them made their way out to the car park.

"We need to take our tent down," Patsy said, dragging at Eddy's arm.

"Urgh. It's going to be all wet and muddy," Eddy said, as if he hadn't been a rugby player, well used to being face down in a muddy field.

The tent was wet, but was quickly disassembled, and packed into the patrol car, along with the paramedic's blanket.

"There's some car keys," Patsy said, bending down to pick them up from where the tent had been. She held them out. "Anyone's?" They all shook their heads.

"I found another set," Charlie said, and pulled the keys out of his pocket. "Hang onto those. Let's fingerprint them, just in case."

"Just in case of what?" Patsy asked. She produced a couple of evidence bags from the patrol car and stashed the keys away safely.

"Just in case, just in case," Charlie said. He didn't know if the keys were significant. The set under the tent could have been spare keys and have fallen out of Hector Powell's pocket, or the paramedics. The set he'd found could have been there for days. But just in case they were significant, he wanted them safe.

THE FOUR LLANFAIR OFFICERS MET, as had become their habit, in the break room at the police station. Patsy had done the honours with a trip to the supermarket for sandwiches and cookies. Not the Sunday lunch Charlie had been expecting, but it was food, and he was hungry.

"So," Charlie said once he'd drunk a cup of coffee and eaten half a sandwich. "Anything to report?"

"Hostility and boredom," Eddy answered. "No one saw anything, or if they did, they weren't going to tell us about it."

The other two nodded in agreement.

"What about the guy who found the body?" Charlie asked.

"Landon Emery. All he cared about was that Bosworth would sack him for sneaking out," Mags said. "I suspect he wasn't the only one to take a smoke break, but no one else admitted it. They weren't supposed to stand outside the door, so they mostly walked down to the end of the car park. The bit that's underwater."

"Find out about him," Charlie said. "He was in the obvious position to have done it. Did he know the dead boy? How long was he outside? Was he wet when he came back in?"

"This is why we need a few experienced officers," Mags said. "We miss things."

You shouldn't have missed that.

"Who spoke to Bosworth?" Charlie asked and got three blank looks in return.

"You?" Eddy said.

"Not to ask him where he was when Lewis was killed," Charlie said, "because that was what you were supposed to be doing. Perhaps it's a good job Ravensbourne isn't here." The three of them looked down, or at their phones, anywhere but at him. "But, we know where to find him. It sounds like we have a good idea of where the staff were, and none of them were on their own for long. What about the guests?"

"Mostly asleep," Mags answered, still looking embarrassed. "If they weren't, they were in the dining room having breakfast. A few said they couldn't remember, and a couple more were on their own. The only one who rang my alarm bells was the father of the bride: Stefan Crane. I don't think he's a murderer, but he's certainly got some issues about telling anyone where he was. He kept ranting about it being his daughter's wedding day and giving me too much information about what it was all costing. Which is a lot. Long story short, he didn't know where he was, or so he said."

"Is there a Mrs Crane?" Patsy asked.

Mags shook her head. "He's a widower. He told me that, too, as a preface to explaining how he'd been left with all the responsibilities of wedding organisation. I don't think he organised much though. He struck me as the sort of man who *outsources.*"

"What about the bride and groom?" Charlie wanted to know. "Can we acquit them at least?"

Mags waved a sheaf of papers around. "I've cross-checked most of them quickly, though we should probably do it again. But you asked about the happy couple. The bride and her matron of honour had a champagne breakfast in her room at seven, and the groom and his best man had the same in his room. Everyone else had to go down to the dining room. We've got fifty guests and twenty staff, and we can probably rule most of them out."

"Who are we left with?" Charlie wanted to know.

"Landon Emery–the waiter; Stefan Crane–the father of the bride; plus one of the groom's friends who was too hungover to remember what day it was, and another one who didn't want to admit to being in bed with someone not his wife, and Bosworth," Mags said.

"And anyone else who was lying, like about taking a smoking break," Eddy added.

"Let's make a chart," said Charlie. "See if Mags is right."

She was. Five people couldn't, or wouldn't, provide their whereabouts between six and eight.

The five names were written up on their battered whiteboard, which Charlie had insisted on retaining during the refurbishment.

"They'll all be too drunk to speak to later today," Eddy said. "Though we could try Bosworth."

Charlie nodded. "But I want to talk to the boys who were supposed to be bullying Lewis. Why don't you and Patsy have a look round the roof of the hotel, and while you're there, see if you can get Landon Emery's movements? Mags and I will go and see the boys." He pulled the names from his memory. "Jack Protheroe and Will Jenner."

JACK PROTHEROE DIDN'T LOOK like a bully. He was a handsome, tall, broad-shouldered young man with a swimmer's physique and neatly styled dark brown hair, wearing ripped jeans and a Welsh rugby shirt. Charlie and Mags were interviewing him at his parents' house with his mother present. From Mrs Protheroe's expression, she wasn't surprised to see them, and her sympathies were not with her son.

"We want to ask you about Lewis Evans," Charlie said.

"Now what's he saying about me? I've already been suspended. That psycho won't be happy until I'm in jail. God, it was only a bit of banter."

"Jack," his mother said, "we've been over this." She sounded tired, and her face was that of a woman who hadn't slept properly for too long. There were dark rings under her eyes, though her hair was clean and brushed, still wet from the shower. Like her son, she wore artfully ripped jeans, but hers were topped with a yellow sweatshirt. Her feet were bare, tucked up next to her on an armchair.

"OK, we got carried away. Sorry. But he doesn't get the hint."

"What hint?" Charlie asked.

Jack rolled his eyes. "He's always there, hanging round, like he fancies one of us or something. Like no one talks to him, but he won't go away."

"Could you tell us where you were this morning? Say between six and eight." Charlie asked.

"Where do you think I was?" Jack rolled his eyes again.

"I don't know. That's why I'm asking." Charlie had plenty of practice at a stubborn expression, allowing eye rolls and snark to roll off him without touching.

"Well, duh, I was asleep."

"Thanks. Now, can you prove you were here?" Charlie asked, anticipating the next outburst.

"He wasn't here," his mother said. "He was at his friend's. Came home an hour ago." Mrs Protheroe's lips were tight. She didn't look at her son, as if she were tired of him and everything he represented.

"Where did you stay, Jack?" Charlie asked.

"What's it got to do with you? I don't have to answer your questions I have rights."

Charlie nodded. "You do, and you don't have to answer my questions, though I'm curious about why you don't want to."

"He was with his mates, smoking weed," his mother snapped. "That's where he was, and that's why he doesn't want to talk to you. Or me, come to that."

"Fuck this." Jack stood up and slammed out of the room, banging the door behind him. Charlie heard him stomping up the stairs, and a few moments later, stomping down again and the crash of the front door closing.

"He comes home for a shower and clean clothes. He doesn't bother to speak to me or his father. At least until last week we knew he was at school in the day if only because he comes home to change. I can't make him talk to you. I can't make him do anything."

Charlie had been taking in the room they were sitting in. Bookshelves lined the walls; two squashy sofas and two matching chairs surrounded the wood-burning stove. Photographs of a happy family adorned the walls—professional photographs showing Jack and his mother with an older man and a young woman. Jack's sister? He wondered when it had all gone wrong, and whether it had gone wrong enough to lead to murder. This was a nice middle-class home, with parents who seemed to care, but he'd seen a lot of teenagers go off the rails, sometimes with terrible consequences. Teenage stabbings weren't restricted to big cities.

Jack and Will would both be going back to school in a couple of days. If one or both of them was involved in this murder, Charlie needed to sort it out before then. Mrs Protheroe's voice broke into his thoughts.

"Why do you want to know where Jack was this morning?" she asked, and for the first time, Charlie saw something other than resignation on her face. She knew something had happened, and she was afraid her son was involved. She would find out soon enough, so he told her.

"We found Lewis Evans's body this morning. We're treating it as a suspicious death."

"You can't think... Jack wouldn't *hurt* anyone. Really, Inspector, he smokes too much weed, and he would have been crashed out this morning. I'll make him come and tell you where he was." She was babbling, all anger forgotten in concern for her child.

"We don't think anything at the moment, Mrs Protheroe," Charlie said. He seemed to be saying it a lot lately. "We know that Jack and his friend Will were suspended because they were bullying Lewis at school. We simply want to know where they were first thing this morning, so we can eliminate them from our enquiries."

Or arrest them for murder.

THEIR ATTEMPT TO talk to Will Jenner was frustrated by his absence from home. He lived in a smaller house, with no visible books. Will's parents were watching football on TV, or rather Will's father was watching, and his mother was attacking a huge pile of ironing in the same room. Both were more relaxed about their son's behaviour.

"Who doesn't smoke a bit of weed, nowadays?" Mr Jenner asked. "They got a bit physical with that Evans lad. I've told Will to pack it in. Won't happen again."

It wouldn't, but the Jenners didn't know why. Charlie thought they'd find out soon enough.

"OUR TWO SCHOOL bullies are still very much on our list of 'persons of interest'," Charlie said, adding their names to the whiteboard when the team met up later. "They may think they can keep out of our way, but they are going to learn that it doesn't work. What about the roof? Anything interesting?"

Patsy perked up, eyes sparkling. "It was great," she said.

Mags sighed. "I'm sure it was, but were there any actual clues?"

"Actually, there were, so no need for a snotty tone." Patsy said.

"We've photographed a lot of footprints, scrape marks, and a few scraps of fabric and string that could have been meant as flags," Eddy said. "There could be reasonable explanations for all of it, but the scrapes and footprints come from the outside walls and then onto the roof, rather from the inside. What we saw bears out Bosworth's story. But it's all been rained on, so nothing is very clear. Might be worth Scenes of Crime having a look, but probably not."

"Do you two want to follow up with the parkour people in the school?" Charlie asked, and the two nodded. The words *Parkour People* were added to the whiteboard. Charlie was sorry that he wouldn't be talking to them himself, but it wasn't as if there was nothing else to do. But it would all have to wait until the morning.

"Come round for dinner," Tom said. "It won't be much, but it'll be better than a sandwich."

Charlie wanted to go. He wanted to see Tom. But he didn't want to meet the twins, and he didn't want to ask if they were still there.

"The girls have gone home," Tom said, as if reading Charlie's mind. "It's a teenager-free zone."

"OK. What time?"

"As soon as you like, and Charlie? Bring some spare clothes. Because we both know you'll be staying the night."

Charlie was on his own, sitting in his car in the police station car park, and he blushed redder than Bosworth.

Half an hour later, he was being enfolded in Tom's arms, overnight bag at his feet. He felt Tom's arousal through their clothes and lifted up onto his toes to kiss and then bite Tom's neck, just beneath his right ear. It never failed to elicit a shudder, and this time was no exception.

"Early night?" Tom asked.

"I was promised food," Charlie said. "But it can probably wait."

FAKERY: MONDAY

From: Kate Brontë
     To: Tom Pennant
     cc: painting tutor team

Hi Tom

I'm writing on behalf of the whole painting team to ask when Inigo Vitruvious is either coming back to work, or if he isn't coming back, being replaced?

We are struggling to cover V's classes and have each taken on several of his personal tutees, which is not ideal given that term is almost over. The students are fed up, and as you know, some of them are not the strongest. If you recall, V had booked several outside painting trips and the London gallery overnighter. The London overnighter includes print and sculpture students so we can manage that, though V did take the lead and we don't have access to his notes. The other trips have minibuses booked, but we don't know what he was planning. The students are expecting the trips to happen, and we don't want to disappoint them. The first is next week, to Borth, and the rest next term (by which time I hope things are back to normal). *We can only resource next week's trip by cancelling other classes, which we obviously don't want to do.*

We're sorry to have to complain like this, but we are struggling.

Kate

To: Kate
Cc: Painting tutors
From: Tom Pennant

DEAR *all*

I'm sorry things are so difficult. I'm afraid I can't answer your question about a replacement for Vitruvious, and I can't give you any information except to say that it is in the hands of the police and college governors. As soon as things are resolved, I will let you know.

What I can do is lead the trip to Borth. Please let me know what day, what time the minibus leaves and ask the students to bring pencils, sketchbooks and warm clothes!

I'm also happy to convene a meeting to ensure the students get the most from the London overnighter.

Best wishes

Tom

BECAUSE A DAY away from here will be balm for my soul. Tom wondered if he could kidnap Charlie and take him along. He imagined sketching Charlie sitting bundled up in coat and scarf on the endless sand in the howling winds that were typical of Borth in autumn. He could hear the wind and smell the salt. He could feel the sand blowing onto his skin and the gulls screaming overhead. Then his email pinged, and the vision shattered.

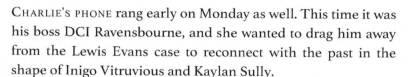

CHARLIE'S PHONE rang early on Monday as well. This time it was his boss DCI Ravensbourne, and she wanted to drag him away from the Lewis Evans case to reconnect with the past in the shape of Inigo Vitruvious and Kaylan Sully.

Inigo Vitruvious was a fake. Tom always insisted that Vitruvious was a talented painter, but he hadn't made his name as a painter. Instead, he was the self-proclaimed 'conscience of art'. He appeared, or rather he *had appeared* on the kind of television programmes that debated politics, the arts, or whatever cultural phenomenon was attracting attention. He dismissed Tom as a producer of 'wallpaper for the middle classes' though Charlie was fairly certain that Vitruvious would be happy to sell as many paintings as Tom sold prints. The other thing about Vitruvious was that he was a murderer. He had allowed Rico Pepperdine to die, so that he, Vitruvious, could draw and paint him as it happened. But it couldn't be proved, not without a confession, or a witness. They had the drawings, but as long as Vitruvious denied making them, they were stuck. He had also been stealing money from the college for years, though he denied that too, and the paper trail had been obliterated. If bare-faced lying was an Olympic sport, Vitruvious would have been a gold medallist.

Charlie and Tom had found Vitruvious's drawings of Rico dying and dead, and Charlie was never going to forget them. Some things couldn't be unseen. Vitruvious's co-conspirator, Kaylan Sully, was in prison awaiting trial for shooting Charlie and kidnapping Tom at gunpoint. Kaylan's testimony could put Vitruvious behind bars, but until now, he insisted he couldn't remember what happened to Rico. But according to DCI Ravensbourne, he'd asked to see Charlie.

"I'm too busy," Charlie had told his boss. There were four of them to provide a police service to the town of Llanfair, and now to investigate Lewis Evans's death. Yes, they had support from colleagues in Wrexham, but it was support, not actual boots on the ground. Charlie wanted to investigate the parkour clique at the school, to find out whether they had allowed Lewis to join their adventures. He needed to talk to Brian Telford, the Family Liaison Officer working with the Evans family. He still hadn't been onto the roof of the hotel. He didn't have information about where Jack Protheroe and Will Jenner had been at the time of Lewis's death, or come to that for Rupert Boswell, the hotel manager. It might only be day two, but already Charlie felt as if they were all running as hard as they could to keep still.

"Tell him yes, but I can't leave here for a few days."

"You're going to have to find the time," Ravensbourne told him. "Vitruvious's lawyer is banging on about how his client is being persecuted. I'm surprised your boyfriend hasn't told you."

Charlie's anxiety spiked. "What?" he asked.

"Vitruvious is threatening to go to the media unless he's reinstated at the college," Ravensbourne said. "We need him off the streets and the only witness we have is Kaylan Sully, and the only person Kaylan will talk to is you. Your appointment is in Liverpool at three this afternoon."

Charlie could hear Tom in the kitchen, making coffee in his posh machine from the smell wafting towards him. He must have known about Vitruvious wanting his job back, but he hadn't talked to Charlie about it. Had Tom not wanted him to know?

The wood floor felt smooth and cool against Charlie's bare feet. He opened the bag of clean clothes he'd brought, and got dressed, packing yesterday's things neatly back into the bag. He sat on the bed, paralysed with indecision. Should he leave? Ask Tom why he hadn't talked about Vitruvious? Tell Tom about his appointment with Kaylan? They had worked together to catch Kaylan and Vitruvious, but was that because Tom was new to his role, and needed Charlie's help? He recognised the pattern in his thoughts, but was powerless to break out of it. His mother's voice in his head telling him he had messed up, *again.* Wanting to do the right thing, say the right thing, terrified of getting it wrong, taking refuge in silence and keeping out of the way. The best thing to do would simply be to go to work.

He picked up his bag and opened the bedroom door, to find Tom on the other side, in a pair of pyjama trousers and nothing else. He held two mugs of coffee in one hand and a plate of cinnamon rolls in the other. Charlie stared.

"Let me in, then," he said.

Charlie stepped backwards.

"I brought us breakfast," he said, as if it wasn't obvious.

"I, um, got a phone call. I need to go."

Tom put the coffee and buns on the desk in the corner of the room. He pointed to the armchair where Charlie generally left his clothes when he stayed over. "Sit. It's not even seven o'clock. You've got time for coffee and cake."

Charlie sat, numbly. The skin on his face seemed to have set, and although words tumbled around inside his head, he couldn't put them into any kind of order. He wanted to ask what Tom knew about Vitruvious, and why he hadn't spoken about it, but he told himself that was Tom's business, not his.

"What's wrong?" Tom asked.

Charlie shook his head.

Tom dropped to his knees in front of the armchair, his hands on Charlie's thighs. "Who rang, Charlie?"

Charlie cleared his throat. "Ravensbourne," he croaked. "She wants me to visit Kaylan Sully this afternoon."

"Why?" Tom looked up at Charlie with big soft eyes. "Why now, when you're in the middle of a new case?"

Charlie shrugged.

"What aren't you telling me?"

"It's your business," Charlie said. "Vitruvious trying to get his job back. Ravensbourne thought I knew. She thinks I might get Kaylan to tell the truth and we can send Vitruvious to jail." Charlie heard his own voice, the words stilted. Now Tom's anger would come, he was sure of it. He tensed in preparation, wrapping his hands around himself. Tom said nothing. He untucked Charlie's hands and held them in his own.

"Charlie, I've upset you, and I don't know what I've done. Please tell me, so I can make it right."

The script was wrong, and Charlie didn't know what to do with it, what his next lines should be. So he said nothing. His throat was blocked in any case.

"Ravensbourne rang you. She wants you to talk to Kaylan so that Vitruvious doesn't get his job back. *She thought you knew.* What did she think you knew Charlie? That Vitruvious was trying to get his job back?"

"You didn't tell me," Charlie said. "But it's your business. You don't have to tell me everything."

Tom's face cleared, and he sat back on his heels. "I didn't deliberately not tell you," he said. "It's been blowing up all week, but there's no way the governors are going to have him back. Getting him sent to jail would help, but he's not getting his job back whatever he does. I'd have told you. It's not a secret. Have some breakfast." And with that, Tom seemed to think it was all over. It wasn't though. Tom had spent the week in meetings with the college governors. Until yesterday Charlie had been filling in reports about stolen cars, someone setting a bin on fire, and returning a lost dog to its owner.

"You're doing it again," Tom said. "I recognise that expression. You're telling yourself that you aren't good enough. You *are.* Who does Ravensbourne think can get the truth from Kaylan? You. If Vitruvious goes to jail, it will be down to you."

There was part of Charlie that wanted to believe what Tom said, but a bigger part that told him his successes—including

Tom—were down to luck, and that one day soon, his luck
would run out.

Tom took his hands again. "It's too early to say this, and you
don't have to say it back, but I love you, Charlie Rees. There,
I've said it." Tom's cheeks went pink above his beard, and he
didn't look Charlie in the eye.

It took several beats of Charlie's heart for the words to sink
in. Then he began to feel lightness in his chest, a tingling in his
skin and an uncontrollable desire to smile. He leaned forward
and pushed Tom backwards onto the hard wooden floor, half
falling on top of him, wrapping his arms around whichever bits
of Tom he could reach, and burying his face in Tom's neck.

When the emotional cuddle became less emotional and
more lustful, Charlie pulled away with a grin.

"I really do have to get in to work," he said. "I'd far rather go
back to bed, but time and crime waits on no man."

"Then get off me and drink some coffee,"

Charlie did as he was told. "I wanted to ask you about
someone who works at the college," he said. "Lewis Evans's
stepdad is your head of campus services."

"Neville. Yes, I know him, though not well. He seems OK, if
a bit military for an art college. The rumour is he was special
forces, no idea if that's true. Obviously, he was appointed under
the old regime. Why?"

"He struck me as a bit odd, that's all. I went round to tell
Lewis's family about his death, and Neville seemed unaffected,
detached even. Yet he told me he'd adopted Lewis and his two
brothers. It's probably nothing."

"If you thought it was odd, it was odd." Tom said. "I haven't
known you long, but experience suggests that your feelings
about people are usually trustworthy. I mean, you liked me and
couldn't stand Vitruvious..."

Charlie grinned and poked him in the ribs.

"I'll see what my spies have to say about Neville Evans,"

Tom said. "My spies being Ann. She's been the principal's secretary for as long as I can remember, and she knows everything."

As Ann was also one of the co-mothers of Tom's twins, Charlie assumed that Tom could talk to her without raising red flags all over the campus.

"Thanks," he said. "We've got a Family Liaison Officer at the Evanses. I'm going to see what he thinks about Neville."

Charlie ate his cinnamon rolls and drank the rest of his coffee in harmony with Tom. He still felt anxious about having to take the time out of the Lewis Evans investigation to see Kaylan, but there was nothing to be done about it. At least he and Tom were OK, and it was Monday morning. Meeting the twins wasn't likely to be on the agenda until the weekend—one more thing he could put away for later.

Brian Telford answered Charlie's call on the first ring. "It's the formal identification this morning," Brian said when they'd done their hellos.

"Not looking forward to it, gotta tell you, Sarge.".

"I suppose there might be worse ways of spending the morning, but none come to mind," Charlie said.

It was a devastating experience for the parents, depriving them of the last vestiges of hope. Until they were faced with the brutal reality, there was always the faint possibility that someone had made a mistake, and their child was still alive.

"I wondered what you thought about Neville," Charlie asked. "When I visited them, he seemed a bit detached."

"They aren't his kids," the FLO said. "But he adopted them years ago, and the two other boys treat him as their dad, so I guess Lewis did the same. There is something off, though. He seems like quite an angry man; angry in general, not just angry that Lewis is dead. He's keeping his anger under control all the time, and it's taking up most of his energy. Obviously besotted with his wife. I'll keep you posted."

Charlie thanked him, feeling reassured about having such a reliable person in the Evans household. One less thing to worry about. Now for the rest of the outstanding jobs.

8

QUACKS LIKE A DUCK: MONDAY

From: J Hartford, solicitor
   To: Prof Pennant
   I'm sorry to have to write to you again about my client Dr Inigo Vitruvious, but I have yet to receive your satisfactory response. The disciplinary code which the College includes in the Staff Handbook makes several references to investigations being carried out in a timely fashion, and without undue delay. My client's mental health is being adversely affected by the persistent delays and lack of communication from his employers.

   I look forward to your response,
   J Hartford

To: J Hartford, solicitor
   From: Professor Tom Pennant, PhD, MA, BA (Hons), RSA
   ~~Your client is not entitled to use the title 'Dr'. He is also a murderer.~~
   Thank you for your email which I have noted. I have passed it to our legal department for reply.

CHARLIE HAD time to call in to the police station for a catch-up before leaving for Liverpool and the visit to Kaylan Sully. He decided to squeeze in a detour to the Castle Hotel, to see whether he could nail down Rupert Bosworth's account of where he was when Lewis was killed. It wasn't that he suspected Bosworth in particular. He didn't like the man, but Charlie's dislike didn't make him a murderer. It was more a matter of being able to scrub a name from their list on the whiteboard. Or something. It was a loose end, and at this stage, they needed the fewest loose ends they could get.

The hotel had a dispirited atmosphere this morning after all the excitement of the day before. The wedding guests were still there—except the bride and groom who had left for their honeymoon. A few suitcases were in a huddle in the reception hall: their battered modernity contrasting with the Victorian Gothic surroundings. The door to the dining room was open, and smells of bacon, fried potatoes, smoked fish and coffee filled the air. There were subdued voices, and the rattle of cutlery against china. Charlie diagnosed hangovers from both alcohol and the previous days overwhelm.

Charlie let himself through the Staff Only door and knocked at Bosworth's office. There was no answer. He tried the handle and the door opened. The office was empty. The corridor beckoned, and Charlie didn't resist, opening doors to several storerooms with things like boxes of toilet rolls, glasses and paper napkins. Another room had shelves with bales of neatly labelled clean linen, another with untidy bundles ready for collection by the laundry. There was a staff break room, not dissimilar to their own at the police station, except that the carpet and upholstery was brown rather than blue. The stack of mugs, used teaspoons and spilled sugar were the same. The next room appeared to be a staff dining room, currently being cleared by a young woman in grubby jeans and T-shirt, wrapped round with a filthy apron in heavy white cotton. Her hair was hidden under a tightly tied bandana. She startled as he came in.

"I'm looking for Rupert Bosworth," Charlie said.

"Try the dining room," she replied without enthusiasm or interest.

"Were you here yesterday?" Charlie asked.

"No," she said, and went back to collecting dirty crockery in a plastic basket. "Try the dining room," she said again.

Charlie gave up and returned to the corridor. Opposite the staff rooms were two small offices with open doors. The desks inside were piled high with papers, but empty of people. The only other doors were to staff cloakrooms, for men and women. A faint scent of disinfectant emanated from each. He turned back towards Bosworth's office and the reception hall, when the door opened and Bosworth himself walked through.

"What the hell are you *doing?*" he snapped.

"Looking for you," Charlie replied calmly.

"This is a private area," Bosworth said.

Charlie ignored the comment and continued with what he'd come to find out. "I need you to account for your movements between six and eight yesterday morning," he said.

Bosworth's face reddened, but Charlie interrupted before Bosworth could bluster and shout. "We asked every member of staff, except you. Now we need to be able to eliminate everyone we possibly can. So, where were you between six and eight yesterday morning?"

"Everywhere," Bosworth snapped. "Kitchen, dining room, reception, my office. Everywhere."

"You weren't in the kitchen," Charlie said. Bosworth's absence from the kitchen meant at least one person had slipped outside for a smoke.

"Then I was in the other places."

"Who did you see? And who might have seen you?" Charlie asked. Their efforts at cross-checking the witness accounts yesterday had begun to produce a comprehensive picture of where almost everyone in the hotel had been during the vital hour. Bosworth was missing.

"I can't be expected to remember everyone I saw, and I can't possibly know who saw me. This is ridiculous."

"A teenager was killed during that time, Mr Bosworth. I'm sure you understand why we need to collect this information."

"You might need it. It doesn't mean I remember."

The door from the reception hall opened suddenly. A young man in a suit with a staff badge on his lapel appeared and a look of relief crossed his face when he saw Bosworth.

"Mr Bosworth, one of the guests says his car keys have disappeared from his room. I've looked in lost property, but they aren't there. Could you talk to him please?"

"Of course." Bosworth pushed his way past Charlie, who was thinking about the two sets of keys they had found in the car park the day before. He looked at the young man.

"Detective Sergeant Rees," he said. "What sort of car does your guest have? The one with the missing keys."

"Sorry, I didn't ask," the young man said, looking puzzled.

"Let's go and find out," Charlie said. But the young man waved vaguely down the corridor and mumbled something about having to go and do something. Charlie let himself into the reception hall. Bosworth was listening to a middle-aged man Charlie recognised as one of the wedding guests. A middle-aged woman, presumably his wife, was part of the circle.

"We can get a locksmith to come ..." Bosworth said.

"The keys were *in our room*," the man said. "On the bedside table."

"Surely it's worth asking the chambermaid?" the woman asked.

Charlie interrupted. "What kind of car is it?" he said, "We found a set of keys in the car park yesterday."

"Then you should have brought them straight in here," Bosworth blustered. Charlie ignored him and waited for one of the couple to answer.

"It's a Lexus," the woman said. "There's one fob and a key for the car, and a set of three house keys on the ring. The fob has a Lexus logo."

"Thank you," Charlie said. "I'll ring my colleague to check if they're yours."

"THAT'S THEM," Mags said cheerfully when she answered his call. "We've had a look for fingerprints and got a lot of smudges and one partial. Do you want me to bring them to the hotel?"

Charlie said that would be great and passed on the good news. He wondered whether the muddy set he'd found had also gone missing from the hotel.

"But they were in our room," the guest was insisting. "How did they get into the car park?"

Which was a very good question. Of course, there was no guarantee that the keys hadn't been dropped by the couple on their way into the hotel. Or that one of them hadn't gone out to the car during the day and dropped the keys on the way back. If someone always puts their keys in the same place, they assume that's what they've done this time.

But if the keys *had* been in the room...how had they got to the car park?

Bosworth was now all smiles, muttering about things ending well, what a relief that they were getting their keys back.

"About the other matter, Mr Bosworth," Charlie said. "I'd like you to think about it, and I'll be back to talk to you again."

The reception hall began to fill with departing guests

collecting suitcases, and the late arrivals for breakfast. Charlie decided it was time he went.

THE PUBLIC AREA of the police station was busy when Charlie arrived. He recognised Will Jenner's father, and the young man next to him was presumably Will himself. He was wearing the ubiquitous grey sweatpants and hoody, and he had his hair buzzed short at the sides and left just long enough on top for a product-enhanced messy wave.

Both were standing awkwardly in the small space. A woman in a black suit was chatting to Eddy over the counter.

"Sarge," Eddy greeted him with evident relief. "This is Will Jenner and his solicitor. He'd like to give a statement."

Part of the police station refurbishment had included bringing their sole interview room into the twenty-first century. Charlie lifted the counter and led the two Jenners and the solicitor into the room. It was crowded with four adults. Will and the solicitor sat opposite Charlie, and Will's father stood behind his son.

"I assume you've no objection to my recording this meeting?" Charlie asked.

"Fine," the solicitor said.

Charlie switched the machine on and introduced the parties present.

"My client wishes me to read the following statement," the solicitor said. Charlie nodded.

"I would like to state that I have no involvement in the death of Lewis Evans. I have been asked to account for my movements yesterday morning. I spent the evening with my friend Jack Protheroe playing computer games in my room. He decided to stay the night and when I woke up at about eleven o'clock, he was gone. I didn't leave the house from Saturday evening until Sunday lunchtime. My parents were also in the house."

The solicitor put her paper down.

"You say Jack had left before you woke up," Charlie said. "Do you have any idea when he left?"

Will shook his head. "No idea."

"You say that you were playing computer games. Were you also using drugs? Is that why you slept so deeply?" Charlie asked.

"No comment," said Will, unable to prevent a smirk turning the corners of his lips upwards.

"Then thank you for coming in," Charlie said. "I'll obviously need to confirm with your parents that you were in the house yesterday morning. I may also have some more questions for you."

This time, the look on Will's face was alarm.

They don't know whether he was in or out.

Charlie wondered if Will was as stupid as he appeared. He had thrown his friend under the bus, in the hope of diverting attention from his own movements. If the two teenagers had been in Will's room getting stoned and crashing out, they could have alibied each other. All Will had done was convince Charlie that both were lying about their whereabouts. Wherever they had been, it wasn't Will's room. Looking at the solicitor, Charlie thought she was as unimpressed with Will Jenner as he was.

As he ushered the group back out to the front of the police station, Mags was coming back in. She waited until the Jenners and their solicitor had left before raising an inquisitive eyebrow.

"The lad was Will Jenner. He says he was asleep at the crucial time, and he doesn't know where his friend was."

"Yeah, right," Mags said.

"I've got to ring the boss, and then head up to Liverpool," he told her.

"She should come and take charge," Mags said. "Or send a proper team."

"Come into the break room," Charlie said. He shouted to Eddy on reception and upstairs for Patsy. They arrived looking puzzled.

"Sarge? Please tell me you've got news about reinforcements," Eddy asked.

That was it, the last straw.

"No reinforcements are coming. There is no Major Incident Team being assembled to take over. The people in this room, that's who we've got. Fucking live with it." He ignored their looks of shock and walked out to call Ravensbourne.

"KEEP INTERVIEWING those lads until one of them cracks," she said. "I doubt it'll take long."

"I'd like to know more about Lewis's stepdad," Charlie said. "And there's something about the hotel and those car keys that's bugging me."

"Occam's Razor, Charlie. Or, put another way, if it quacks like a duck, and swims like a duck it's probably a duck."

"Boss?"

"The simplest solution is probably the right one. You've got two lads already in trouble for bullying the victim. Neither of them has an alibi worth the paper it's written on. Don't make it more complicated than it is. Go and charm Kaylan Sully into giving up Vitruvious."

"Yes, boss," was the expected response, but he didn't give it.

"I think it *is* more complicated, boss. I'm not writing the two lads off, but I'm not giving up on the other suspects either. And I'm not going to *charm* Kaylan Sully. He's playing games and we shouldn't be falling for it."

There was a snort of laughter from the other end of the line. "it seems like you've given your charm a time out," she said and ended the call.

Now he just had to argue with Tom, and he would have a full set.

In the meantime, Liverpool.

9

LIVERPOOL: MONDAY

Notes from an interview with David Yarrow, Finance Director, Llanfair College of Art.

Present: David Yarrow, Madeleine Tempest (union representative), Cainwen Parry-Jones (Head of Human Resources), Elizabeth Sparrow (representing college auditors), Ann Hathersage (note-taker).

DY: I have no knowledge of any donations paid to general college funds by international students or their families.

ES: Here is a signed affidavit from the parents of a student who joined the college last year. In it they say that they were asked to donate $50,000 to secure a place for their daughter. They have also provided a certified copy of a bank statement. You can see that in addition to tuition fees and the cost of board for the autumn term, an additional $50,000 has been paid as a separate transfer.

DY: It must be for the rest of the year. Lots of people pay in advance.

ES: There are other certified bank statements showing the rest of the year's tuition and living cost payments.

DY: I can't explain it, then.

ES: Then allow me to show you another affidavit from another parent. *Again, a bank statement has been provided. In fact, I have ten other affidavits all saying the same thing.*

DY: *I have no idea where these came from.*

ES: *They came from the families of international students. This money was paid into the college accounts. Are you saying that half a million dollars was paid to the college and you, as finance director, had no knowledge of it?*

DY: *You're making it up.*

MT: *I think Mr Yarrow needs a break.*

C P-J: *That seems like a good idea.*

THE INTERVIEW ROOM in Liverpool Prison where Charlie met Kaylan Sully wasn't that different from the interview room (pre-refurbishment) at Llanfair police station. Table bolted to the floor, walls and floor grey with the dirt of ages and a single window letting in almost no light. Except for the smell. The smell was awful. Cigarette smoke, male sweat, disinfectant, drains, boiled cabbage. Charlie supposed that if he had to stay there, he would get used to it, but given that he didn't have to, he planned to go straight home for a shower and a change of clothes. He could feel the smell clinging to him, taste it in his mouth as well as his nose. At least it wasn't noisy. The wings where the prisoners lived were noisy, but the interview rooms were quiet, except in this one where Kaylan Sully was sobbing loudly.

Charlie wasn't convinced the sobs and tears were genuine. Not much about Kaylan was genuine, Charlie thought, apart from his own self-importance. It seemed that Kaylan really did think the world revolved around him, and if he needed any more evidence, well, he had demanded to see Charlie, and Charlie had appeared.

The cause of the sobbing was a visit Kaylan had received

from "some Federal spooks" who had—according to Kaylan—threatened to have him deported back to his home country of the USA.

"They'll lock me up in one of those Supermax prisons and I'll never get out or be allowed to talk to anyone. People go mad in those places."

Charlie shared some of his horror at that aspect of the American prison system, but he had little sympathy for Kaylan. He had let his friend Rico die so that Vitruvious could paint an authentic dying man. But the US authorities weren't interested in that. They cared about Kaylan's abilities to make computers do what he told them. Charlie suspected that if deported back to the States, he would be put to work rather than sent to jail.

"What do you think I can do about it?" Charlie asked as the sobbing eased.

"You tell me," Kaylan said. "What do I have that I can trade?"

"You shot a police officer. You won't be getting out of here before your trial, and then you'll go straight back to jail."

Kaylan looked at Charlie from red-rimmed eyes and a tear-stained face. "But that's *here*. I can cope with it here."

Think you can persuade someone to let you out, more like.

"What you're saying is that in exchange for not being deported, you will offer us something?" Charlie asked.

Kaylan nodded.

"What? Evidence against Vitruvious? Tell the truth about what happened to Rico?"

Kaylan leaned forward across the table.

"I have money," he said.

Charlie leaned back. "I'm sure you do. But I'm also sure you have enough sense not to try to offer it to a serving police officer."

"I could offer it to the art college," Kaylan said. "We both know they need it."

"Just tell the truth about Rico's death. That's what you have to negotiate with, Kaylan."

"Yeah, right, then I get a longer sentence. Not gonna happen."

Charlie stood up. "Your choice."

He knocked on the door to be let out.

"Wait," Kaylan called.

"Get in touch when you're ready to tell the truth about Rico," Charlie said, and left.

CHARLIE PUT Kaylan out of his mind on the way back to Llanfair. Either he would tell the truth, or he wouldn't.

He rang Brian Telford.

"Hang on a sec, Sarge," Brian said. "Just taking the phone outside. Now then, what can I tell you?"

"Anything about our victim," Charlie said.

"I can tell you that he is defo Lewis Evans," Brian said. "Identification this morning. I took them to Wrexham. Mrs Evans—Gina—was hoping it wasn't him, but of course she really knew it was. Poor bugger. Poor them too. Lewis sounds like a bit of a strange one. Bit of a loner. Then those two toe rags at his school started and no one would stick up for him in case they got bullied instead. Gina and the two lads are devastated. But I've gotta say that Neville almost seems relieved. Kept saying *You don't have to worry about him any more, love,* to Gina. All the way back from Wrexham."

"That's kind of insensitive."

"You're not wrong, Sarge. But Gina kept nodding. And then crying some more. She said one odd thing: 'Lewis respected you, Neville.' Neville pinched her arm, and if I'm not mistaken, it was to shut her up. I'd like to talk to the brothers, but I can't get them on their own. Neville sticks to me like glue. I'm wondering if he's got a temper. He's got that air about him, y'know? Secrets. Wives who fall downstairs a lot."

Charlie did know about men *with a temper*. Domestic abuse was a big part of police work. He knew about *secrets* too. Secrets concealing domestic abuse. Brian was an experienced officer, and if he was getting the vibe from Neville, it was worth paying attention.

"I can't stay with the Evanses much longer," Brian said. "But I've arranged to go back every day to keep them up to date."

Charlie thanked him and they ended the call.

With a few badly signposted motorway junctions coming up, Charlie concentrated on driving. It hadn't rained today, so the roads were dry, but he was heading west into the setting sun. Fine when he was behind a lorry, or a stand of trees, but every few hundred yards bright orange light almost blinded him. All around him, drivers had their sun visors down as far as they would go, but he noted that no one went any slower. He had planned to ring Eddy to ask about the parkour people but decided it would have to wait until he turned south and out of the sunset. He hated this time of year. Nothing to look forward to except endless days of grey skies and rain. If they got unlucky, it might even snow. His mind ran to images of Caribbean beaches, lying on a sun lounger, feeling the sun soaking into his skin and occasionally getting up and going for a swim in the warm ocean. He wondered whether Tom could be persuaded...

Eventually he turned south for Llanfair and rang Eddy to see how they had got on with the parkour crew. The plan had been to ask for an informal interview with the most committed *traceurs* and a teacher as an appropriate adult.

"The headmaster sat in," Eddy said, "Dr Ellis. Impressive guy, knows all the kids. Put them at their ease, so they forgot he was there, and we learned a lot."

"Don't keep me in suspense, Eddy, mate."

Eddy laughed.

"Are you sure you don't want a bit more of an introduction? Like who was there? Where the meeting was held? All important information."

"Which I'm sure you've written down. Now tell me."

"If you insist."

"I insist."

Eddy laughed again. "We saw four people, three boys and one girl. They've been doing parkour for the last few years, and they're into skateboarding and climbing walls and all sorts of other stuff. They were obviously the ones who changed the town clock, but everyone very carefully skirted round that. They're very serious about not doing any damage when they go out to climb things, or do whatever it is they do. I got loads of guff about self-discipline, and doing lots of practice until all the moves could be done safely. Quite interesting. There are some movies about it. I'm going to rent one."

"Did you ask them about Lewis Evans at all?" Charlie asked, not bothering to keep a lid on his snark.

"Of course we did. Lewis was dead keen on parkour, could do all the moves, but they said he was hard to be around. Apparently he could be rude—asking intrusive questions one minute or saying nothing at all for ages after that. They said they couldn't get a sense of what he was like. He would follow them around so he could join in with their training, except when he was there, they couldn't relax. One boy said it was as if he wanted to be part of the group without bothering to get to know any of them first."

"No small talk?"

"More than that. These guys have been mates since nursery, and now everywhere they went, Lewis was waiting for them. It wasn't so much that they didn't like him, it was just *awkward*. That word came up more than once. They also said Lewis kept saying stuff like how parkour would let them look in people's bedroom windows, and they said that was awkward too."

"Because that's not the point of parkour."

"Exactly. To be fair, they didn't think he wanted to look in people's bedroom windows, it was *awkward*. They didn't want to tell him to shut up, because they aren't that sort of kids, so they tried to avoid him as much as they could."

Not that sort of kids implied they weren't likely to have murdered Lewis to avoid awkwardness.

"Did they have anything to say about Jack and Will?" Charlie asked.

"The girl, Kelly, said she felt sorry for Lewis. Implied that so did everyone else in their year. But again, *implied* rather than said. No one wanted to stick up for Lewis and get on the wrong side of Jack and Will. It's like Lewis being bullied took the pressure off everyone else. I did notice Dr Ellis taking notice at that point."

Charlie thought it was a good job someone—Dr Ellis—was prepared to deal with Jack and Will, who appeared to be terrorising a lot of people. He wondered whether being suspended over their behaviour towards Lewis had been enough to push them over the edge to real violence. Murderous violence.

BY THE TIME he reached the outskirts of Llanfair, the sun had all but gone. He drove past the newly built council sponsored co-working space which bizarrely appeared to be doing very well. Bizarrely, because Charlie thought it was one of those ideas that looked good on paper but fizzled in real life. Apparently the desire to rent a short-term office space was alive and well in Llanfair. Another reason to keep a lid on crime in the town. They had the art college, which was enough to keep the shops open, where other little Welsh towns were struggling. Llanfair had suffered so much bad publicity in the last year that it had to be putting people off, and he had started to care. He'd never wanted to come here, but here he was, and Charlie wanted the place to thrive.

The phone rang as he parked outside the police station. It was Ravensbourne. His heart sank. He wasn't going to be able to give her the news she wanted: that Kaylan would tell the truth.

"Boss," he said. "I saw Kaylan, if that's why you're ringing..."

"Of course it's why I'm ringing."

"He tried to bribe me, not too seriously, but I told him what we cared about was the truth about Rico's death."

There was a growl from Ravensbourne.

"Maybe you should have tried charm," she said and laughed.

"He doesn't bring out my good side, boss, and I do think he's playing games to keep the boredom at bay. Or possibly he seriously thinks he can negotiate his way out. He's not going to give a witness statement about Rico's death."

"He thinks he's smarter than he is. Happily, you are smarter than you think you are. Keep chipping away and you'll get a result."

Had Ravensbourne paid him a compliment? This time he gave the expected answer: "Yes, boss."

10

GENERIC TEENAGER: MONDAY

Notes from reconvened interview with David Yarrow, Finance Director, Llanfair College of Art.

Present: David Yarrow, Madeleine Tempest (union representative), Cainwen Parry-Jones (Head of Human Resources), Elizabeth Sparrow (representing college auditors), Ann Hathersage (note-taker).

CP-J: *Thank you for coming back everyone. David, have you anything to add to what you said earlier?*

DY: *I have been contacted by Clwyd Police, and I have arranged to talk to them in the next few days.*

MT: *I think the police investigation takes precedence, Chair.*

C P-J: *I think so too. So, we'll adjourn until the police have concluded their investigation. Mr Yarrow will remain suspended until further notice.*

MT: *On full pay?*

C P-J: *Of course. Perhaps you will contact me when the police have finished?*

· · ·

ANN HAD LEFT the notes on Tom's desk, as well as emailing them. At the bottom of the page, he sketched a picture of a dragon with David Yarrow's face, sitting on a heap of gold coins.

LLANFAIR POLICE STATION had closed its doors to the public for the night, but there was a light on upstairs in the room they worked from, and where Charlie had his miniature office. He threw his coat onto his desk and returned to the main room. Mags was frowning at her computer, a notepad beside her on the desk. Eddy and Patsy were looking over her shoulder. They all looked round as Charlie came in.

"What's up?" he asked, half expecting the cold shoulder after his earlier outburst.

"Burglaries, Sarge." Eddy said, "Email analysis document from on high showing that our policing area has more burglaries than almost the rest of Clwyd put together. Seriously. Like, there's no commentary or anything, but the charts are pretty clear."

Charlie joined his colleagues in peering over Mags's shoulder at her screen. A bar chart with different colours for each policing area did appear to show that Llanfair was the burglary capital of north Wales. Admittedly, the coastal resorts were close behind, but Llanfair was in the lead. Eddy exaggerated, but for a small town, there were a lot of break-ins. Like they needed something else to worry about.

"Shit," Charlie said. "I knew we were getting a lot of reports, but to be honest, I thought it was because we were open more often. Let's face it, our predecessors did a brilliant job of training people not to bother reporting anything. Who fancies looking into what's been stolen and where from and looking for patterns? Because if we don't, we'll be getting more than emails."

"Late to the party, Sarge," Eddy said. "While you've been living it up in Liverpool, we've been working hard finding out who's been robbed and what they've been robbed of. No flies on *this* team."

"Burgled, not robbed," said Patsy. "Robbery implies a threat of violence. These are burglaries, aka breaking and entering."

"I know the difference between burglary and robbery, thank you," Eddy said. "I said robbed, not robbery, which is an idiomatic use of English, not a legal definition."

"Shut up," Charlie said. "Someone please tell me who has had what stolen from their houses? Or stolen from other places. Without threat of violence, thus earning the perpetrators a sentence of up to two years inside, rather than the much more severe penalties for robbery. Just tell me."

Patsy opened her mouth to speak and earned a nudge in the ribs from Mags.

"Mostly cash and cards," Mags said. "Plus car keys, mobile phones and some jewellery. Mostly stolen from bedrooms or home offices. Generally stolen at night. None of it recovered."

"Car keys? Were the cars stolen too?" Charlie asked.

"Some were, some weren't. No surprise that it was the expensive ones that disappeared. But there were only three of those. It's possible that one of the sets of keys was used to steal that souped-up Fiesta that we found in the river last month."

"All things our burglar could put in their pockets," Charlie said.

"A car won't fit in a pocket," Patsy said.

"*Patsy!*" Three people said simultaneously, and she got another poke in the ribs from Mags.

"How many burglaries are we looking at?" Charlie asked.

"Almost thirty," Mags said. "One every couple of days for the last two months. A few more before that. And there are bound to be some that haven't been reported. Probably because we were closed such a lot. Most people only come to us for a crime number so they can claim on their insurance."

They had found the keys to an expensive car in the hotel car park. Did that have any significance? If it did, Charlie didn't know what it was.

"Next steps?" Charlie asked. "Are any of them recent enough to go and take fingerprints?"

Mags shook her head. "Last one was almost a week ago."

"Find out what happened to the loot," Eddy suggested. "It's a small place, small enough that I bet we could find out who's been buying phones and credit cards. Ask around in the pubs."

Patsy flopped down into a chair and laughed. "Because no one would guess you were a copper, Eds. Eddy Edwards, under-cover giant."

"Listen, *Pats*, there are other ways to find things out than pretending to be a villain. We can ask the landlords. They don't want us thinking there are dodgy deals going on," Eddy began. He appeared to be getting into his stride.

Charlie held his hands up. "Enough. It's worth an hour talking to publicans. The pubs will be quietish now, so you can both go once we've finished. What about Landon Emery?"

Mags produced her chart of where everyone had been during the period around when Lewis died. "He's missing for ages, and more than once," she said pointing to the blank spots on the chart. "I asked around, discreetly, of course. No one thought he was sneaking off to murder Lewis Evans, because they all thought he was sneaking off to play casino games on his phone. Apparently he's an addict. Always arguing about it with Bosworth. One of the kitchen staff said she was surprised he was still working there."

"Not a lot of friends, then?" Charlie asked.

"He knows the father of the bride," Patsy piped up. "At least to say hello to."

"I think everyone did by yesterday lunchtime," Mags said. "The man was everywhere."

"We need to keep looking," Charlie said. "Landon Emery had the opportunity, he found the body, and he could easily have got hold of a knife. To my mind he's a lot more credible than Jack Protheroe or Will Jenner."

CHARLIE WANTED to send Mags home. Partly because he couldn't rid himself of the idea that pregnant women needed special treatment, but mostly because he wanted the place to himself so he could think without distraction. But he was too late. She'd logged back on to her computer and was concentrating hard. He decided to make himself a drink and stare at the whiteboard for inspiration. Perhaps the gannets he worked with might have left something edible in the fridge. They had. A box marked *Sgt R ONLY!!!!* contained a chocolate chip muffin of the kind with gooey chocolate inside. He sighed with anticipation as he waited for the kettle to boil.

Lewis's relationship with his adoptive father warranted further attention. He added Neville Evans's name to the board with a note that Brian Telford had concerns.

Charlie's instincts were also flagging up the Castle Hotel and especially Rupert Bosworth. There was no reason to connect Bosworth to the murder, except his lack of alibi. Charlie had heard a lot of lies in his time in the police, and he was certain Bosworth was lying. He could have obtained a knife easily enough, and no one had seen him when Lewis was killed. Lewis had no obvious reason to be at the hotel, yet he had been there. Lewis was a parkour person; he'd told his fellow *traceurs* that parkour would let him look in bedroom windows. They had been talking about thefts from bedrooms, including the theft of car keys. Was Lewis the thief? Was he at the hotel to steal? It sounded credible. Could Bosworth have caught Lewis stealing and killed him for it? Less credible. He would have called the police, surely?

Charlie put an asterisk next to Bosworth's name, and added the word Burglaries to the list, and underneath it, *Lewis, parkour, bedrooms?*

Then there was Landon Emery who had found Lewis's body. The time frame for the death was a couple of hours, probably even less. The car park wasn't big, not with half of it under water. It would have been half dark, but if someone other than Landon had been outside for a smoke, surely they would have seen him? Charlie put an asterisk next to the waiter's name.

There was a clatter in the corridor. Charlie started, and checked the time. He'd been pondering for over an hour, but even so, he was surprised that Patsy and Eddy had finished their pub crawl so early. He heard footsteps on the stairs. It seemed that Eddy and Patsy's return had disturbed Mags too.

"Any luck?" he asked.

"Bingo at the second attempt," said Eddy. "Even Patsy was impressed by my knowledge of the Llanfair underworld."

"You mean the pub you could get served in when you were fifteen?"

"That's the one."

"Go on then," Charlie said.

"The Yew Tree."

Charlie sent him a puzzled look. He hadn't come across a pub with that name.

"It's the one behind the old post office. You can't see the pub, but there are a few tables outside under an archway," Eddy said. "It always used to be the underage drinkers' pub, and apparently it still is."

Mags nodded.

"And the dealers' pub, and the stolen goods pub," Patsy added.

"We had a chat with the landlady, and she was very keen to

help. Turns out her licence is up for renewal soon. She has seen a few dodgy deals, though of course she gave us the usual flannel and run-around. What it boiled down to is that a teenage boy has been meeting a known villain most weeks for the last few months. *Obviously* she didn't know the boy was underage. *Obviously* she had no idea that the guy was a crook."

"I recognised the description," Patsy said. "As you know, our previous boss didn't go in for arresting people when he could take a bribe instead, but this guy pushed it too far. He's got a record for receiving stolen goods—like buying razor blades and electric toothbrushes from shoplifters right outside the pharmacy. The Yew Tree landlady admitted she'd seen him buying stuff in the pub including credit cards, and she's hoping that now she's told us, we won't oppose her licence."

"He's called Huw Leader," Eddy said. "Fence of this parish. The landlady was going to ban him. I told her no way. We want to know where to pick him up."

"What about the teenage boy?" Charlie asked.

"Short brown hair, black or grey trackies, black or grey hoody." Eddy said.

"Lewis Evans," Patsy said. "He's our burglar, and it got him killed."

"It's also a description of Will Jenner," Charlie said. "And not just those two. I bet half the lads in The Yew Tree looked like that."

From their expressions, Charlie knew he was right.

"There's something else," Mags said. The three of them turned to face her. "Sarge, you wanted to know what happened to the loot. Eddy and Patsy found out where some of it went, but I sent some emails, and had some replies. Only a couple so far. Two people who had their cards stolen told me that the cards had been used for online gambling. They got their money back—in the end—and it's only two out of thirty or so. But it's interesting. Usually, stolen cards are used to buy things that can be turned into cash."

11

SENSE OF HUMOUR FAILURE: MONDAY

From: Cainwen Parry-Jones, Head of Human Resources
    To: Professor Tom Pennant, Principal

Hi Tom

I'm afraid we weren't able to get anything from David Yarrow (notes attached). It's up to the police now.

We do need to start a similar series of interviews with Dr Vitruvious, unless the police are dealing with him, too. Do you know?

Best wishes
Cainwen

FROM: Tom Pennant
    To: Cainwen Parry-Jones

I will enquire of the police re Vesuvius.

Please note that he is not entitled to use the title of Dr. I'm not even sure he's got an art GCSE.

Ann already sent me the notes.

Tom

From: Tom Pennant
To: Cainwen Parry-Jones

Sorry, Cainwen, getting a bit of a sense of humour failure about Vitruvious. He's not even here and he's causing me more work than anyone else. Don't mean to take it out on you.

Tom

~

"I want you to meet my girls," Tom said. "They want to meet you."

He and Charlie were on the sofa in Tom's living room. Tom was stretched out with his head on Charlie's lap and his feet on the arm of the sofa. Most of the house had hardwood floors, but this room had a carpet and there were also rugs, and cushions on the sofa, and walls painted blue and covered in pictures. The dark blue velvet curtains were drawn against the night, and Bach's Goldberg Variations were playing softly in the background through concealed speakers. There was a tiled fireplace with a convincing fake wood-burner, in front of which lay Tom's black cat, Billy. The coffee table in front of the sofa held two glasses and an empty wine bottle. Charlie could smell the wine, but he couldn't reach it without moving Tom, and he didn't want to. He would rather play with Tom's hair, which was long enough to curl over his collar.

"I can't commit to anything until this case is over," Charlie said. "That's the reality of police work."

Tom raised his eyebrows. "You're here now. They could have come for dinner, and you could have met them."

It was true. But Charlie had spent the last few days trying to decide if one teenager had killed another. He had spent time listening to the parents of teenagers who had no idea what their offspring were getting up to, except that it included using illegal drugs. Not that he necessarily thought those drugs should be illegal, but they were, and he wasn't supposed to ignore it. Though surely two thirteen-year-old girls wouldn't be smoking dope?

"Charlie?" Tom asked.

"Nothing," Charlie said, because *Do your daughters smoke weed?* probably wouldn't go down well. So he asked, "Did they meet your other boyfriends?"

Tom smiled. "Are you trying to find out about my disgraceful past?"

"Just how disgraceful are we talking about here?" He stroked Tom's hair and considered tickling his ears.

"Hardly disgraceful at all. Pretty dull in fact."

"But you're an artist. I thought artists were hedonists with crowds of groupies, or whatever the groupie equivalent is for printmakers."

"Not this artist. No groupies anyway. I lived with a guy for a few years. The girls met him. He was another printmaker. An amazing artist, and sometimes an amazing guy. He died just over eight years ago."

"Shit. I'm sorry."

"We argued pretty constantly for most of the time we were together, and he killed himself."

Charlie thought Tom said the words as if they weren't describing an event that must have knocked him sideways. How had they got from imaginary groupies to this?

Tom was still speaking.

This is important. Tom is telling me something that changed his life.

"He was seriously depressed. I think he had been abused. I don't know. He had all the PTSD symptoms, but like I say, I don't know. I try not to diagnose things I don't understand." Tom closed his eyes. "Anyway, I knew he was ill, but I couldn't persuade him to get help. And I was too guilty to kick him out. We argued, and made up, and argued some more. It got violent sometimes. Ann and Orianna didn't want the girls near him, and in the end, that's what made me decide to tell him to leave. Christmas was coming up, and I planned to talk to him after that. But he killed himself before I could."

"That must have been awful. The poor guy. And terrible for you and everyone who knew him." Charlie well knew the fallout from suicide went far deeper than simple guilt and anger.

"I've had a lot of therapy, which I have to say, I bloody needed. And no more boyfriends until you. Ann already likes you. The girls will like you. Ori will like you. I'm hoping you will like them." Tom turned on his side so he could look at Charlie. "This isn't a bit of a fling for me, Charlie. I don't think it's one for you, either."

"It isn't," was all Charlie could manage to say, a little croakily. The way he felt about Tom was different to the way he had felt about anyone before. He had had plenty of what Tom called 'flings' and crushes galore. He'd even thought he was in love once or twice. But he thought about Tom all the time. Mostly about sex, because Tom was sexy AF, but he also thought about listening to Tom talk about art, and about pottering around the kitchen together, walking in the hills, watching a movie. And, OK, sex. Tom grounded him, and he was beginning to believe that Tom really didn't care that Charlie was a small-town policeman, without a degree, and who didn't know a Picasso from a Poussin. "You like looking at pictures," Tom had said. "That's enough for me." It was true. Since meeting Tom, he had started looking, and seeing. He was developing ideas about the kinds of images he liked, and if he and Tom didn't work out, he would carry on looking at pictures.

But meeting Tom's children? That was another thing. Meeting the kids suggested they were serious and had a future together. Which at moments like this he could almost believe; at moments like this he could ignore the nagging voice that told him he wasn't good enough for a man like Tom.

CHARLIE REMEMBERED that he'd promised to ring Ravensbourne. He was pretty sure she wouldn't have forgotten. Also, he wanted something. Search warrants for Jack and Will's rooms. He forced himself to sit up and picked his phone off the table.

"Sorry," Charlie said. "I have to ring my boss."

Tom stood up to collect their glasses and the empty bottle, then took them into the kitchen. Charlie heard the rattle of the dishwasher opening and reflected that there was no censure in Tom's demeanour, just acceptance that this was Charlie's job.

"I thought you'd forgotten me, Charlie," Ravensbourne said when she answered.

"No, boss. Sorry it's a bit late."

"Never mind that, tell me about those two bullies."

"We've spoken to them, and to their parents, and they're not cracking, boss. But if it was one of them, they won't have had time to get all their clothes in the wash. They may still have the knife. Jack's mother would have noticed anything unusual, like blood. She's always looking for things to paint him in a bad light. Probably Will's mother would as well. And there's always the chance of finding the knife. Maybe we'll find Occam's Razor"

"Are you being cheeky with me, Charlie?"

"No, boss," he said.

"Yes, you were. But it's a good idea. Try for a voluntary search, but I'll get the warrants underway, and you can tell them that to concentrate their minds. It'll be interesting to see how they react."

"First thing in the morning, boss."

"I'll try to get you the warrants by then."

Charlie wondered if she ever stopped working. He suspected not. He remembered a female friend in the sixth form telling him that women had to work twice as hard to get half as far. His experience in the police showed the truth of that statement every day.

Tom him from the kitchen door when Charlie ended the call and put the phone down on the dining table. "Do you want to go to bed, or can I bend you over the back of the sofa? Because you being all business-like and police-y is having an effect. Plus, I made dinner, so you ought to put out."

Charlie felt all the blood in his body run to his groin. Tom in 'let's fuck' mode was the Tom who had tried to pick him up in the Rainbow bar when they first met. It was a different, more laid-back Tom. Charlie liked 'let's fuck' Tom as much as Tom the artist, and even Tom the college principal was much sexier than Tom probably realised.

"Keep your shirt and tie on, and you can choose," Charlie said.

"Trousers? Waistcoat?"

"Fuck, yes," Charlie could barely get his breath. He closed his eyes and tried to calm down.

"How long have you had this fantasy of me fucking you over my office desk?" Tom had sneaked up behind him to whisper in his ear. "And in your fantasy, do we close the blinds?"

Charlie groaned and felt the wetness of pre-come leaking into his underwear. Strong arms slid round his waist and big hands opened the button and zip on his jeans.

"Oh my, what's this?" Tom pulled Charlie's jeans and underwear down, freeing his cock. "Someone is eager. Are you naked in your fantasy?"

Charlie was incapable of speech.

"Then let's go with no," Tom said, "because there are all those people in the outer office, and the court is full of students. If they looked up, they might notice a naked man. Maybe you'd be safe if you just gave me your arse."

"Oh, fuck," was all Charlie could say, as Tom opened his arse cheeks and inserted the very tip of his thumb into Charlie's hole.

" I've always wanted to fuck someone over my desk," Tom said, and pushed Charlie over the table, face down, arms stretched out to hold himself steady.

Tom reached round and stroked Charlie's cock with a featherlight touch, then pumped it gently.

"Don't," Charlie gasped.

"Don't? I'm the college principal. I'm the one in the suit. You don't tell me what to do in my own office."

All Charlie could do was whine. He felt Tom back away, and then he was back, rustling plastic and dripping cold lube between his arse cheeks. A slick finger found its way in, and then another, and with every thrust, Tom stroked Charlie's dick until the sensations blurred and he was desperate to come. And also not, because he wanted to feel Tom inside him.

"Tom. I'm going to come."

"No you're not." Tom stopped stroking and gripped the base of Charlie's cock hard. "Not till I've had my evil way with you. Remember you asked for this. Keep quiet or people will hear. We don't want them having any reason to look up at the windows, do we?"

"Hurry up then," Charlie gasped. The table was hard against his body, and he could feel Tom's tie fluttering around his face. The wool of Tom's suit was soft, but also hairy against his arse, and he was overwhelmed by Tom's size and his voice, and the image of them fucking in front of those acres of glass panels. He heard Tom unzip his suit trousers and push his briefs down, and then the slap of a condom and the wetness of more lube, and then...

"Oh, Jesus, Tom, please,"

Tom responded by pushing in, a millimetre at a time, holding Charlie steady with one hand, and stroking his aching cock with the other. When Tom's cock found his prostate, Charlie couldn't control his cry. Tom pulled out an inch and hit Charlie's prostate again, and again, until there was nothing Charlie could do to stop the waves of ecstasy rolling over him, leaving him stunned and helpless. Tom grabbed Charlie's hips and held him as he fucked hard and fast until Charlie felt him lose control, and the pulsing as Tom came in his turn. He collapsed on top of Charlie, gasping for breath.

"This table is fucking hard," Charlie said with the last bit of breath left in his lungs, "and you're squashing me."

Tom pulled out carefully, and dropped the condom on the floor as he stood up. Then he started laughing.

"I don't think I've been that turned on since I was sixteen," "I'm never going to look at my desk in the same way again." He helped Charlie to his feet.

"That's not as easy as it looks in porn movies," Charlie said. "But fuck, it was unbelievably hot. I'm going to be covered in bruises by morning. Ask me if I care."

Somehow they made it back to the couch, mopped themselves up and lay together kissing and giggling until it was time for bed.

12

TOM FORD SUNGLASSES: TUESDAY

F rom: Tom Pennant
    To: Bryson Carroll, Chair of Governors
    cc: Elizabeth Sparrow
Confidential

DEAR BRYSON

I've copied Elizabeth into this, because she needs to be aware of our possible liabilities. I asked for a report of the possible consequences of repaying the fraudulently obtained 'donations'. I looked at two main scenarios: firstly, the worst case, in which we are required to repay everything, and we recover none of the stolen money, and secondly, a best case, where we do recover half the stolen money. I can't imagine a scenario where we recover it all, because informal conversations with the police suggest that Kaylan Sully (who claimed to have this year's 'donations') is highly skilled at hiding money, even from the FBI. Recovery of the previous two years' money depends on a successful prosecution of the conspirators, and the seizure of their assets — neither of which is either guaranteed or speedy.

You will see from the calculations that we will be short of £1.5 million in the coming financial year. It would be reasonable to use up to £750,000 of reserves, but the Finance Committee should be consulted, along with colleagues from the Department for Education, as we are obliged to keep a substantial reserve for contingencies (such as this one, I would argue). Even so, we could be looking at finding considerable savings. Current student applications for the coming year are below average at this point. Our Painting students do not have a Senior Tutor, meaning that the other tutors are struggling, and this is affecting the student experience. We should expect this to have an impact on our league table positions.

We have a number of options, none of which are palatable (see attached for costings).

Options include: a staff recruitment freeze, staff redundancies, lowering requirements for applicants to increase student numbers, increasing revenue from postgraduate recruitment, short courses and similar, obtaining short-term help from either loans or grants, merger with other institutions. As you see, none of these options is attractive.

In my opinion, we should begin discussions without delay with the staff, the trade unions and the funding bodies, not least because they may have other, better ideas. ~~Or I could disembowel myself with a rusty spoon~~

... continues ...

~

FROM: DCI Ravensbourne
To: DS Rees

PLEASE FIND ATTACHED *Search Warrants for both the Protheroe and Jenner houses. That is the whole house and outbuildings, not just the boys' rooms. Note that you are only able to look for the murder*

weapon and anything else specifically pertaining to the murder. Get
in there!
      FR

CHARLIE PICKED up Ravensbourne's email on the way into the
police station. She must have been bothering magistrates late
into the evening, so he hoped it would prove useful, one way or
another. They needed to arrive at both houses simultaneously
to prevent one teenager warning the other, so Charlie had to
wait impatiently with Patsy for Eddy and Mags to arrive.
Neither was due in yet, but that didn't stop Charlie pacing
around the office, slurping too-hot coffee, reading and re-
reading the warrants. Eventually they both arrived, well before
eight-thirty. Charlie decided he couldn't face any more of Mrs
Protheroe's negativity, so he and Mags headed for the Jenner
house, leaving Jack for Patsy and Eddy.

   Armed with their warrant, Charlie checked with Eddy that
he and Patsy were outside the Protheroes' before walking up
the path to bang on the Jenners' front door.

   "Search the house? Search the fucking house? Will! Get
your arse down here!" Fair to say, Mr Jenner wasn't happy.
Judging by his outfit—a Llanfair College Campus Services
fleece and navy-blue trousers, Jenner was leaving for work. "Do
I need a solicitor?" he asked.

   "No," Charlie said, "but providing Will and your wife come
into the room with us, I'm more than happy to wait while you
talk to one on the phone. You can read them the warrant."

   "Give it to me. Wife's at work. Will, get down here!"

   Will appeared in his usual sweatpants and hoodie, giving
the impression, from the scent of sweaty teenager, that he'd
dragged them on moments before. "What now?" Will said,
belligerently.

"What now is that the police have a warrant to search the house looking for evidence of your involvement in the murder of Lewis Evans, that's what now."

"Fuck off. I need to ring Jack. This is bullshit."

"You will find that my colleagues are in the process of serving the same warrant on the Protheroe household," Charlie said blandly. "Your father is deciding whether to call your solicitor. I'd like you to stay in here, please, though you are both at liberty to watch us search once we begin."

"You can't make me," Will said. Then he looked at Charlie's face and sat down, in an armchair. "My phone's upstairs." Another look at Charlie's face, and he threw his head back, rolling his eyes upwards and mumbling "Fucking bullshit," under his breath.

Jenner senior put the warrant on the coffee table. "Is this legit?" he asked Charlie. "Because it looks right, and I don't want to waste any more money on solicitors. We can watch you search?"

"You can watch us search. If we remove anything, we'll give you a receipt. You can even film us if you want. We're only allowed to look for things to do with the murder, so if we found, say, evidence of another offence, we couldn't seize that evidence, unless it was a very serious offence. For instance, if we found a firearm, or a very large quantity of illegal drugs, or a stash of child pornography. Then we'd arrest you anyway." In other words, forget about that bit of weed, assuming that's all there is. If you've got a greenhouse full, all bets are off.

Jenner nodded slowly. "I need to ring work and tell them I'm going to be late."

Charlie and Mags started in Will's room and worked together, so that Will and his father could watch. Will stayed for five minutes and then began to mutter *bullshit* and stormed off, stamping down the stairs and slamming into the kitchen. Will's bedroom was the second largest of the three, around ten by ten feet. The walls and carpet were grey, and the bedding on the double bed, now crumpled and smelling powerfully of sweat and cheap cologne, was a darker grey. A wardrobe and matching chest of drawers faced the bed. There was a modern computer desk, scattered with headphones, boxed computer games and games consoles. Instead of a monitor, a big TV screen dominated one wall of the room. Mags looked carefully at the things on the desk and photographed them individually.

Charlie looked in the wardrobe. He wasn't surprised to see the clothes had been ironed and folded neatly, remembering the towering pile of ironing on his first visit. He was surprised at the number of shoeboxes with pairs of expensive trainers in the bottom of the wardrobe, and the sheer quantity of designer sportswear. There were shoes and garments Charlie recognised from his own shopping expeditions, meaning he knew what they cost. The sheepskin flying jacket wasn't a cheap imitation, and even the carefully folded jeans were all top brands. At a conservative estimate, there were several thousand pounds worth of clothes in the wardrobe of a teenage boy whose father worked as a concierge/caretaker/security guard.

"May I ask what your wife does as a job?" he asked.

Jenner looked surprised. "Checkout at the Co-op. Why?"

"Does Will have a job?"

"He does a bit for me and his mum and mows the grass for a few neighbours. Nothing regular. We give him an allowance, why?"

"Because there are a lot of expensive clothes and shoes in here, Mr Jenner."

"He gets things for Christmas and his birthday, and I think he shops online. Lots of cheap stuff if you know what to look for on the auction sites and that."

Charlie nodded. Will would have to be one hell of a good internet shopper to get this lot for the money he had coming in.

He doubted that his allowance plus mowing some lawns paid for a shearling flying jacket or anything at all from Tom Ford. They needed to have another chat to Will.

The search of the rest of the house produced nothing of interest. If the Jenners had a stash of weed, they must have buried it in the garden because Charlie and Mags looked everywhere, including the loft, the garage and the garden shed for the knife or evidence of blood. It took all morning and at the end they were both exhausted. Thankfully Mrs Jenner's housekeeping standards were so high that they were still almost as clean as when they began. Even the garden shed seemed to have been regularly dusted. It was possible they had missed something, but Charlie doubted that Will was particularly imaginative when it came to hiding places. That he had left so many expensive items on display didn't suggest he was well versed in the ways of concealing crime.

"Could we have a word with Will, Mr Jenner? With you there, of course. Just informally at this stage."

Jenner was generous enough to make them both a coffee, for which Charlie was very thankful. Perhaps the sight of a pregnant woman had brought out the gentleman in him. Charlie thought it was beginning to dawn on Jenner that Will had been less than honest about his internet shopping.

They found Will back in the living room, watching TV.

"The coppers want a word, Will," his father said.

"Fine with me," Will shrugged, though he didn't sound like it was.

Charlie drank some coffee, wishing it had come with a biscuit. "There's a lot of expensive gear in your room, Will. How do you afford it all?"

"What's it to you?" Will said.

"I can't afford four pairs of Vans, or a new PlayStation. How are you paying for it all?"

"I have jobs."

"Will, there is stuff worth over ten grand in your room. Probably more. Tom Ford sunglasses? A thousand-pound jacket? Bose headphones? You're fifteen. You don't even get the minimum wage."

"Christmas presents," Will offered, unconvincingly.

"I'm assuming you've got receipts for it all?" Charlie asked.

"Oh, yeah, right, 'cos I keep all my receipts for the taxman," Will said with a sneer.

"Good. Because we'd like you to bring them to the police station. Say later this afternoon? With a better explanation of where you found the money to pay for all those things. We'll be in touch." Charlie stood up and resisted the urge to help Mags to her feet. Will was still managing to look defiant, but his father had gone as white as a sheet. Charlie decided to turn the screw.

"When I called in before," Charlie said, "you told me Will smoked a bit of weed. Have you been dealing, Will?"

At this, Will's dad blushed red, and both he and Will said, "No!" simultaneously.

Charlie raised an eyebrow. "You seem very sure of that."

Mr Jenner shuffled on his chair and looked down at his hands like a toddler sent to the naughty step. "Look, I know it's illegal and all, but Will gets his weed from me. I'd rather he gets it from someone I know than from some stranger on the street. You know what you're getting, like."

Ho, hum, Charlie thought. Do you know what you're getting because you're growing it on an allotment somewhere? Or because you know someone else who's growing it? Something for another day.

"So, if he's not dealing, where is he getting this stuff? Are you stealing it, Will?"

"No way. We didn't raise him to steal," Mr Jenner said.

"Then where?" Charlie asked, but there was no answer.

There would be an answer at the police station, under caution, with a solicitor.

"Thank you for the coffee, Mr Jenner. You might want to talk to your solicitor again."

Jenner nodded wanly.

BACK AT THE POLICE STATION, Eddy and Patsy had a series of photographs of designer sportswear, games consoles, games and accessories, an e-scooter and a modest amount of cocaine. The cocaine was in an evidence bag rather than a photograph, sitting on the table in the middle of the break room. Jack also had a phone that his mother denied ever having seen before, despite Jack insisting it was the one she had bought him. Jack also had about two hundred pounds in cash. Jack Protheroe's mother immediately accused her son of dealing drugs.

Eddy had asked about whether Jack might have a job.

"He's stoned all the time. No employer would put up with it," his mother had said. "Anyway he's too lazy."

"What about Jack's dad?" Eddy had asked, "Would he be giving Jack money?"

"Do you see Jack's dad?" She'd said. Then she answered her own question, "No. And nor do I most of the time. He keeps out of the way, so he doesn't have to deal with Jack. Can't say I blame him, but I haven't got the handy excuse of going to work." The bitterness had apparently rolled towards Eddy and Patsy in waves. Charlie knew the Protheroes' house was comfortable, spotless, warm and filled with books, art and music. It should have been a place of refuge, somewhere to unwind at the end of the day. Somewhere like Tom's house. Except this one was filled with loneliness and misery. He wondered why Mrs Protheroe didn't have a job. None of them had asked.

Charlie thought Jack was probably hell to live with, but he guessed most teenagers were. He didn't say any of that. Instead, he told Patsy and Eddy to arrange an interview with a solicitor and an appropriate adult for Jack.

13

LEADERBOARD

FROM: PROFESSOR ALI COOMBES, SOUTHWEST WALES
UNIVERSITY

To: **Professor Tomos Pennant**

Hi Tom

How are you?

I was at a meeting yesterday with the Welsh Government's Higher Ed people. They suggested that I talk to you about a possible merger between our two institutions. I'm assuming this isn't news to you, though I have to confess that I'm surprised – I always thought Llanfair was determined to remain independent. Anyway, I'd love to talk. Can we get our secretaries to set something up? Say lunch one day soon?

Best Wishes

Ali

Tom threw the pen he'd been doodling with across the room. What the actual fuck was this? He heard Ann walking from the outer office.

"What's up?" she asked.

"This," Tom said, turning the laptop towards her so that she could read the email.

"Bryson Carroll stirring the pot," she said. "And you know

the politicians love pointless and destructive change. A marriage made in heaven."

HUW LEADER HAD his name on the white board with a big star next to it in red pen. At the very least he could identify which of the teenagers he had been meeting in The Yew Tree, but if they played their cards right, they could persuade him to tell them what said teenager was selling. Charlie didn't expect Leader would cough up everything he knew without something in return, but a search on Leader's name produced the information that he had previously acted as a confidential informant. It would be worth trying to recruit him again. As Patsy had said, Eddy was clocked as a copper everywhere he went. Patsy herself wore a uniform to work. Charlie wondered whether she would be recognised without it. She was headed for a detective's job sooner rather than later, so why not see if she could recruit Huw Leader? Charlie had outlined the plan to Patsy, and she had promised to go to The Yew Tree that evening.

The other thing Charlie had planned for the evening was a meeting with Ann's partner Orianna, the other mother of Tom's two children, and the daughter of a long line of high-ranking soldiers. He was hoping the old boys' or should it be girls, network would turn up something useful about Neville Evans.

"He had an honourable discharge, after serving with distinction for many years," was all the information Charlie could get from the MOD about Neville Evans. The consensus at the police station was that Neville had been in the SAS, but neither Charlie nor anyone else, including Ravensbourne, could get it confirmed.

Maybe it didn't matter. All soldiers were trained to kill. It was the nature of the job. Did he think Neville had killed his adopted son? He could have done. He had the expertise, and if he'd been to one of the wars in Iraq, Syria or Afghanistan, he had probably killed people. The motive was less obvious. Lewis might be the troublesome child, the one who worried his mother, and Neville was solicitous—very solicitous—about Gina's wellbeing, but Charlie doubted it was enough.

"Orianna might be able to find out," Tom said. "I know she's a poet now, but her father was a general. Probably still is."

Orianna Wildwood was a poet even Charlie had heard of. When he'd found out she was one of the mothers of Tom's children, he'd bought a book of her poetry. He'd expected to find it entirely beyond him, words on a page to make him feel even more inadequate and uncultured than he already did. But he had loved it. She wrote about Wales, and about landscapes he knew. Her words moved him in ways he hadn't expected, so much so that he'd carried the book around in his pocket until he was afraid someone would see it and think him pretentious. She worked in the art college library, because as Tom said, "If you think art is badly paid, try poetry." Could she really find out about a single ex-soldier? Charlie asked, without much hope.

"Worth a try," Tom said, "she can always say no."

She said yes.

BUT BEFORE THAT, Charlie had Will and Jack to talk to. Again.

BOTH TEENAGERS HAD BROUGHT A PARENT. Will came with his dad and Jack brought his mother. Charlie was beginning to wonder if Jack's father existed, despite having seen his photograph in the house. What kind of parent runs away when their kid is in this much trouble? Charlie knew about those kinds of parents. He recognised his own parents in the Protheroes: absent father and hypercritical mother. Though in his case, his father was hiding at the bottom of a bottle rather than in the office. Tom would be a better father, he thought, and then felt guilty because one of the things Tom wanted was to show off his kids.

Soon. I'll see them soon.

The bad news was that regardless of the more intimidating atmosphere of the police interview room, Jack still maintained that the things in his room were honestly come by. Charlie produced a photograph of the bag of cocaine in its inadequate hiding place under the mattress.

"It was planted," Jack said.

"Your mother watched us search," Charlie said mildly.

Jack shrugged. "Maybe she put it there," he said.

His mother mirrored his shrug, but Charlie saw the flash of pain on her face.

That was the high, or low, point of the interview. Every time Charlie started feeling some empathy with Jack, the teen would blow it by behaving like a total turd. They gave it up as a bad job after half an hour. Jack's smirk as he left the interview room made Charlie want to thump him.

Will was more polite, and less obnoxious to his father, but continued to maintain the fiction that he had paid for all the items they'd found in their search.

"You do know," Charlie said, when he'd had enough of listening to lies, "my boss thinks you and Jack are good suspects for Lewis Evans's murder? You bullied him at school, so much so that you've been suspended for a week. And you've both got rooms full of expensive stuff that you refuse to explain. Your story about where you were at the time Lewis was killed is thin to say the least. It's up to you. My advice is to tell the truth."

It did no good. Will sat in silence, staring at his own feet, and his father looked as if the world was about to end.

But Charlie couldn't visualise Jack and Will as killers, whatever Ravensbourne said. He remembered the wound; so small and precise. Whoever stabbed Lewis had to have been up close and personal. There were no defensive wounds, no evidence of a struggle. Could either of the boys have done that? "Got lucky" with the first blow, as Hector Powell had said? There had been no evidence that either Will or Jack had any interest in weapons. No hunting knives or gun magazines in their rooms. The video games included plenty of the shoot 'em up variety, but then, so did his own. Dr Ellis the headteacher reported verbal abuse and shoving, but no threats involving stabbing. For certain, the two were lying about something major and illegal, but Charlie didn't think it was murder. Convincing Ravensbourne would be quite the task, but she hadn't met them. Perhaps she should, because if he didn't frighten them, Ravensbourne might.

14

HONOURABLE DISCHARGE: TUESDAY

F rom: Bryson Carroll, Chair of Governors
To: Tom Pennant
Confidential

THIS IS to let you know that I've now had extensive conversations with the people at the funding bodies, and the Welsh Gov, as we discussed. No joy I'm afraid. The consensus is that if we can't get ourselves out of this hole, we will have to merge the college with a bigger institution. I pointed out that would mean the loss of our identity as well as our independence. In vain did I rehearse our many achievements. I'm afraid the bean counters aren't interested. The fashion is for STEM subjects, the arts can go to hell, because they don't bring any money in. Apparently. And yes, I gave them all the examples we came up with from the Hay Festival to Dr Who! You won't be surprised to hear that selling the buildings was suggested and moving everything to the site of one of the bigger universities. I said I would resign first.

.   .   .

FROM: **Tom Pennant**
   To: **Bryson Carroll**

IT'S WHAT WE EXPECTED. Back to the drawing board. I have no desire to be principal of the art department of Big Uni. Put another way, I'll resign first, too. We will just have to find the money. I'll open discussions with the senior staff and Academic Board.

"THE DAY he resigns over a matter of principle is the day pigs fly." Ann said, reading over Tom's shoulder.

ORIANNA'S FATHER was not called Wildwood; he was General Percival Gordon. Tom told Charlie that Orianna had phrased her request in terms of her finding Neville Evans 'a bit odd' and, as she had to work with the man, could her father please find out more?

Orianna had taken notes, and now she was round at Tom's house to share the information. Charlie wanted to know, but he was terrified of meeting Orianna. He wanted to say he'd read her work, but he wasn't sure he'd be able to get the words out. And what if his reading of the poems was wrong? What if there was some hidden meaning he hadn't seen? Tom would be there, and Tom would know he hadn't understood. It would have been better if he'd never bought the book. Charlie sat in his car in the police station car park and told himself to turn the ignition on and drive to Tom's house. Ten minutes of indecision later, he managed it, and five minutes after he arrived, he forced himself out of the car and up the path to Tom's from door.

Tom opened the door and took Charlie by the hand into the living room. A small, dark-haired woman dressed in jeans and an art college sweatshirt bounced out of one of the armchairs and kissed him on the cheek. She smelled of face powder and flowers. He saw that her fingers were covered in rings, and bracelets rattled on her wrists.

"You must be Charlie," she said, sounding like a member of the royal family. Charlie blushed, feeling the heat rise up his neck until his cheeks burned. She took his other hand and stepped back, smiling. "We have been *dying* to meet you, absolutely *dying*. And now here you are. Look at you. As lovely as Tom said." Charlie was incapable of speech. Hector Powell, the pathologist, sounded like this, and Charlie told himself firmly that Hector was a nice bloke, an ordinary bloke who just happened to have an expensive accent. Orianna would be the same. *But she's a poet.*

"Ori, don't gush," Tom said.

Orianna dropped Charlie's hand. "Sorry. I do get carried away. I am pleased to meet you though, and I am ridiculously excited to be involved in your case, even just a little."

"You're not involved," Tom said firmly.

"I am," Orianna said. "I'm a source. A secret source. Aren't I, Charlie?"

Charlie cleared his throat, but no words came out. He nodded instead, hoping the coolness on his face meant the redness had receded.

"Drinks. I've got a bottle open," Tom said. "Sit down, Ori. Charlie, come and give me a hand."

As Tom could easily carry three glasses and a bottle of wine, Charlie knew his help wasn't needed. He tried not to think about how he was embarrassing Tom in front of Orianna.

In the kitchen, Tom put his arms around Charlie, and kissed the top of his head. "I will kill that woman one day; I swear I will. Secret fucking source. It's a miracle the children have turned out as well as they have."

"But she's a poet, aren't poets allowed to be..." Charlie wasn't sure what words to use.

"She's a trial, that's what she is. Ori would try the patience of a saint."

Charlie looked up at Tom, who was grinning. He realised that Tom's exasperation was with Orianna, not him. "Sorry," he said, not altogether sure why. Tom kissed him again.

"She is a nut job, and she promised she wouldn't embarrass you, but she's OK under all the Swiss finishing school exterior."

"I love her work," Charlie said without thinking.

"Me too," Tom said, "but don't tell her, it'll go to her head." It took a moment before Charlie realised Tom hadn't reacted to Charlie's revelation that he had read Orianna's poetry. As if it wasn't a big deal. *Oh.*

Tom carried the glasses and an open bottle of Shiraz into the living room. There was a plate of snacks on the counter, so Charlie brought them. Orianna was curled up in the armchair, reading from the same book of her own poetry that Charlie had.

"I always worry this is sentimental," she said, waving the book.

"I didn't think so," Charlie said. "I liked it. I recognise those places, and that's how they are." He couldn't believe how bold he was being, but if Tom liked the poems... No, he told himself. He had liked them before he'd known Tom's opinion. Screw this overthinking. He was allowed to like things. Even poetry.

"Thank you," Orianna said. "They weren't meant to be sentimental, simply descriptions of places and how they made me feel." She put the book down on the arm of her chair. "Now then, our mysterious Neville Evans." Her face was shining with excitement. She reached onto the floor by her chair and produced a battered leather bag, and from its depths, a large notebook. "I wrote it all down."

"Is this classified information," Charlie asked. "By which I mean, are we going to jail if it gets out that we have it?" Charlie had been caught with classified information before—though he hadn't known it was classified at the time.

"I've no idea," Orianna said. "But Daddy asked for it as a favour. There won't be a paper trail. Plus, I will deny everything, and so will he."

"I did ask through official channels," Charlie said, "but all I got was *honourable discharge*."

Tom poured the wine and pushed glasses and the plate of snacks towards Charlie and Orianna. Then he lay back on the sofa with his own glass.

"An honourable discharge is what he got," Orianna said. "Special forces, as you suspected, served in Afghanistan, Iraq, Afghanistan again and even a bit of counter-terrorism stuff here, but that *is* classified. A long and distinguished career according to the records."

"I'm sensing a 'but'," Charlie said.

"Gambling. That's the 'but'. Gambling to the point of mental illness. So bad that his colleagues reported him, and complaints were received—note passive voice—that Neville borrowed money which wasn't repaid, and also sold things which may or may not have been his to sell. A brilliant soldier with a serious problem, Daddy says. It's usually drink, or drugs, but Neville gets his rocks off by betting with money he doesn't have."

It was Orianna's turn to lay back and sip her wine with a look of satisfaction on her face.

"I've had no complaints about him borrowing money," Tom said.

"But would they come to you?" Orianna asked. "That's why you have an HR department. They'd only tell you if he needed sacking. Maybe not even then. You're strategy, this is operations. Something like that, anyway."

"Strategy? Is that what it's called?" Tom put his wine glass on the table. "I'd call it firefighting. All I do is deal with people moaning about Vitruvious. Half of them want him back, the other half want him gone. No one is ever happy. We've got no money, and student recruitment is down." He rubbed his face. "Sorry. It's been a day. I've agreed to take a bunch of first year painting students to the seaside for a day's sketching next week, just to get out of the office and away from the computer."

Charlie could see the tiredness in Tom's face, and in the way his chin dipped towards his chest.

"Which seaside?" Charlie asked. "And why painting students?"

"Borth. Which is a good challenge. Windy and flat, and an absolute bugger to draw. The students are Vitruvious's. As long as he's still officially on the staff we can't replace him, so the remaining painting tutors are having to cover all his work and they're kicking off about it."

"Now I could fancy a day out in Borth," Orianna said. "Even if it is the middle of winter. It's a shame I have to work."

Tom laughed. "This will be work, trust me. Trying to get a bunch of not very talented painting students to draw sand dunes and marram grass while standing in a force nine gale trying not to be blown over. But they'll be better artists for it, and I will be less bad-tempered."

Orianna finished her wine and stood up. "I'm expected at home for dinner. Don't worry, Charlie, I shall give A to Z a glowing report, saying how wonderful you are."

Charlie decided to ask for clarification about A to Z later.

"Thank you for the information," he said.

"You're welcome. I'll see myself out." And she was gone, the front door slamming behind her.

Charlie moved from his armchair to the sofa and Tom. "Is work really that bad?" he asked.

"Worse. I shouldn't have taken the job, but now I have, I can't leave without making things a hundred times worse. The college needs time to recuperate, and it needs rid of that blood-sucking vampire, Vitruvious."

Charlie instantly felt responsible. He'd been supposed to persuade Kaylan to turn Vitruvious in and he'd failed. But this wasn't about him.

"What can I do, apart from murder Vitruvious?"

"Nothing," Tom sighed, "so you may as well give me a kiss."

Charlie did, and then another one. A few moments later, Tom had kicked his shoes off and wriggled down to lie on the sofa, pulling Charlie on top of him. Charlie felt his skin begin to buzz with the need to feel closer to Tom. His hands tingled with the desire to touch and be touched. He pushed himself up until he could unbutton Tom's shirt and then he leaned forward to trace the lines of Tom's tattoos with the tip of his tongue. He stopped to suck each of Tom's nipples in turn, and then resumed tracing the patterns, over Tom's shoulder where the patterns ended. Tom's shoulder seemed eminently biteable, so Charlie ran his tongue over the indentation above the collarbone and then bit the fleshy part of Tom's shoulder. He tasted delicious. *And I can think of something else that would be delicious ...* Charlie shifted his body to get access to Tom's zip, wanting to feel Tom's dick in his hand, to give Tom pleasure. Because Tom was ... everything. Tom saw the best in Charlie, never judged, always expected Charlie to succeed. That Tom was gorgeous was simply an added bonus.

But Tom turned away.

"Let me sit up a minute and swig a bit of that wine. Want to make some dinner?"

"Sure," Charlie said, wondering what had gone wrong. He told himself not to overthink it. Tom was just tired and hungry.

Not everyone was sex mad. He'd misread the signals that's all. But he felt the lump of dread in his chest expanding until it was squeezing his ribs. Nonetheless he got up and helped make pasta and even managed to eat some of it.

When they'd eaten. Charlie suggested he might go back to Dilys's—his nominal home. He suggested it most nights, but Tom usually insisted he stay. Not tonight.

"Sorry, Charlie," he said. "It's crap, but I must do some work. You may as well go home and get some sleep." It wasn't as if he hadn't known this was coming, so he smiled and said he would. Tom kissed him goodnight. Charlie held onto the kiss as he walked through the town. Tom just needed to get some work done. It would be OK. But his heart still ached.

BACK IN HIS ROOM, he called Patsy about her visit to The Yew Tree, rather than sit on his own feeling miserable. "No sign of the guy," Patsy said. "I had a drink, chatted to a few people at the bar. Stayed about half an hour. I hung around outside until almost closing, but he never showed."

"Hung around?"

"Car across the road. No one could see me, don't worry."

Charlie hadn't been worried and said so. "I didn't know you had a car, though."

"I borrowed my friend's car. It's a bit of an old banger, but it's dark. Did the job."

"Was there any curiosity about why you were looking for Leader?" Charlie asked.

Pasty shook her head. "I wasn't the only one asking for him," she said. "The barman seemed surprised that he wasn't in. I got the impression he uses the pub as his place of business."

"We should go and visit him at home then," Charlie said.

There had been an address in the files, and it was a local one. Worth a trip.

"Do you want me to go?" Patsy asked.

"Come in civvies tomorrow, then go to his address just before lunch. You should catch him getting ready to go to go to work. If buying and selling stolen goods can be considered as work. Take a pepper spray. He's got no history of violence, but just in case."

15

BOSWORTH FIELD: WEDNESDAY

N otes of informal meeting between Tom Pennant, Principal and College Department Heads (Ann Hathersage, note taker)

THE PRINCIPAL EXPLAINED that the college faced substantial losses due to criminal fraud. Staff asked whether college management had been sufficiently vigilant so that the fraud could have been prevented. The principal pointed out that he had been handed this mess on taking up his post, but that it would have been reasonable for previous senior management to have noticed — however he was also clear that this was the subject of a police and US FBI investigation, and that if the fraud had been easy to spot, someone else would have spotted it before he did.

The meeting became acrimonious.

A time was agreed for a reconvened meeting at which options would be discussed.

·   ·   ·

"I NEED A DRINK," Tom told his secretary.

He told himself: I need to talk to Charlie and say sorry about kicking him out last night. I need to get over myself. The mess is here and there is fuck all I can do except deal with it. But I still need a drink.

THE SECOND CALL about a dead body at the Castle Hotel came at the same early hour as the first. As before, it woke Charlie from sleep, though he was alone in his bed at Dilys's, and as before it was Mags on the phone, it still being her week on phone duty. But this time, she knew exactly who the victim was and the cause of death didn't seem in doubt.

"It's the waiter, Landon Emery, he's lying in a pool of blood and there's a knife on the ground next to him," Mags said, "I've called Eddy and Patsy and they're bringing the tent and I think it's worth sealing the whole area off for Scenes of Crime people. They called me from Emergency Services and please can my turn be over? Because I don't want to see any more dead young men." Charlie heard the despair in her voice.

"I'll call the boss and the pathologist," Charlie said. He sat on the side of the bed and rubbed the sleep out of his eyes.

Twenty minutes later he climbed into a white paper suit and shoe covers and walked to the newly erected tent. Mags was waiting for him, looking decidedly green. Eddy and Patsy were stringing blue and white tape in a big circle around the area.

"I've called the boss, and she's on her way," Charlie said. "So is Hector Powell. I'll just look in from here, and then we'd better start talking to people. Are you OK?" He put his hand out to Mags who had swayed and then stepped forward to keep her balance. "Come and sit down."

She nodded, but gingerly. Charlie took her arm and led her to the patrol car. "Just lean on it for a second and I'll open the door." He helped her into the passenger seat.

"Sorry," she said, "I feel a bit pale and interesting. It's the shock. I was convinced he'd done it. Killed Lewis Evans I mean. It was just too convenient him finding the body like that. I admit he had no motive, but he had the best opportunity, and he'd every chance to get a knife from the kitchen and then slip it straight into the dishwasher when he went back in."

Charlie disentangled her words and rearranged them to make sense.

THE WAITER, Landon Emery, was dead.

The waiter, who had the means and opportunity to kill Lewis Evans, was dead.

Dead in the same place that Lewis Evans had died, killed in the same way.

"DO YOU NEED TO GO HOME?" Charlie asked Mags, concerned about her, but hoping she'd say no and make a miraculous recovery.

"I've got a flask of mint tea," she said. "Leave me here to drink a cup and think happy thoughts, and I'll be fine."

"Sure?"

Mags smiled. "I'm sure."

"You'd better be. I don't want Mr Mags on my case."

BY CHARLIE'S CALCULATIONS, they had around forty minutes before Ravensbourne, Scenes of Crime and Hector Powell arrived. Charlie told Mags to stay in the car and stop anyone crossing their tape, while he, Eddy and Patsy started asking questions. Once again, they had arrived slap bang in the middle of the breakfast service, and once again, Charlie didn't care. The waiter had been older than Lewis Evans, but he was still a young man with his life in front of him, and he'd been robbed of it.

This has to be where it ends.

Charlie decided to do the hardest thing first and talk to Bosworth. No doubt the man would go red and deny everything, but he was the manager. Charlie sent Patsy and Eddy to get everyone's names and contact details, plus details of their movements from the moment they woke up until now. He told them to start in the kitchen and take no nonsense.

"If a few people get a cold breakfast, I don't care. This comes first. When you've done the kitchen, start on the dining room." Charlie felt the anger in his set jaw, and tight shoulders, and he saw the same anger on the faces of his colleagues.

"This is getting out of hand," Eddy said, for once not making any attempt to lighten the mood. "Come on, Pats."

BOSWORTH WAS IN HIS OFFICE, looking as if he was about to throw up: face pale and slightly sweaty, throat working as he swallowed repeatedly.

"We're in the middle of a corporate event. I don't have time for this. It's nothing to do with the hotel," he said as Charlie sat down in front of the desk.

"No? So how do you explain the death of a second person in your car park?"

"I can't. How could I? I have no idea."

"Try harder," Charlie said. "That is one of your staff members lying dead out there. If I have to close this hotel down to find out what happened, you better believe that I'll do it. Corporate event or no corporate event. Let's start with where you were from getting out of bed until half an hour ago." Charlie got his phone out, set it very obviously to record, and put it in front of Bosworth on the desk. "Start talking anytime," he said.

Bosworth was as vague and unhelpful as he had been when asked to account for his movements when Lewis Evans was killed. There were a couple of checkable encounters: one with the breakfast chef, one with a waitress, but for the rest of the time, he claimed either not to remember, or said he was alone.

Charlie changed tack. "Tell me about the man who has been killed," he said. They needed to stop thinking of the victim as "the waiter" and instead start thinking of him as a human being, whose life might hold clues to his death. Bosworth relaxed, though only a little. He ran his fingers around the inside of his collar as if it was making him sweat.

"His name is, sorry, was, Landon Emery. But you know that. He's been here for almost a year, saving money to go travelling now lockdown is over. He told me he applied because he can live in—not many places do that. It works for us, because he's here if we need someone to cover a shift. I think he came from Manchester. I've got his parents' address on file." Bosworth ran his fingers round his neck again. He'd need a clean shirt before much longer. "Oh, God, someone will have to tell his parents..."

"The police will deal with that, Mr Bosworth. We will need to search his room. Perhaps you'd like to take me there now?"

Bosworth's eyes registered shock, and he went, if it were possible, even paler.

"Mr Bosworth?"

"Search his room. Yes." Charlie wondered why Bosworth's reaction to this death was shock, when the reaction to Lewis's death had been fury. Sure, he had known Landon Emery for much longer, but they hadn't been friends. Nothing about Bosworth suggested that he would be friends with any of his employees, especially not one as lowly as a waiter. But

Bosworth stood up and opened a key cabinet in the wall behind him, snagged a key and told Charlie to "Come on, then."

The route to the staff accommodation involved traversing the kitchen to an inconspicuous staircase covered in aged blue vinyl. Above the kitchen a corridor had several closed doors and an open one, through which Charlie could see pipes and blue and white tiles. Bathroom, he guessed. The staircase continued upwards.

"Staff rooms. Manager's flat upstairs." Bosworth waved his hand vaguely. He led Charlie to the second door on the right, immediately opposite the bathroom, and unlocked it.

Charlie hadn't known what to expect, possibly something austere like a servant's room from the eighteenth century: a wooden floor with a rag rug, an iron bed with a single mattress, and a small closet. The room itself could easily have fulfilled that fantasy, but the furnishings were uncompromisingly modern. There was a double divan bed, made up with white sheets and duvet. A fitted wardrobe had been built against one end of the room, and there was a desk with a big TV and an easy chair. Instead of the wooden floor, there was a grey carpet. In other words, it looked like an anonymous hotel room. The impression was strengthened by the room's tidiness. There was a tablet computer on the desk, and a pair of trainers next to the bed. Jeans and a sweater had been folded on the back of the easy chair. But apart from that, there was little sign that the room was inhabited.

"Please stay by the door, Mr Bosworth," Charlie said. He put a pair of disposable gloves on and stepped in. He would have the room properly searched by Scenes of Crime, but he feared there would be nothing to find.

The wardrobe contained a middle-sized wheelie suitcase which was being used as a laundry hamper, plus a rail of ironed shirts and black trousers — presumably for work — and generous shelves with jeans, T-shirts, sweaters, hoodies. Some drawers held underwear and socks. The bedside table held condoms, lube, paracetamol, car keys, a passport, various letters, opened and put back in their envelopes and a pile of loose change. Charlie picked up the letters. Bank statements.

He opened the top one. Landon Emery had an extremely healthy bank account. Either he was very good at saving almost everything he earned, or he had another source of income. Given the goings-on in the hotel and the town, Charlie thought it could be either. He put the pile of envelopes aside to take with him.

"Are you going to be much longer?" Bosworth asked from the doorway. Charlie didn't know whether to be pleased or annoyed that the man's face had begun to return to its usual red colour, and his voice reverted to irritation.

"I'm about done, but colleagues from Scenes of Crime will be here soon to do a more thorough search." Charlie picked the car keys out of the bedside cabinet drawer. "Do you know where Landon's car is?"

Bosworth went white again.

"He hasn't got a car."

CHARLIE'S PHONE buzzed with a text from Mags to say that Ravensbourne, Scenes of Crime and Hector Powell had arrived.

"I need to lock this door," he told Bosworth. "And I need to keep the key. Are there any other keys?"

Bosworth shook his head. "Emery had one. This is the spare." He held it out to Charlie who locked the door and pocketed the key. The keys he'd found in the waiter's bedside table went into an evidence bag. He thought Bosworth looked defeated, as if all his dreams had crumbled around him. Perhaps they had. Two murders in a single week were not going to do much for the hotel's future bookings, and it was happening on Bosworth's watch.

"My colleagues are here, Mr Bosworth," Charlie said.

"Right." Bosworth looked round as if he wasn't sure what to do next. Then he led the way back down the stairs and through the kitchen. "I'll be in my office," he said. Charlie almost felt sorry for him. Almost.

16

IN LESS THAN A WEEK: WEDNESDAY

N otes of (reconvened) informal meeting between Tom Pennant, Principal, and College Department Heads (Ann Hathersage, note taker).

THE PRINCIPAL INTRODUCED *a series of options previously discussed with the Chair of the Governors. He also explained that the Chair had met with representatives of the funding bodies, but that no money would be available unless the college agreed to a merger. Department Heads described this as blackmail. The principal said he would resign first. It was pointed out that the principal might be able to afford to resign, but that others could not. Department Heads asked whether the principal was proposing compulsory redundancies. The principal said that nothing was currently proposed. He had simply introduced options and would be keen to hear others. A pay cut was suggested for the Principal, Board of Governors and senior management. The principal agreed to a personal pay cut, and pointed out that everyone in the room was senior management, and that the Board of Governors were volunteers.*

The meeting became acrimonious.

Department Heads agreed to consider the presented options and contact the principal by email with their responses.

DCI Freya Ravensbourne was back to her usual dishevelled self: hair un-brushed, jacket leaking its padding, the smell of cigarette smoke competing with mint chewing gum. Charlie wondered at her tidier appearance on Sunday morning. Could she have been going to church? Or like him, planning to go out for lunch, until she was dragged away by murder? He found her by the entrance to the white tent they'd erected to cover the body. Hector Powell was crouched down beside the dead man.

"Boss," Charlie said.

"Two in less than a week, Charlie? What's going on?"

"I'm sorry, boss," he said, and was rewarded with one of Ravensbourne's less than gentle pats on his arm. The bruises from the last time had hardly faded. Or were those the bruises from Tom fucking him over the table? Not a thought he was going to pursue.

"No one's blaming you," Ravensbourne said. "Not yet anyway." She gave a slightly croaky laugh. "Seriously, what's going on?"

"Seriously? I think someone has been stealing credit cards, phones, jewellery and car keys, and selling them on. The keys for the most expensive cars—the Mercs and the Range Rovers and so on—are then used to steal the cars. Lewis Evans might have been the thief, but we don't have any hard evidence for that. Or, it may have been someone else—maybe even this guy." He pointed at the body in the tent and produced the evidence bag with the keys he'd found in Landon Emery's room. "These were in his room, and Bosworth, the manager, says Emery didn't have a car. There are car keys turning up everywhere." Charlie paused to organise his thoughts. "The obvious supposition is that Landon Emery saw something on the morning of Lewis Evans's death, and that something got him killed. That's the first thing I want to find out about. Did he tell anyone else that he'd seen something?"

"Or," Ravensbourne suggested, "someone *thought* he'd seen something."

Charlie nodded. "Known unknowns, and unknown unknowns, that's how this feels, boss."

"I got your notes from the interviews with Will Jenner and Jack Protheroe. What's your take? Have they got anything to do with this?"

"Yes, and no. They were bullying Lewis Evans. Was he stealing to pay them off? Or were they the thieves, and the bullying was what they did for extra fun? What I can't do is connect Will, Jack or Lewis to the Castle Hotel. It can't be a coincidence that the two bodies were found here, but I'm damned if I can see why. And then I keep finding random car keys."

"Then follow your car key trail," Ravensbourne said. "But Kaylan Sully wants to see you again, and if there's any possibility he's going to crack, you need to see him, too. As soon as you can. The prison is expecting you today." And wasn't that the boss he knew? *Hey Charlie, run the enquiry your way, but not until you've done something horrible for me.*

"Emery's family are in Manchester, boss. I could go and see them on the way back from Liverpool Prison." It wasn't on the way back, or anywhere near Liverpool Prison, but at least it would keep him working on Lewis Evans and Landon Emery, instead of wasting all his time with Kaylan Sully, who simply wanted a break from his boredom. He saw Ravensbourne lift her hand to give him another encouraging pat on the arm and managed to side-step before the blow landed.

"I'll tell Manchester you'll be on their turf. If you left now, you could go straight to Emery's family and break the news."

Charlie absolutely should have seen that one coming.

"Can I hear what Dr Powell has to say first?" he asked.

There was some rustling and a quiet grunt from inside the tent. "Dr Powell has nothing unexpected to say," Hector said. "Just that the older he gets, the harder it is to crouch on the floor and then get up without groaning."

Ravensbourne stepped inside the tent as if to lift Hector herself, but finding him already on his feet, settled for a slap on the arm. "You're not that old," she said.

"Thanks, I think," Hector said. "You probably won't be surprised to hear that in my opinion, this bloke was stabbed, and not very long ago. I'll be taking that with me,"—he pointed to the knife, now safely in an evidence bag--"and I'll be very surprised if it didn't cause the fatal wound."

"Anything in the pockets?" Ravensbourne asked.

"Wallet with bank cards, in the name of Landon Emery. He's also got a name badge on his shirt." Hector handed them an evidence bag with the wallet. There wasn't any photo ID, but they didn't need it. Landon Emery had been interviewed only a few days before. And now Charlie had to go and break the news to his parents.

HE WAS ALMOST BACK to his car before he remembered Huw Leader, who was probably part of the car keys trail. He went in search of Patsy, who had turned up in uniform to the crime scene. He found her taking a statement from a member of the kitchen staff. When she finished, he drew her aside.

"I still want you to try to find Leader. Pack it in here in an hour and nip home to get changed," he told her. "Don't forget your pepper spray. If anyone asks, I'm going to see Emery's next of kin. Patsy's face showed her sympathy.

. . .

THE DRIVE to Landon Emery's home address had taken longer than Charlie hoped, thanks to hitting commuter traffic from the Expressway onwards. Was it unreasonable to hope that murderers would consider these things before stabbing people in the early morning? His sat nav led him to a nineteen- fifties semi-detached house in an unfamiliar Manchester suburb. Hundreds of thousands of these houses had been built in the years after the Second World War, and Charlie, who had been brought up in a town full of them, thought they were a blight on the landscape. He suspected when they were first built, they had been much better. It was the paving over of all the front gardens for parking, the addition of dormer windows in the lofts and oversized extensions... He told himself to stop being so negative. Those thoughts were the voice of his mother in his head: always ready to condemn and complain about things that she couldn't control and that only left her unhappy and dissatisfied. Who was he to obsess about where people chose to live? He had lived in one room in a Bed and Breakfast for *months* because he couldn't bring himself to do the adult thing and get a mortgage. Thoughts whirled because he didn't want to leave the warm car, knock on the white UPVC door and spoil someone's life. For the second time in a week. He forced himself out and up the neat brick path.

There was a car—yet another Golf—parked on the brick-paved front garden, and after the first knock, he'd heard a toilet flushing. On the second knock a dog barked, and he heard a man's voice telling it to shut up. He knocked again. A few moments later, the door opened to a man in a pair of pyjama trousers and a sweatshirt with the Manhattan skyline on the front.

Charlie already had his warrant card out, and he showed it to the man as he introduced himself.

"Are you Mr Henry Emery?" he asked.

"Harry," the man corrected. "What's this about, because I've just finished a twelve-hour shift."

"Could we go inside please, sir?" Charlie asked.

Harry Emery focussed, and Charlie could see the pieces begin fitting together in his mind. His jaw went slack, and all the sleepy anger faded. He held the door open and led Charlie into the kitchen at the back of the house, where he pulled a chair out from the table and flopped down into it.

"Tell me," he said. "How bad is it?"

"This morning we found the body of a young man we have identified as Landon Emery..." Before Charlie had reached the end of his sentence, tears began to roll down Harry Emery's cheeks. He pressed his fingers into his eyes, trying to control the sobs shaking his chest and shoulders.

"Sorry," Emery stuttered between sobs, his body rocking as if unable to contain his grief.

Charlie saw a roll of kitchen paper and wordlessly passed him several sheets, then moved to the kettle, filled it and began the ritual of making a hot sugary drink. The coffee stood next to the kettle, and the tea bags were at the back of the cupboard. Charlie chose coffee.

"Thanks," Harry Emery said. Then he blew his nose and mopped up the tears. He took a deep ragged breath, and Charlie saw the effort it took for the man not to break down again.

"I'm a paramedic," he said, which explained the twelve-hour night shift. "What happened?" Before Charlie could answer, Emery put his head in his hands and said, "I'll have to tell my wife...ex-wife... Fuck, fuck, fuck."

"We could--" Charlie began, but Emery shook his head.

"She's a bitch, but he's our son. I'll tell her."

"Can you tell me about Landon?" Charlie asked.

There was a long silence. Emery's eyes seemed to focus on something inside himself, and he shook his head slowly.

"I can't believe this. Why has a detective has come from Wales to break the news," Emery said. "And no 'suspicious circumstances' rubbish, please."

OK then, Charlie thought. This guy is going to have seen as many, probably more, terrible things as I have, and he's going to find out anyway.

"Your son was stabbed. He was found in the grounds of the Castle Hotel where he worked. Earlier this week, a young man was discovered in the same place, also stabbed. Landon found that victim. We're treating both deaths as murder."

The kitchen roll in Emery's hands was a soggy mess. He unrolled another few sheets and headed them over, getting a watery smile in return.

"He wanted to go travelling. Last time I spoke to him, he said he'd almost got the money together," Emery said, after he'd blown his nose again and got himself under control. "He said he could make a lot of money working at that hotel. I said he could stay here—God knows I don't need a house this size, and it wasn't as if I was going to charge him rent—but he said he'd finish up spending all his wages on tram fares. Complete bollocks, of course, but he wanted to get away from me and his mother. Can't blame him. We gave everyone a bloody awful time, and she's got another bloke that she met somewhere or other, and I had someone round and he came in, and... You don't need to know this stuff. We drove him away. That's the long and short of it." There was another burst of sobbing. Charlie pushed the mug of coffee towards Emery, who picked it up and took a gulp..

"There's biscuits in the tin next to the kettle," he said. Charlie collected them and put the kettle on again. Once their coffee cups were refilled, and a biscuit eaten (Charlie was glad of the calories), he asked Emery if Landon had any siblings.

"One was enough," Emery said. He took a sip from the hot coffee. "That sounds awful. Me and his mother, it was a mistake, but we decided to keep the baby and raise him together. We even got married." Emery rubbed his hands through his hair and pulled at his sweatshirt. "The whole thing was a mistake from start to finish." There was a pause. "The only thing you need to know is that between us, we alienated our only child, and now he's dead. Some fucking parents we turned out to be."

Charlie didn't know how much more of this he could bear.

17

BRIGHT PINK DRESS: WEDNESDAY

Tom should have been writing an email about the lower-than-usual level of applications for the coming academic year. He had plenty of ideas for things they could do to boost their numbers, but he had a bad case of the donwannas when it came to writing them down. His pencil moved across the page of his sketchbook as he drew the disapproving expression on the face of his black cat, Billy. Possibly Billy's breakfast had been delayed by a few moments or hadn't consisted of the right flavour of expensive cat food. Maybe Billy hadn't wanted to be left alone when Tom left for work. Whatever, Tom was usually in the wrong when it came to the cat. Billy liked Charlie, he liked the twins, he liked Ann and Orianna; it was just Tom he disapproved of. Or so it seemed.

The phone rang. With a sigh, Tom pushed the sketch book aside in favour of a pad of lined paper.

"Tom!" Bryson Carroll shouted into his ear. "About this vote of no confidence against you."

"What vote of no confidence?"

"It's only the staff trade unions. Nothing to worry about. The governors will support you whatever the result."

"The unions are proposing a vote of no confidence in me?"

"Some of them. Hotheads. At the whole college meeting, yes. I assumed you knew. Like I say, nothing to worry about. Just Vitruvious and his friends causing trouble."

AT THE END of the call, Tom looked down at his pad. It held a few notes about student numbers and a drawing of Billy, grown to Godzilla-like size, stalking a figure with Bryson Carroll's features. There was no sign of disapproval on the cat's face. Billy was having fun.

THE DRIVE from the Manchester suburb to Liverpool Prison would have been impossible without satellites and the disembodied voice coming from Charlie's phone. Streets of houses like Emery's ran into one another, leading to parades of shops and cafes, then more suburban streets, another "village centre" and then a bit of green space and a fifty mile an hour dual carriageway. Rinse and repeat. He had no idea where he was, or if there might be another route, but forty minutes after leaving Harry Emery's house, he saw the first sign for the prison. His stomach was painfully empty, and he decided he had to eat, regardless of his need to get Kaylan dealt with and get back to Llanfair. The decision to eat, and the entrance to the drive thru McDonald's were a happy coincidence. In the event, he had plenty of time and no need to have gobbled his food, because the prison officers kept him sitting around in an interview room for over half an hour before ushering Kaylan in. It gave Charlie time to wish he'd ordered more and taken his time eating. Next time he would bring a paperback to these visits. Phones weren't allowed into the prison, and all he had to do was think about Harry Emery and his grief.

"You wanted to see me?" Charlie said to Kaylan. "Getting bored?" Yes, it was unprofessional, but Kaylan seemed to know what buttons to press to get a reaction from Charlie. The young men, Rico, Lewis, and Landon had all been robbed of their lives. They clamoured for justice in Charlie's mind, along with their grieving parents. Kaylan hadn't killed Lewis or Landon, Charlie knew that, but Harry Emery's grief had affected his good sense.

"Fuck you too," Kaylan said. Which, Charlie thought, was a good summary of how he felt about Kaylan.

"Not going to tell the truth, then?" he asked, "I may as well go back to Maccies and get another burger." Charlie went to push his chair back to stand up, except it was bolted to the floor.

"I'm not going to keep you away from your urgent police business," Kaylan sneered. "I *do* have some information, but it's the last you're getting unless I get a guarantee of no deportation."

"Let's have it then." Charlie was tired, still hungry and sick to death of being jerked around by this, well, jerk.

"Photographs. Vitruvious took photographs."

Suddenly Charlie was awake and alert.

"What did he take photographs of?" he asked.

"You'll see when you find them," Kaylan answered. "I want a guarantee. No deportation. My fucking mother has been lobbying for me to *come home*, like I'll be in some dinky neighbourhood jail in Chicago, where she can come and bring me cake."

"I'll tell my boss," Charlie said. "That's all I can do." Because it really was. Decisions about whether to deport someone were made by politicians, not police officers. "What did he use to take the pictures?" he asked. "Camera? Phone?"

"Like I say, you'll see when you find them."

"That's it? You've dragged me all the way here to tell me

there are photographs? We knew there were photographs."
They didn't, though Tom had always maintained that there
would be, that Vitruvious would have taken them alongside his
drawings.

"You didn't know. You perked up like a dog seeing a rabbit
when I told you," Kaylan said.

"Thanks for the image," Charlie said. "Perhaps it would be
more accurate to say that I am not surprised there were
pictures. You're confirming what we expected. Now, why don't
you tell me how I can find the pictures?"

"You're the detective. Detect."

"Kaylan, this is part of detective work. If you know where
those photographs are you have a duty to tell me. Are they in
Vitruvious's studio?"

"Maybe. Haven't you searched it yet?"

"So, you don't actually know where they are?"

"Mr Policeman, I watched those pics being taken. I know
exactly where they are."

Which meant that Kaylan had watched his fellow student
die and done nothing. Charlie had told Rico's parents that their
son was dead and had listened to them cry from the other side
of the world. He was spending too long listening to grieving
parents.

No matter how Charlie worded his questions, Kaylan just
smirked and said nothing helpful. He remembered that Tom
had kicked Kaylan in the ribs when they had overpowered him
and had him in handcuffs. It was a completely non-Tom thing
to do. But he'd spent a long time tied to a chair, listening to
Kaylan talk. After half an hour in a locked room with Kaylan,
Charlie understood the urge.

The stink of the prison and the smirk on Kaylan's face were
suddenly too much. He wanted to get out, into the air outside
the walls, to talk to people who weren't psychopaths, and to
drive away from all these endless rows of houses and dual

carriageways with confusing signs to places he'd never heard of. He wanted to go home to Tom. He'd got the single drip of information Kaylan was prepared to impart, and there was nothing keeping him. He stood up and banged on the door to be let out. He had nothing to say to Kaylan, so he said nothing.

The 'fresh' air outside the prison was full of the revolting smell of a nearby brewery. Charlie felt sick instead of hungry, and even more desperate to get home. The sun had come out, and his car was hot and sticky. All around him were industrial buildings, most long abandoned. The walls of the prison were constructed of huge blocks of roughly cut stone, twenty feet high, topped with razor wire and inset with green-painted steel doors. He was on the outside, but the smell had come outside with him, and suddenly his nausea couldn't be ignored. He grabbed an evidence bag from the passenger seat and retched.

CHARLIE COULD HAVE MADE his phone calls from the prison car park, but the need to get away was too strong to do more than check he had his phone on charge and collect a bottle of water from a package on the back seat. He would stop, he told himself, as soon as he had crossed the border into Wales. It wasn't as if Ravensbourne knowing that Vitruvious had taken photographs couldn't wait an hour. He wanted to talk to his team, to find out what they had discovered about Landon and to share what he knew. But that could wait an hour, too. Landon was dead.

He could even wait an hour to talk to Tom, assuming Tom wanted to talk to him. They hadn't been in touch since Charlie left for Dilys's last night. Let him get back into the hills and the forests, away from these walls and stinks, and he would feel better, and then he'd make all his calls, including to Tom, like the grown-up he was pretending to be.

He didn't get the chance. Before he could turn on the ignition, his phone rang with a call from Ravensbourne. How did she know he was sitting outside the prison deciding to keep her waiting?

"Boss," he said. "There are photographs. That's all he said. Vitruvious took photographs. Wouldn't tell me any more, just that we'd know when we found them."

"That wasn't why I was calling, Charlie, though thanks for telling me. No, I was going to ask about Landon Emery's family."

Charlie didn't know whether to be pleased that Ravensbourne didn't have a drone following him about, or annoyed that he'd made himself sick getting information she didn't seem to want.

"Harry Emery confirmed what Bosworth told us," Charlie said. "Landon was supposed to be saving up to go travelling. According to Harry, Landon could have made as much money staying in Manchester as by moving to Wales."

"So why move?" Ravensbourne asked.

"Harry said he and his ex-wife made life uncomfortable for Landon. It sounds toxic to be honest. But he also said that Landon claimed to have almost all the money he needed– which is borne out by his bank statements."

"Hmmm. Another young man with unexplained resources? Or is it possible he could have saved the money?"

"I can't see him getting more than minimum wage, boss."

"Nor me," she answered. "And he would have had to pay for his accommodation and food. Worth a good look at those bank statements when you get back."

"Will do, boss."

Ravensbourne ended the call.

With a sigh of relief, Charlie started the car and headed home. For the first half of the journey, he could have been anywhere in the developed world. He slotted into the stream of traffic heading west: lorries making for his home town of Holyhead and the ferry to Ireland, tradesmen and delivery drivers going who knew where, and then anonymous people in cars, people like him. He'd chosen to listen to his thoughts rather than music or the radio and his thoughts said: *I'm doing all the right things and it's all going wrong.*

The words took on a rhythm of their own, echoing around his mind until they became a meaningless chant. Automatic pilot took the car back towards Llanfair until the sight of the hills clothed in trees brought him back to himself. There was a stretch of road with tall beech trees on each side, their trunks proud of the earthen field boundary. They were beautiful whatever the time of year, even now, almost leafless. He and Tom had talked about who had planted the trees, and as he drove, he wondered about it again. Then he was into the next set of bends and the drop down into Llanfair and the police station car park. He opened the car door and smelled the damp autumn air, chilly against his skin. The town clock chimed, though he forgot to count the chimes. There was nothing to do but keep going: ask questions, collate information, look for evidence. *Persistence*, Charlie told himself and went inside.

Patsy turned up a few minutes after Charlie, looking very un-Patsy-like in a bright pink jersey dress and even brighter pink tights. Her boots and jacket were black, but the jacket was almost covered by a huge pink scarf. She unwrapped it and folded it carefully. Then she took the jacket off and gave it a shake before hanging it over the back of a chair. The blonde hair she usually kept tied back hung loose and shiny down her back. Charlie realised he'd only ever seen Patsy in her uniform and had had no idea what her personal taste was. Now he knew, and he liked it a lot.

Mags said what they were all thinking. "Wow, you look great."

"Thank you," Patsy said and smiled. She looked at Eddy, as if daring him to speak.

Eddy nodded. "What Mags said." Patsy looked surprised, probably at the lack of an insult, Charlie thought, and smiled. She drew a pepper spray from her coat pocket and put it on the table in front of Charlie.

"I took it, like you said, but I didn't need it. Huw Leader wasn't at home. None of his neighbours have seen him for the last couple of days. I couldn't interview them, because I wasn't being official, so the 'last couple of days' is as close as I could get. No one knew where he'd gone, but they appeared used to people coming and knocking on the door to find him. One bloke suggested The Yew Tree. I said I'd already been there, and the bloke just shrugged."

Mags got a pen and wrote "Missing?" next to Huw Leader's name.

"There's more," Patsy said. "I had a look at the DVLA before I left. He's got a car, a Golf, like everyone else around here." At this Eddy growled under his breath, signalling the return of business as usual between him and Patsy. "I got the deets and went looking for it. No car. Not on his street or any of the neighbouring streets or in any of the car parks he might reasonably use."

Mags wrote "Car missing" on the whiteboard.

They all stared at it, as if hoping for inspiration.

"To sum up," Eddy said, "the one person who could tell us who was selling stolen credit cards has disappeared."

"Not necessarily," Mags said. "We can get pictures of Will and Lewis and ask in the Yew Tree. The bar staff should be able to recognise which one of them it was. Jack has dark hair and it's longer, so I think we can rule him out."

Charlie nodded. It was something they could do in the short term "We can also run Leader's number plates through the ANPR system, see if it tells us where he's gone." But Charlie had wanted more from Leader. He'd wanted to know if Leader had any ideas about the car keys, and he wanted to know who was buying the credit cards and who was stealing them—because stealing them and selling them didn't need to be done by the same person.

"Right," Charlie said, "Let's go through everything we've got and work out the next steps."

It took them two hours. Charlie was exhausted from driving, and from trying to work out what he could have asked Kaylan to get some actual answers as opposed to endless lies and evasion. His colleagues looked like he felt, so he sent them home. He sat in the empty police station for a bit longer, thinking about Lewis and Landon. That they had been killed by the same person seemed like a working hypothesis, but he struggled to get any further. If Landon had witnessed Lewis's murder—or had evidence of the murderer—why had he kept it to himself? The answer was that he hadn't felt in personal danger, which raised another series of possibilities. Had he confronted the murderer and died as a result? Was he in some way implicated? By the time Charlie had finished writing down his thoughts, his notes looked like spiders with inky feet had been fighting on the page. Frustrated, he rang Tom, hoping for an invitation for wine and cuddles. He'd even bring the wine. His call went straight to voicemail.

18

SILENT NIGHT: WEDNESDAY

The hammering at Tom's front door raised him from a miserable stupor. Billy the cat had stalked off to the kitchen, possibly because Tom's bad mood was infecting the atmosphere or possibly because no one had turned on the fire. Come to that, Tom hadn't turned any lights on either. Enough light seeped out of the kitchen for him to see the outlines of his living room, a room he had hoped would change if he could persuade Charlie to move in. Except that if the no-confidence vote went against him, no one would be moving in with anyone. *Fuck*. Who was banging? He dragged himself off the sofa and out to the hall.

Ann and Orianna pushed past him when he answered the door.

"Jesus, Tom, its freezing in here." Orianna shivered theatrically. By the living room door, Ann put the lights on, then moved over to the fireplace and turned on the fake wood-burner. Orianna produced a bottle of wine from her bag and put it on the coffee table.

"I'll get some glasses," she said, heading for the kitchen,

returning a moment later with three glasses in her hand and a purring Billy on her shoulder. "No Charlie?" she asked.

"No Charlie." That was the worst of it. Not the humiliation of having lost the confidence of his staff, people he had thought of as colleagues and friends, though that was bad enough. He couldn't stay in the town to see Vitruvious brought back, and a new principal doing the job he hadn't wanted, but hadn't wanted to fail at either. He'd have to leave Llanfair, which meant leaving Charlie. Printmaking wouldn't pay the bills. He needed a studio with a big etching press, which meant another art college, and with a vote of no confidence against him, he'd be lucky to get a job as a technician. He could finish up anywhere and he could hardly expect Charlie to up sticks and follow. It wasn't only that he loved Charlie, though he did, more than he'd thought he would ever love again, it was that Charlie would be forced to endure Tom's disgrace. Charlie was making a difference in the town, getting his life back together after his own humiliation and Tom was about to rip up all that progress. He groaned, shaking his head. His heart ached, a physical sensation inside his chest, and he felt the beginnings of a headache.

"Tom!" Orianna's voice cut into his despair. "What is *wrong* with you? I've been trying to give you a glass for the last ten minutes."

"Perhaps thirty seconds," Ann countered. "Listen, we've got an hour while A to Z are at the swimming club. We thought we'd come and have a private moan about the no confidence crap."

"It isn't crap though, is it? It's that murderer back in the college and me out of a job." Tom rubbed at his beard and pushed the hair away from his face. "I never wanted to be principal. I should have said no. It's not like I know what I'm doing. God knows where I'll finish up now." He picked up the glass of wine Orianna had pushed towards him and took a long swallow. He heard the buzzing of his phone. It was Charlie, and Tom wasn't ready for that conversation. He didn't think he'd ever be ready. It buzzed again with a text.

THINGS OK? Xxx

TOM PUT the phone face down on the table. In an unusual show of affection, Billy jumped silently from Orianna's lap onto Tom's own.

IT COMES *to something when even the cat feels sorry for me.*

∽

CHARLIE RANG Tom twice more and left a text. It was possible Tom was in a meeting. The previous night, Tom had complained about the pressure of work and until the third unanswered call, Charlie could go along with that. After all, he, Charlie, was the person who'd missed lunch with Tom's children because of a work call. It wasn't reasonable to suppose that coppers were the only people whose work took longer than a regular nine to five. The college had been struggling to cope with the events of the last year. Charlie could come up with a dozen good reasons for Tom not answering his calls, none of which stopped him worrying that the real reason was that Charlie had done or said something wrong.

He locked up the police station, leaving his car in the car park. His walk home to Dilys's took him along one of Llanfair's main streets, past the pub where he'd eaten curry with Tom on their first 'date'. Then he cut into a narrow street to bring himself out to the site of the cattle market, mostly used as a car

park. It was lined with small terraced houses on three sides,
looking cosy under the streetlamps. Clouds obscured the moon
and stars, promising rain to come. Charlie was halfway across
when his phone rang.

It wasn't Tom, it was his mother, but it was too late, he'd
already answered.

"Tom?" Charlie asked.

"Who's Tom? It's your mother, Charles. Why haven't you
been answering my calls?" And that was it, she was away.
Charlie found a bench and sank down on to it, holding the
phone away from his ear as his mother rehearsed a familiar set
of complaints: business was terrible, the only guests at their
bed and breakfast were lorry drivers who didn't want to pay the
going rate but still wanted an early call and a big breakfast, if
they made any money his father drank it, and above all, why
didn't Charlie give up that ridiculous job and come and
help her?

There had been a time when Charlie might have argued.
His mother had no need to remain married, or to run a business she hated.

"You could always get a divorce," he would say.

"Your father would never manage on his own, and anyway,
we can't afford it," would come the reply.

Counselling, was "not for people like us, and anyway we
can't afford it."

Given the frequency with which his mother pleaded
poverty, Charlie wondered how the business was supposed to
support him as well as his parents. But he had long since given
up trying to suggest that his mother could make different
choices. He sat on the bench waiting for her to wind down. The
seat was cold, and probably damp. The earlier autumnal smell
was enhanced by wisps of woodsmoke from the nearby houses.
He could see the flickering blue light of televisions between the
edges of drawn curtains and hear two people chatting in Welsh

on one of the doorsteps. A single car went past, bass thumping in a way that boded ill for the driver's hearing.

"Charles," he mother was saying, "when are you coming to visit and who's this Tom?"

"I'm in the middle of a case, Mum." And Tom is the man I'm in love with who doesn't want to speak to me.

"You're always in the middle of a case."

"That's the job," Charlie said, and then, "Sorry, Mum, I have to go." His legs felt stiff from sitting too long in the cold, but the blood had begun to circulate by the time he let himself into Dilys's. Dilys's had nothing in common with the bed and break-fast where he'd grown up, except that they both had rooms to rent. Where his parents' house was aggressively beige and plain, Dilys went in for colour and warmth. Unlike his mother Dilys was always ready with a smile, a cup of tea, and a morsel of town gossip. His mother would have charged extra for all of them.

Tonight, Dilys took one look at him and dragged him into the kitchen and into a chair at her own table.

"You look done in, lovely," she said. "I bet you've eaten nothing but cake all day."

Charlie smiled wearily. "I had a burger for lunch," he said.

"Then it's a good job I didn't finish the soup," she said and went over to the stove to turn the gas ring on under a large saucepan.

She sat with him while he ate, telling him funny stories about her other guests and then asking him about Tom.

"I haven't seen him for a couple of days," she said. "I keep waiting for you to come and tell me you're moving in with him. Not that I want you to go, mind."

"He hasn't been answering my calls, Dilys. I think I've blown it."

"As if," she said, grabbing his bowl and re-filling it. "He looks at you like you walk on water. I'm hearing that the college is in an uproar about something or other. That's what it'll be. It's one crisis after another over there. Don't worry."

But Charlie did worry. He watched the news with Dilys on the TV, trying not to let her see him checking and re-checking his phone for a message that never came. Then he went to bed and lay awake going over everything he had said and done that had made Tom shut him out.

19

DISINTEGRATION: THURSDAY

"There is a huge banner hanging over the side of the art college. It says Bring Back Proffessor Vitruvious." Ann's call caught Tom just as he was leaving home.

Tom wanted to pull his beard out. He considered getting in his car and driving to Blackpool, or Brighton or any other seaside resort beginning with 'B'. Bournemouth, perhaps, or Bridlington. Anything to get away. Then he remembered that he was going to Borth. All he had to do was get through a few more days, and he could get into a minibus with a bunch of students, some pencils and a sketch pad and he could have his wish. It would be furiously windy and would probably rain. But the chip shop would be open, and if the students were all half-wits, he would be able to talk to the minibus driver.

"Tom," Ann said again, "there is a huge banner hanging over the side of the college."

"It's an art college. Banners are art," he said. He suspected this one wasn't, because otherwise why would Ann be calling him at home?

"It says *Bring Back Proffessor Vitruvious, with two fs,*" Ann said. "If it was made by any of our students, their tutors need to talk to them about their spelling."

"Is my resignation an option?"

"No."

"Then we'd better get the banner down."

"The thing is, it's hanging from really high up on the roof. We're going to need scaffolding."

"Or we need whoever put it up there to take it down."

"Right."

Tom ended the call. Could he ring Charlie and ask for help? He owed Charlie an apology and an explanation, except it wasn't an explanation Charlie was going to like. But maybe the banner was a crime, and even if it wasn't, he needed to hear Charlie's voice.

"Charlie," Tom said. "Could you help me with something?"

Charlie's voice was hesitant. "Of course," he said.

Tom felt like a louse.

AFTER THE PHONE call from Tom, Charlie walked down to the art college with Patsy. The banner was as uncompromising as he'd expected, and as inaccessible.

They looked up at the college roof. The sky was blue between racing clouds, the sun shining on the banner like a floodlight. Most of the roofline was castellated, accessible from the inside, and according to Tom consisted of lead and cement. A fragile roof out of bounds for anything except repairs. At the front of the building there was a tower with a steep pitched slate roof. Tom had said there was a room within the tower, but it wasn't used for anything—in order to keep people off the flat roof. Again, it was accessible from the inside, but only with keys, and the keys were kept in a key cabinet in the Campus Services office. Even supposing that whoever had put the banner up had access to either the roof or the tower room, they would still have to climb the slate tiles to the ridge and balance there for long enough to hang the banner.

"It was dry last night, so for experienced climbers, it probably wasn't that difficult," Patsy said. "It's possible they did it for fun. Could be students, could be the parkour people."

"No art student made that banner," Charlie said. "They would have made a better job of it, but the parkour people haven't got any skin in the game. They don't know Vitruvious from Adam—as far as we know. Someone put them up to it, and we need to find out who. And why."

"Back to the shop, and start finding out about the *traceurs*?" Patsy asked. Charlie nodded. Once they had some basic information, they would be doing another set of interviews with teenagers.

A dark cloud rolled overhead, blocking out the sun. It began to rain, gently at first, and then in huge, heavy drops. As they watched, the letters on the banner began to run.

Patsy and Charlie ran for shelter under the awning of one of the shops. Together with several shoppers caught out by the rain, they watched as the words "Bring Back Proffessor Vitruvious" turned into long black streaks like non-waterproof mascara running down someone's cheeks. Charlie thought that now it did look like an artwork, one designed to demonstrate the progress of decay. There was a flurry of wind, and the banner tore in half; the two sections flapping wetly against the roof.

Charlie texted Tom.

CHARLIE: *Banner is disintegrating in the rain. Completely unreadable.*

. . .

He saw that his message had been received, and the three dots wobbled across the screen, then stopped. Charlie watched for a few more moments, but there was no answering message.

Charlie: *We will still follow it up. We've got a good idea who hung it, and we'll be talking to them.*

Again, he got the "message received" notification, but there was still no reply. Maybe Tom was in a meeting. Or maybe all Tom wanted was Charlie the police officer, not Charlie the boyfriend.

Charlie rang the school and arranged to meet Dr Ellis and the four parkour people.

He took Eddy with him in the hope that two detectives, plus the headteacher, should convince the kids that this was serious stuff. Not so much the danger of climbing onto the roof of the college, though that was bad enough. What concerned him was that they had been either persuaded or coerced to support Vitruvious, a man who had allowed someone not much older than them to die horribly. Which of course the parkour kids probably didn't know. If they did, all bets were off. But he didn't think they did.

Charlie was right. The kids knew nothing about Vitruvious. He was also right that they were apprehensive at the sight of the two detectives and their own headteacher.

"I'm reasonably sure that one or all of you climbed on to the roof of the college last night and hung a banner from the roof," Charlie began. "Obviously it was a potentially dangerous thing to do, and you could be charged with trespass. However ..." Charlie waved at the window, currently obscured by raindrops running down the outside. "The banner is in the process of being washed away, so it's not like the college is going to have to spend any money getting it removed. What we want to know is why. Not why you climbed onto the college roof, but why you hung a banner demanding the reinstatement of Mr Vitruvious."

The four looked at each other, at the floor, at their own hands, anywhere except at the two police officers and Dr Ellis.

"I don't know how DS Rees can make it any clearer," Dr Ellis said. "You aren't going to get into any official police trouble for your escapade. The decent thing to do would be to answer his question."

More shuffling, more evasive stares. No answers.

CHARLIE'S PHONE RANG. He recognised Tom's number.

"Excuse me just a moment," he said, and went outside. It wasn't Tom; it was Ann.

"Charlie," she said, "I'm worried about Tom. He's not himself, sitting staring into space and he's probably got a hangover. Maybe you could drop in if you have time? Update him on the banner business? Cheer him up?"

"I'm a bit busy," he said. "And to be honest, I'm not sure Tom wants to see me."

"Yes, he does," Ann said. "He's just too stubborn to admit it. Please, Charlie."

Charlie had no reason to drop everything and rush back to the college. Tom had been giving clear signals that Charlie wasn't wanted. But Ann was no fool, and she had sounded concerned. Most of all, Charlie wanted to see Tom so he could find out what he'd done wrong and whether he could put it right. It wasn't as if Eddy couldn't manage on his own.

He went back into the head teacher's office. "I need to nip off, I'm afraid. I'll leave you in DC Edwards's capable hands."

· · ·

CHARLIE WALKED BACK ROUND to the college through gentle rain, with no idea what to expect. What he found was a worried-looking Ann in her office, with Tom's office door closed.

"Go straight in," she said, brightly. Too brightly?

Tom was staring at his computer, or possibly in the direction of his computer.

"Tom?" Charlie asked.

"What? Why are you here? I'm busy."

This was so far from Tom's usual behaviour that Charlie barely stopped himself taking a step backwards.

"I came to see if you wanted to go out for lunch," he extemporised wildly. He didn't even know what time it was. Tom was wearing a black wool suit and beautifully pressed white shirt but was somehow managing to look less well-put-together than usual. His hair and beard looked untidy which they never did (except after sex, and better not go there).

"May as well," Tom said. "It's not like I'm needed here." He slammed the laptop closed and stood up. "Going out," he called and marched through the outer office without another word.

Charlie followed and Ann shrugged as he walked past her desk. He caught Tom up at the top of the stairs. "Wait for me."

He didn't. Tom headed for the car park, long legs at full stretch. He did wait in the car, and as Charlie caught up, leaned over to open the passenger door. He spun the car out of the car park, and onto the bridge and a narrow road into the mountains. He didn't say anything, and after a few attempts to make conversation elicited no response, Charlie shut up. About twenty minutes later they reached a car park with a view back towards Llanfair in one direction, and deep into the Carnedd mountains in the other. Tom pointed the car towards Llanfair. A couple of red kites circled lazily above their heads. The sky was grey, and the clouds low, but Charlie told himself that he could see the tip of the clock tower, and the college buildings beyond. Or rather, he knew he would have been able to see them on a better day. There was a battered picnic table for that better day, but they wouldn't be sitting at it today. Tom had thrown his head back against the head rest and his eyes were unfocused. If Charlie was forced to describe Tom's expression, he would have said *helpless,* but Tom didn't do helpless.

"What's happened?" he asked, afraid to reach for Tom's hand in case he was rebuffed.

Tom stared into space for another few heartbeats before he started to speak. He didn't look at Charlie.

"I know it's not your fault. I *know.* There's nothing anyone can do." There was a pause. "I thought between you and that woman, your boss, that you could get it sorted out. *Hell,* Charlie. I'm going to have to resign from the place I've worked all my life, and probably Ori and Ann will resign too out of stupid solidarity. I'll have to move. Well, I won't have to, but it'll break my heart to stay and see it ... And I don't want any of this and it's making me ill."

"You're not making any sense. Something's happened, but I don't know what. I thought..." *I thought we were boyfriends.*

Tom turned his face away to look out of the side window. The clouds were getting lower, beginning to swirl around the car, cutting the views down to glimpses of green between the tendrils of mist.

"Vitruvious has egged his supporters on to put a motion of no confidence in me to the whole staff meeting. If—when—it passes, I'll have to go. He's had all that money, and the college is going to have to repay it, even though we never had it in the first place. And he'll get his job back, and his reputation, and I'm not entirely sure how I'm going to get past it. I kept hoping that you would get Kaylan to come clean, and maybe you will, but it will be too late."

Charlie took a deep breath. "I rang you last night," he said, "and texted, but you didn't answer, and then this morning I'm trying to find out how that banner got there. I'm trying to help, Tom, but I'm not sure what to do."

"Sorry," Tom said, "I am literally drowning in meetings, and it's all about Vitruvious, or David Yarrow, stolen money, and staff up in arms about having to fill in for people we've suspended pending police investigations. Which look like continuing for the rest of my time on earth."

Charlie thought that Patsy would point out that it was impossible to literally drown in meetings, and the merest hint of a smile touched his lips. Of course, that was the moment Tom turned round.

"I'm glad one of us thinks it's funny," he snapped.

"Tom. It isn't funny at all. None of it is. I've got two murders to investigate, and Ravensbourne keeps sending me off to Liverpool to talk to Kaylan."

"At least she hasn't forgotten about Rico Pepperdine."

"None of us have forgotten about Rico Pepperdine. But I can only be in one place at once. I can't forget about Lewis Evans or Landon Emery either."

They stopped. Charlie felt the world was tilting. The tipping point hadn't been reached yet, but if they carried on, they'd get there, and he didn't want to.

"It's taking forever because there aren't enough of us to do everything. We haven't forgotten. I went round to the school to find who put the banner on the college this morning. Because that must be one of Vitruvious's minions. And I got some information from Kaylan yesterday. He admitted that Vitruvious took photographs."

Tom gripped the steering wheel as if desperate to be moving again. But his face was set and angry.

"*I told you there would be photographs.*" His voice was as tight as if he were speaking whilst being strangled.

"I know. But we don't know where they are, or if we'll have

the same problem we had with the drawings. All Vitruvious has to do is claim he didn't take them, and there's nothing we can do to prove it."

"Come for a walk," Tom said, and got out of the car.

Charlie had no great desire to blunder round in the mist, but he wanted to make things right with Tom. If he could. All his feelings of inadequacy were making acid in his stomach. He didn't know how to make the police investigation into Vitruvious and David Yarrow move any faster. He felt guilty for resenting the visits to Liverpool prison. How was he supposed to choose between loyalty to Tom, and loyalty to the families of Lewis and Landon?

When Charlie got out of the car, it was as cold and damp outside as he'd expected. He had a hat in his pocket, so he put it on and pulled it down over his ears before hurrying after Tom.

"Tell me what's going on at the college," he asked.

"I already did." Tom was striding down a forestry trail, no more than two parallel strips of flattened gravel. On either side, abandoned logs were decorated with lichens and fungi: some looking brown and slimy, others in bright colours, red and white, gleaming in murk. The grasses were wilting in the cold and the bracken had begun to turn brown. The air was damp on Charlie's skin, and everywhere smelled of earth.

"Slow down and tell me again. I didn't understand what you said about paying money back."

"We've had some letters," Tom said. "From the parents of some of the students who were admitted because they paid donations to the college. They want their money back. If we have to pay back everything that was stolen...we could have to make people redundant, or merge with a bigger university."

"I didn't know. You didn't tell me until now. I'll talk to Ravensbourne." It was all he could offer. But that wasn't going to make things right for Tom, who had never wanted to be college principal in the first place.

"Tom," he said and Tom turned. Charlie put his arms round the big man, and hugged as hard as he could through their thick coats. "I am doing what I can, I promise. And I will try harder with Kaylan." He felt some of the tension leave his lover's body, but only some.

"I love it here," Tom said. "I don't want to leave, but I can't stay if Vitruvious comes back. And it's looking like he's going to."

They walked back to the car in silence. They weren't back to normal and Charlie didn't know if they ever would be.

20

LEMON CUPCAKES: THURSDAY
FROM: NORTH WALES COURIER AND POST WEBSITE

L ocal Art College to Merge?
Is Llanfair College of Art about to lose its identity? One of the most prestigious art colleges in the UK could be forced to merge by its funding body. Merger would mean the college would be no more than an offshoot of another university. Redundancies are also threatened.

"We risk the loss of everything that makes the college special," said Inigo Vitruvious, Senior Painting Tutor. "Current college management don't seem to know what they're doing." Dr Vitruvious is currently suspended, pending a police enquiry. He denies any wrongdoing, and told this newspaper that he was the victim of a personal vendetta.

"I'm a human rights activist, as well as an artist and an educator. I'm afraid that doesn't sit well with the conservative college management. People like me are getting ready to fight to keep our college. We will do whatever it takes to stop our college being sold to the highest bidder."

Approached for comment, a spokesperson for the college said that there were no plans for the college to merge, or for redundancies.

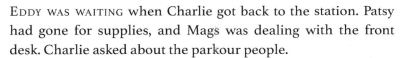

EDDY WAS WAITING when Charlie got back to the station. Patsy had gone for supplies, and Mags was dealing with the front desk. Charlie asked about the parkour people.

"They gave it up in the end," Eddy said. "One of them has a sister in the sixth form, and she's going out with a student from the college, and this student kept going on about how Vitruvious was this brilliant painting teacher, and he'd been sacked because he was too left-wing. Long story short, one of them came up with the banner idea, and the four musketeers used it as an excuse to climb onto the roof. They made the banner themselves out of some leftover wallpaper and poster paint. The art student was supposed to make it, but he was taking too long."

"No direct link to Vitruvious, then. Dammit,"

Charlie couldn't stop thinking about Tom's words. *I can't stay if he comes back.* What did that mean for them? Tom said he loved Charlie, but Charlie's job was here, in Llanfair. He hadn't wanted to ask Tom, because he was afraid of the answer.

He told Eddy what Kaylan had said about the photographs. "We need something to link him to Rico's death."

"Or the fraud. Surely that's easier?" Eddy asked.

"You'd think so, but Vitruvious just denies everything. Says all the arrangements were made by phone, he didn't make the phone calls, he never met any of the parents who paid the money, and anyway the money was paid to the college."

"Either Kaylan needs to tell the truth, or that Finance Director. It's not looking good for the send-Vitruvious-to-jail project."

"Think about it," Charlie said. "That man let one of his own students die of dehydration, and the fraud could end up with the college having to sack people, or even close." The closing bit might be an exaggeration, but Tom said a merger might as well be closure in that all the decisions would be made some-where other than Llanfair.

Charlie went down to the break room to make more coffee, then into his office and closed the door. There had to be some-thing they hadn't thought of.

A KNOCK BROUGHT his thoughts back into the present moment. Patsy put her head round the door. "Cupcakes, Sarge, and we have news." Then she disappeared. Despite Charlie having offered to take Tom out for lunch, neither of them had actually eaten anything, so a cupcake sounded good. He stood up wearily, limbs aching from the tension he'd been holding, feeling slightly sick from the endless cups of coffee.

Down in the break room, he asked for mint tea. Mags swore it settled her stomach, and Charlie's stomach needed all the help it could get. He chose a lemon muffin, the kind filled with lemon curd. It had a blob of buttercream on top. Patsy ate one too.

"Not lemony enough," she said. "It needs lemon zest, but they probably use some pretend flavouring, and not enough of it. I won't be buying these again."

"I thought it was OK," Charlie said, though if he was honest, he would have said the same about any form of calo-ries. He reached for a chocolate chip cookie, and took a drink of his mint tea, which was surprisingly pleasant.

Eddy cleared his throat and gave the whiteboard a poke with his foot.

"If we're ready to turn our minds from cake," he said. "We've found Huw Leader's car. But still no sign of the man himself."

"Where?" Charlie swallowed hastily, adding heartburn to his problems.

"Well, that's where it gets interesting. It's been left on the edge of a quarry over towards Dolgellau. A quarry known for the number of people who have drowned in it. To be fair, most of them were accidents rather than suicides, and we aren't talking about that many people, but whatever, it does have a bad reputation." Eddy unfolded a paper map, pointing to the quarry in question.

"Let me guess, keys and mobile left in the car?" Charlie asked.

"Yup."

"Do we get the divers down to look for a body? Or are we being led up the garden path? Who called it in?"

"Local copper. The car park is on a semi-regular patrol because of fly tippers and the like, and the car was spotted. The PC saw it was empty and called it in. It's been sent to Wrexham on the back of a low loader."

Charlie looked at the map. The quarry was on a seemingly empty mountainside. A track led in and out, and there were what looked like forestry trails close by. The nearest road was the kind marked as "other road or track" on the map's legend. He calculated that it would take well over an hour to drive there; not because it was very far, but because the roads would be appalling, especially in bad weather. Plus, you would need to know exactly where you were going.

"Easy enough to drive there in tandem with a mate, leave the car and get a lift to wherever," Eddy said. "You could even walk away if you had good boots, though it'd take a few hours to the nearest bus stop."

"I don't see Leader as a suicide risk. We've been asking a couple of questions in the pub, but that's got to be expected given his trade. He's been an informant in the past. He's not scared of us, I'd put money on it," Charlie said.

"He could have been pushed," Eddy said. Which was another alternative, and not one that filled Charlie with any pleasure.

"Right," he said. "I want those two lads in. Jack and Will. If Leader can't tell us who he was buying from, one of them is going to tell us who's been selling. And I'll ask the boss about whether we get the divers in, but my gut says he isn't in the quarry."

"The other thing we can do, Sarge," Eddy said, "is to look at the cameras going out of town. We know where he's going, but we don't know when he left. If we could get his car, we could see if anyone else from our whiteboard of shame left around the same time."

"You should be a detective," Charlie said. "Let's do it."

Charlie rang Ravensbourne to bring her up to date. "No divers," she agreed. "Or not yet anyway. I'll get one of the civilian staff to look at the ANPR cameras and get back to you."

"How long, boss?" Charlie asked, wondering what he'd have to pay for the answer he wanted. For once, there was no price.

"Straight away. It's not like there are many cameras in Llan-fair." Which was true.

By the time they had all finished their drinks and cakes, they had their answer. Leader had left Llanfair closely followed by Rupert Bosworth, or at least Rupert Bosworth's car.

BEFORE THEY COULD DECIDE what to do about Bosworth, Char-lie's phone buzzed with a text from Brian Telford, who was still visiting the Evanses in his role of Family Liaison Officer. It said simply: *Ring pls*. Charlie rang.

"Hi, Sarge," Brian said, in a chirpy voice. "Sure, let me just go outside." A moment later, he was back. "Thanks. I needed an excuse to get out for a minute. I thought you would want to know the Evanses are on their uppers. Gina Evans is crying her heart out because they haven't got enough money for a funeral for Lewis, and they haven't paid the rent for months. They've had the summons to court, and she's expecting to be evicted. Credit cards all maxed out. They spend all their income on food and heating, and I think they owe money for the heating."

"If I said I'd discovered Neville had a gambling problem, would that make sense?"

"Perfect sense. Gina says Neville keeps telling her he's sorted it all out and not to worry. No idea what he means by 'it'. He's gone back to work. Bastard. Sorry, Sarge. She also said that Lewis gave her money sometimes. Always in cash, twenty quid, or sometimes fifty, once a hundred. She didn't ask where it came from. She didn't want to know. I'll suggest the gambling thing and see what she says."

Charlie thanked Brian. It was confirmation of Orianna's revelation. Then he called Brian back. He could hear Gina's voice, so Brian was back in the house.

"Just a yes or no should do," he said. "This idea that our man had, quote, sorted it out, unquote, was that recent?"

"I don't like what you're asking, Sarge, but I'll find out."

The one-word text came through a couple of minutes later: *Recent.*

"THE ODDS just shortened on Neville Evans," Charlie said. "Except it isn't funny." He realised that Patsy and Mags didn't yet know about Neville's gambling problem, so he told them about Orianna, and what Brian had said.

Mags nodded vigorously. "I'm friends with one of their neighbours. I say friends; I've known her a long time and she's a dreadful gossip."

"One person's dreadful gossip is another person's rich source of information," Charlie said. "Tell all."

Mags smiled. "There were a lot of arguments according to my friend. *Terrible temper, he has, that Neville. Disappears off all night sometimes. And they've had the bailiffs round more than once.*

She is a dreadful gossip, but I think her information is accurate."

"Disappearing all night suggests gambling in person rather than betting shops, or online," Eddy said. "Casinos maybe."

"Are there any casinos near here?" Charlie asked.

Everyone looked blank. Patsy got out her phone. "Towards Manchester Airport, there's a place. The Ringway Hotel, Spa and Casino," she said. She fiddled some more. "Only take an hour at night without the traffic."

That was the route Charlie had taken to see Landon Emery's father, and he could attest to the level of traffic in the day.

"He wouldn't need to go that far," Mags said. "They do poker nights at the hotel. My husband went once. He likes poker, and he's good at it, but he said the other people weren't very interesting. One of them was Vitruvious, and there were a couple more from the college."

"Playing for money?" Charlie asked.

Mags nodded. "He lost a hundred and thirty quid. Which is probably the real reason he didn't like it much. Also, the whole college and Vitruvious thing started happening, and I found I was pregnant."

They all contemplated the loss of a hundred and thirty pounds in the context of a family about to be evicted, and without enough money to bury their child.

"But Evans is in the hole for thousands," Eddy said.

"Worth looking into, though," Charlie said. Because gambling was the only connection, however tenuous, they had between the hotel and Lewis Evans. "Bosworth was more upset by Landon Emery's death than I expected," Charlie went on. "Not angry, like he was about Lewis; upset, white, sweating, distracted."

"That sounds like scared more than upset," Mags said.

"Though given two people have been murdered in his car park, he's probably afraid of losing his job."

Patsy was closest to the whiteboard, so she added "Casino?" to both Bosworth's and Neville's names. Charlie was still disconcerted seeing her out of uniform, and even more disconcerted when the marker pen she produced was a sparkly purple. Still, it cheered the whiteboard up, and made them all smile. If he lost Tom, he'd be glad of his team. Even thinking the words made his stomach turn over and his heart ache. *Stop.*

"I think we should look at the hotel itself," he said. "Who owns it? Is it profitable? Are the poker nights legal? That kind of thing. Let's get ourselves organised."

"Hotel please," Mags said. "I can look online and staff the front desk at the same time." She put her hand up like a school girl asking a question. They all looked at her. "I meant to say that we've had no reports of burglaries this week. I don't know if that's significant. The people who did the statistics in Wrexham will probably know."

Patsy wrote "Burglary statistics" on the board in sparkly purple.

"I'll ask Ravensbourne to find out. Actually, could you do that, Mags?" Charlie said. "I'll also ask Neville about his gambling habit. Brian Telford is there now, and hopefully he can stick around. Eddy and Patsy can go and find out why Bosworth was following Huw Leader out of town, and where Leader is now."

"We'll ask about poker nights while we're there," Eddy said. "Because that doesn't sound ever so legal to me."

Patsy was playing with her phone again. "Stefan Crane, father of the bride, holds the license for the Ringway Hotel and Casino. I'm not sure if it's important."

"It's important if he's been involved in illegal poker games at the Castle Hotel," Charlie said.

"Did Mr Mags have to pay to go to the poker night?" Patsy asked. "Because there's the first red flag."

Mags shrugged. "Dunno. But I'll find out. Also, my husband is called Dylan." She left the room. Not flouncing exactly, but irritated. "Mr Mags" was so ingrained that learning to call him anything else was going to be a strain. But Charlie thought it was probably important.

"Sounds like Mr Mags is a bit of a dark horse," Eddy said.

"Dylan," said Patsy, "and lots of people like poker."

When Mags came back, Charlie asked if Dylan had anything to add about the poker night at the Castle Hotel. She nodded.

"He did pay to get in, a tenner he says, which included snacks and drinks. The other thing he says is that one of the gamblers was Stefan Crane, but he was just another punter, Dylan said I made him tell me all the names he could remember. Bosworth was the dealer."

21

IF "ANGRY MAN" WERE A COLOGNE: THURSDAY

F rom: Bryson Carroll
To: Tom Pennant

I'M ASSUMING you saw the article in the Courier and Post? We need to talk.

~

CHARLIE RANG Brian Telford and asked him to stick around. It was well past any reasonable going-home time, but that was the job. They met outside the house.

"Is Neville in?" Charlie asked.

"Just back from work," Brian said. "He's all full of some newspaper story that's going round the college about how it's going to close down, and that's sent Gina into meltdown. Even more meltdown."

Charlie decided not to ask about the newspaper article. He was there to find out about Neville and his gambling habit.

Lewis's mother was indeed having a major meltdown, clinging to her husband and sobbing into his shoulder. The two boys looked on, visibly upset. The older one patted his mother's back. "We all miss Lewis, Mum," he said.

Neville looked up and saw the two police officers. "What now?" he asked, arms round his wife. Charlie would have been touched if he hadn't known that Neville had brought the family to the edge of financial ruin.

It's an addiction. Don't be judgemental.

"I'm sorry," Charlie said, "but I need to talk to you, Mr Evans."

"Won't it wait?"

Charlie shook his head. "I wouldn't bother you if it wasn't important." In the background, Brian Telford was filling the kettle and buttering slices of fruit cake.

"I'll stay here, Sarge, if you want to take Mr Evans into the other room. Now, who's for tea and cake?"

The situation was surreal: the sobbing woman, the two boys looking upset and awkward and the middle-aged police officer bustling round making tea and cake.

"If we could..." Charlie said to Neville Evans. Neville helped his wife onto a chair, gave Brian a filthy look and followed Charlie into the living room and closed the door.

"What the actual fuck?" Evans said, stepping into Charlie's personal space. Charlie remembered telling Patsy to take a pepper spray with her to see Huw Leader. He should have taken his own advice. Evans seemed to have increased in size between the kitchen and the living room, and his face had a focussed expression Charlie didn't like. They were in a completely ordinary room: TV over the fireplace, three-piece leather suite, side tables by the seats, scatter cushions on the sofa, rug on the floor. A half empty crisp packet sat on one of the side tables, and there was a bulging school backpack by the door. So far, so mundane. But there was an air of menace in the room making the hairs stand up on the back of Charlie's neck. If "Angry Man" was a cologne, Evans was drenched in it.

"Gambling," Charlie said, keeping his voice level by a great effort of will. "The kind of gambling that is causing your wife a great deal of distress. I'd like to know where you go on your nights out, Mr Evans, and whether you owe money you can't pay."

Despite the air of barely repressed fury, the blow still took Charlie by surprise. His feet flew from under him, and he landed on one of the leather armchairs, shocked into immobility. There was no sign of a baseball bat in Evans's hand, but Charlie imagined that's how it would feel. Or like being hit on the chin by a professional boxer. A big one. It was going to hurt like a bitch in a minute.

Evans was breathing like a bull at a gate, sounding hoarse and threatening, though Charlie was helpless.

"Leave my family alone," Evans wheezed. He sounded to Charlie like a man at the end of his tether, a man with nothing to lose.

Somehow Charlie found the breath to answer, though his entire face was on fire. "You're under arrest for assault on a police officer," he said. It wasn't much of a threat, given that Charlie was sprawled out in one of the armchairs.

"Fuck that noise," Evans said and slammed out of the room, the door to the hallway banging against the wall as he went. The sound of the front door followed.

Brian Telford was first out of the kitchen.

"Sarge," he said, rushing over to see what had happened to Charlie.

"He just knocked me over. I'll be OK." Charlie said, though he wasn't sure about when. He struggled to sit upright and wiggled his jaw experimentally. It felt pulverised, but there were no ominous clicking sounds and when he ran his tongue around his teeth, they all appeared to be in the right place. He could feel the effects of the blow at the back of his neck as well as on his chin. Whiplash. "Dammit."

"Shall I go after him?" Brian Telford asked. Charlie shook his head and wished he hadn't.

"He's unstable and has a punch like Mike Tyson. It's going to take more than one of us to arrest him. He hasn't taken the car, so he won't get far."

The three remaining Evanses crowded into the room. Gina's faced was puffy and tear-stained while the boys simply looked terrified.

"Your husband assaulted me," Charlie said to Gina. "We'll be taking him into custody."

"Good," one of the boys said, and Gina collapsed into tears again.

"SORRY TO BOTHER YOU, SARGE," Mags said, as Charlie leaned his head back, very, very gently, against the back of his office chair. He'd taken the two paracetamol suggested by the NHS helpline after refusing to go to the nearest hospital. The blow to his chin had been hard, and he was going to have serious neck ache, but he hadn't lost consciousness. There was the small matter of not being able to move his head or touch his face, but it could easily have been worse. Paracetamol would have to do.

"I've sent Patsy for frozen peas," Mags went on, "but that's not why I'm bothering you. Will Jenner's dad is downstairs. He says Will has been threatened, and he wants to talk to you. And I've had a message from DCI Ravensbourne to say she's on her way."

Charlie began to get up and thought better of it. "Bring him up here," he said. "He doesn't strike me as the kind to kick off."

"I bet you thought that about Neville Evans, too" Mags said.

"No, I knew he was a nasty bastard. I just thought he had more sense."

. . .

JENNER WAS STILL DRESSED for work, in his jacket and fleece with the college logo, navy trousers and black boots. His hair was buzzed short, like his son's, though his had the odd streak of white, and his skin was the skin of someone who spent a lot of time outside. He looked muscular, fit, healthy and worried to death. The sight of Charlie, obviously in pain simply added to his worried expression.

"I was assaulted, Mr Jenner, by someone connected to this case," Charlie said. "One of my colleagues is going to bring me an ice pack, but it's not as bad as it looks." It was worse, but Jenner didn't need to know that. "What can I do for you?"

"My boy Will," Jenner began. "I think he's being threatened. I don't know, because he won't say." Jenner stopped and blushed. "I'm not proud of myself, but I listened at his door. Ever since you found all that stuff, he's been foul. Snaps at me and his mother for nothing, won't eat with us, or watch telly. He's supposed to be back at school next week, but he says he's not going. It's like we got him in trouble. God only knows, I'd get him out of whatever mess he's in, if he'd tell me what it was." There was another long pause. "I work at the college, and people talk." Another pause, another blush. "Tom Pennant, the new boss, he's a decent bloke. He talks to people like me, always has, as if we're normal people. Some of the senior staff treat us like we're servants, do this, do that, won't look you in the face. Anyway, the gossip is that you and Tom... So I thought... perhaps you were a good bloke too, and I could ask for your help with Will."

The last words came out in a rush, tumbling from Jenner's lips after the doldrums of trying to talk about Tom having a boyfriend. If Tom still wanted a boyfriend.

"If your son is being threatened, Mr Jenner, then that's wrong, whatever else he may have done. Threats are police business. I'm guessing you overheard a threat when you were listening?"

Jenner nodded. "Well not exactly, but it sounded like it."

Charlie adopted his most patient expression. "Tell me exactly what you heard," he said.

"Will was on his phone, shouting, well, talking loud, like, but angry like he was shouting if you see what I mean. He was saying things like 'I'm not going to tell anyone,' and 'I haven't told anyone.' I could hear another voice but not the words. Then Will said that this other person didn't need to threaten him, and that he'd get his money. He—Will—said people were watching him. Then he said to stop ringing him."

"That does sound like Will is in trouble," Charlie said, aiming to sound sympathetic. Charlie knew perfectly well that Will was in trouble, but it sounded like he was in trouble with more than just the police.

"That's not all of it," Jenner said. "He made another call, to Jack Protheroe. Piece of shit that lad, for all his dad's money. Will told Jack that 'he' had been on the phone." Jenner made air quotes around the word "he". "He said 'he' wanted to know if Will had told anyone, and that if he had, he should watch his back. Then he started on about money, and about how 'he wanted his money back' but that they couldn't sell anything because me and his mum were watching him all the time. Which we are. He went over it a couple of times and then put his music on, so that's all I heard. I told his mum, and she said I should come to you, because of, you know, Tom Pennant."

It was something else making Charlie want to shake Jack and Will until they rattled. They were in over their heads, in some kind of debt with a secret they couldn't tell. Jenner wasn't a stupid man. He must be wondering whether Lewis Evans had the same phone call and had been in the same kind of trouble.

"You've got no idea who this 'he' is?" Charlie asked. "Could you make a guess?"

Jenner shook his head. "We've racked our brains, me and his mum. The only one of his friends we know well is that Jack, and we don't like him. There are plenty of good kids in this town, but Jack isn't one of them."

"My boss is coming in later and I'll see what she thinks, but my suggestion is that you sit down with Will, tell him what you heard and ask him to tell us the truth. Boys his age get into trouble. We just need to stop it getting any worse." Charlie didn't need to spell out how things could get worse for Will and Jack. Jenner's face said he already knew.

"Once we know who this man is, we can stop the threats. Even if Will owes money, there are laws about threatening people. I don't know how well you get on with Mr and Mrs Protheroe, but maybe involve them too? And I've met Dr Ellis, the headteacher. I know he suspended Will and Jack, but I think he would help if he could."

Jenner didn't look any better than when he arrived, but Charlie couldn't do any more. Parenting advice was so far out of his skill set that he wouldn't be able to see it from space. Not only that, he didn't have much time for either Will or Jack, though he felt sorry for their parents, and it was true that lots of lads got into trouble, from inexperience rather than malice. He wished Jenner good luck and called Mags to show him out. Not something he'd usually do, but his head ached so much that he didn't want to stand up. He wondered if it was time for more paracetamol, and if Patsy really had gone to buy frozen peas.

The good news was that she had, and she brought them in as soon as Jenner left the office. The bad news was that she was followed by Ravensbourne.

Please don't pat me. I'm already bruised.

She sat down across the desk and scowled at him. "Can't have this, Charlie. You getting attacked. Not good for the investigation."

The smell of cigarette smoke clung to Ravensbourne's clothes, but it didn't stay there. It filled the air between them, adding to his nausea and his headache. It was well into the evening, he hadn't eaten properly all day, and he'd done exactly nothing to help Tom.

"I didn't get thumped on purpose," he said. The peas were cold against his skin, and just because they were doing him good, didn't mean it was a pleasant sensation. His stubble itched against the plastic but touching the skin was painful. "I am doing my best without enough people."

"That's why I'm here," she said, as if she hadn't noticed his irritation, and that made him even crosser.

"What are we doing to help the college?" Charlie asked. He meant Tom, not the college, but he wasn't going to say that. "I want to look for those photographs, and I want to be in on the interviews with David Yarrow about what happened to the money." Perhaps he was being unreasonable, given the objections he'd made to visiting Kaylan Sully, but he didn't care. Tom had helped the police uncover what had happened to Rico Pepperdine, and he, Charlie had been shot. And then everything had gone into slow motion. "Vitruvious is trying to get his job back, and if he does, he will basically have got away with murder and millions of pounds in fraud."

Ravensbourne slid her arms out of the sleeves of her torn jacket and leaned back against it.

"Have you finished?" she asked. She wriggled a hand into her trouser pocket for the packet of chewing gum she kept there and got a piece out to start chewing.

"For now," Charlie said. Being angry with Ravensbourne was like poking a bear and Charlie knew it. But he'd be spending another night on his own at Dilys's and he could feel Tom slipping further and further away. If he had to poke the bear to keep Tom, it was worth the risk.

"We're interviewing Yarrow tomorrow. You can come."

"Thank you."

"Now tell me about this Evans. If I like your answer, I won't tell Chief Superintendent Kent that you criticised his investigation."

The bag of frozen peas was thawing. Water dripped down Charlie's neck, wetting his shirt collar. He tried turning the bag over to get a cold bit next to his chin, but all that happened was it dripped from the other end. He put the bag down on his desk, finding an old cardboard file to absorb the moisture.

"Sorry, boss," he said. "Do you mind if I take a couple more paracetamol?"

There were the remains of a mug of coffee on the desk. Cold, but it would do. He got the paracetamol from his top drawer and pushed two white tablets through the plastic. They caught in his throat going down, a mixture of chalk and cold coffee. It was too early to take them, he knew that, but his headache wouldn't let him think, and thinking was important. Ravensbourne wanted an answer, and he knew she wasn't going to like it.

22

IN THE WIND: THURSDAY

F rom: Tom Pennant
      To: Bryson Carroll, Chair of Governors

IF THE NO confidence vote happens and goes against me, I'll resign then and there.

FROM: **Bryson Carroll, Chair of Governors**
      To: **Tom Pennant**

I AM WONDERING if we could avoid the worst of this by reinstating Vitruvious. Obviously keeping a close eye on him. Maybe an agreement that he doesn't go to the press. An NDA if that's possible.

FROM: **Tom Pennant**
      To: **Bryson Carroll, Chair of Governors**

. . .

Not to be dramatic, but if he comes back, I leave. You and the rest of the Governors must decide which of us you would rather have. Of course, it may be moot if the no confidence vote goes against me. I'm not prepared to discuss it any further.

~

"Neville Evans is in the wind, boss." Charlie said. "He's ex-SAS, he's getting desperate and he's scarily violent. He's dangerous. There's only four of us and a Family Liaison Officer. I couldn't risk going after him."

Ravensbourne wasn't happy, he could see that, but he thought she understood his problem. "What about keeping a watch on his house?" she said.

"Same issue. Not enough officers," Charlie replied.

Freya Ravensbourne had been a good and supportive boss. She might smell permanently of cigarettes, and she might give with one hand and take away with the other, but overall, Charlie liked her a lot. He wasn't seriously worried that she'd slag him off to Mal Kent. Kent had saved Charlie's bacon more than once, stopping him resigning over the Lanzarote affair and sending him to Llanfair. That Kent was taking an interest in the art college made Charlie feel fractionally better. He wanted to tell Tom, except Tom wasn't talking to him. *Don't think about Tom. Don't think about Vitruvious, think about Lewis Evans and Landon Emery.*

"What you're saying is that you have no idea where Neville Evans is right now?" Ravensbourne asked.

"No, sorry, boss. It stinks, but I don't know what else I could have done."

They talked round it a few more times and got no further.

Neville Evans could be hiding out at his soon-to-be-repossessed home. He could have taken to the hills around the town. He could be anywhere.

"Go home, Charlie," Ravensbourne said. "You're no use to anyone in this state. Get some sleep and don't take any more paracetamol." He argued for a bit, until he realised that everyone else had left except him, Ravensbourne and Ravensbourne's driver.

BY THE TIME Charlie got back to Dilys's, the house was in darkness. There were a couple of other people staying at the small Bed and Breakfast, so Charlie made his way upstairs quietly, using the torch on his phone rather than switch the lights on. He was hungry, and Dilys wouldn't mind if he raided the kitchen, but he was just too tired. The headache had receded a little, settling into a steady pain in his jaw and an ache in his neck from the whiplash. Dilys would have made his bed, tidied his few things and given the room a once over with duster and vacuum. The bathroom would be spotless and smelling of lemons. Charlie had been living in one room for months, but on nights like this, coming back to comfort and cleanliness was almost as good as coming back to Tom.

Except when he closed his bedroom door and switched the light on, there was a dark-haired, bearded man asleep in his bed. The figure stirred at the light. Charlie switched it off and felt his way to the bedside table to put a lamp on instead. Then he undressed as quickly as he could, trying not to whimper as he wriggled out of his shirt, got into bed and switched the lamp off.

Tom rolled onto his back, and Charlie snuggled into his shoulder. His neck and head hurt, but the tension flowed away and disappeared like water into dry sand. Tom's arms came round him and held him close, breathing just audible, their hearts beating together in the quiet room.

"I'm sorry," Tom said. "I needed to see you, and Dilys let me in."

"Don't be sorry. Just..." Charlie didn't have the words he needed, so he kissed Tom's skin, warm from the bed and soft from sleeping. He wriggled closer, feeling the muscles in Tom's thighs against his own, their chests together, one covered in thick hair, the other smooth. They were both naked, and Charlie was glad.

"I think I'm going to go mad," Tom said.

"Me too. So let's not think about it." He kissed Tom's lips, running his tongue between them, feeling Tom's beard against his bruises, and not caring how much it hurt. He reached up to grasp Tom's hair and pull him into the kiss, until he forgot about everything outside this room, this bed.

Charlie felt Tom's cock hard against his own thigh. He wanted to lick it, to play with Tom's balls and suck him until he begged to come, but he didn't think his injury was compatible with his desire. Next time. Because Tom's being here meant there might be a next time.

Tom's hand caressed Charlie's arse cheeks, and then Charlie felt a finger in the crease, just touching his hole. He sighed with pleasure and desire. He wanted to feel Tom inside him, to feel the weight of Tom's body covering his own.

"I'm injured," he said. "You'll have to be gentle with me."

Tom pulled away and Charlie imagined his look of alarm.

"Be gentle, I said. I didn't say don't fuck me, because I need you to fuck me."

"Where does it hurt?" Tom asked, his breath soft in Charlie's ear.

"Here," Charlie took Tom's hand and wrapped it around his own dick, loving the feeling of the big warm fingers. He thrust into Tom's hand and enjoyed the wave of pleasure. "head and neck are

"You can always fuck me," Tom said.

"I think that would be even more painful."

In reply, Tom rolled over and scrabbled around for the lube and condoms. Around them the house was quiet, and all Charlie could hear was his own sighs as Tom opened him up with his fingers, and his stifled cry as a finger touched his prostate accidentally-on-purpose. The pain in his neck had receded to the point of irritation when he tried to move.

"Tom," he whispered. "I'm ready. More than ready."

Tom fucked him with long, slow strokes. Charlie felt the final remains of the day's troubles fade to nothing. He existed in the moment, and only in the moment. In his body and only in his body. If this was mindfulness, he wanted more of it.

AFTER THEY'D CLEANED UP, quietly, not wanting to wake the rest of the household, Charlie lay on his back with his hand in Tom's. "Thank you for coming round tonight. It's been a shitty day on top of a shitty week, and it's been worse for you. I was worried..."

Tom rolled onto his side to face Charlie. There was just enough light for them to see each other. "I am going to leave the college if they take Vitruvious back, or if they have this no confidence vote and vote against me. But I'm not leaving *you*. I don't know what we'll do, but we'll think of something."

Something settled in Charlie's mind. He didn't see how they could stay together if Tom left the college and the town, but that Tom wanted him was enough for now.

"I came round to see you because I wanted to see you," Tom said. "But there was something I found out about David Yarrow that might help."

"Perfect timing," Charlie said, "I kind of persuaded Ravensbourne into including me in the interview with Yarrow tomorrow. And the good news is that Chief Superintendent Kent, who is a very big noise, is leading the investigation. I don't know if that means interviewing Yarrow, shouldn't think so, but it means the powers that be are taking the business seriously. It might seem slow, but it hasn't been forgotten. It was Kent who sent me here, to get away from all the attention after my fuck up in Spain. He's been good to me."

"People are good to you, Charlie, because you are a good man."

Charlie winced.

"You are."

"Come on, what did you have to tell me?" Charlie asked. Anything to change the subject.

"Something Ann told me, which I'm sure she expected me to tell you. Because she likes you too, just saying. Anyway, David Yarrow got divorced a few years ago. He and his wife had a lot of children, five, I think, and his wife had an affair. It was horrible, lots of gossip and backbiting. His wife looked after the kids full time, and there was never any question of them leaving the family home. Paying for the house and the kids took all David's salary, so he was essentially homeless and penniless. Ann says he was crashing in someone's spare room. I kind of knew a bit of this because I was on the academic board and a load of other committees with David and he just looked dreadful. But we aren't more than colleagues, so I never knew the details."

"But Ann did?"

"Ann knows everything." Tom said it as if there could be no argument, and perhaps there wasn't. If Ann was as well networked in the college as Mags and Dilys were in the town, then together they would make a formidable team.

"What did she want me to know?" Charlie asked.

"That about six months after he and his wife split up, he bought one of those new houses down on the Aberystwyth road. Only a small one, but apparently he made a big down payment and the mortgage is paid off. Do not ask me how Ann knows that, but I've never found her to make a mistake."

"Would I be right in supposing that these events took place at about the same time we think Vitruvious started his bogus donation scheme?"

"You would be right. I got Ann to help me check all the dates, and they align perfectly. Two painting tutors retired, we took on two new ones, the same painting tutors who told me that they were disappointed in the quality of the international students. That's when I think Vitruvious began his donations-for-places scam. Because before that, it was only possible for international students to get a place here if they were really talented. But the two newbies didn't know what to expect. And that was the same year that David Yarrow got divorced and bought a new house, despite apparently having no money."

Charlie squeezed Tom's hand. "It's circumstantial. He could have won the lottery, or inherited money, or just be very good at saving. He's the finance director after all."

"Could be. Except I do know they bought the big family house with an inheritance, or rather Ann says they did. Can't speak to the lottery or savings though."

"It's a coincidence, and coincidences ring alarm bells. If that money was paid to the college, someone had to move it out, and David was the best placed to do it." Charlie yawned, and that set Tom off yawning too.

"Go to sleep," Tom said, and kissed Charlie goodnight. They slept, wrapped around each other, as if all was right with the world.

23

PERFECT AUTUMN MORNING: FRIDAY

HMP Liverpool
Dear Professor Pennant
My name is Kaylan Sully. I expect you will remember me. I was until recently one of your students, but am now awaiting trial for, among other things, holding you and Inigo Vitruvious hostage, and shooting the policeman—Detective Rees—who came to help. I think the policeman is a friend of yours, maybe more.

I am writing to you to ask for your help. This might seem unreasonable, given what happened, but here's the thing. I don't want to be deported to the United States. I think you may have some influence with the people making those decisions. I would like to see the college thrive, and I might be able to help with that, by way of an apology for my actions. Should you wish to visit, please contact my solicitor.

Thank you for reading!
Kaylan Sully.

TOM REMEMBERED Kaylan making him tie Vitruvious to a chair. He'd threatened to hurt Vitruvious unless Tom had tied himself to another chair. Kaylan knew exactly what buttons to push in order to get what he wanted. He'd been dripping information out one tiny snippet at a time so that Charlie would visit. Now he wanted to try the same thing on Tom. Yes, Tom wanted the money, but Kaylan had no method of getting it back without access to the internet. *Not going to happen.* Tom crumpled the letter and threw it in the bin.

IT WAS the most perfect autumn morning. The leaves underfoot were crunchy instead of soggy. The sky was the hard bright blue of summer, but the chill in the air spoke of pumpkin soup, bonfires and the last grass-cutting of the year. Llanfair glowed in the sunshine, the coloured houses on Charlie's route to work blending harmoniously. Even the police station didn't look too bad from the outside.

Inside, it was as dark as ever. Charlie put all the lights on and filled the kettle. While it boiled, he stared at the whiteboard. He seemed to spend a lot of his life staring at the whiteboard, but if it meant Tom would be OK, he would stare at it forever. The interview with David Yarrow was in Wrexham after lunch, so there was time to stare at the whiteboard some more, and in an ideal world, cross some things off. He wanted to know how the search for Huw Leader was going, and whether Bosworth was prepared to tell them anything. Then there were Will and Jack, and the mysterious "he." The rest of the team would arrive soon, and they could get started. In the meantime, coffee, whiteboard and thoughts of Tom's hands on his body.

The thoughts were interrupted by a call from Will Jenner's dad, asking for a meeting round at the Protheroes' house. Charlie waited for the rest of the team to arrive and then he and Eddy went to see what Will and Jack had to say.

. . .

THERE WAS enough room for all of them in the Protheroes' living room, but it was a tight fit: Mrs Protheroe in skinny jeans and a baggy white sweater; Jack in similar clothes, but his jeans were ripped. Will and his parents. Will dressed like his friend; his parents in their work uniforms. The Jenners looked a lot more worried than their son, but even Will wasn't wearing his usual "whatever" face. With Charlie and Eddy, there were seven of them. Jack ungraciously brought two dining chairs in from the kitchen so the detectives could sit down. Eddy produced a notebook and a stolid expression, sitting outside the rough circle of bodies.

Charlie was not surprised that Jack's mother opened proceedings with her usual passive aggression.

"I suppose I should thank you for coming," she said. "Jack is finally going to tell the truth, though I don't expect he will make a habit of it."

Charlie smiled, as if she had said something pleasant, but he couldn't resist asking whether Jack's father would be joining them.

"Yeah, right," Jack said. "Like he cares."

The older Jenners looked unhappy. Possibly not surprised at the absence of Protheroe senior, and certainly not surprised by Jack's words. But still, unhappy.

"Perhaps we could get on," Will's dad said. "I talked to Will like you suggested last night, and then we both talked to Jack, and they've decided to tell you what's been happening."

"Thank you," Charlie said. He looked at Jack and Will in turn. Both avoided his eyes, but if they'd agreed to tell the truth, one of them needed to make a start. "Jack? Will?" The teenagers looked at each other.

"It was Mr Evans," Jack burst out. "Lewis's dad. Will's dad's boss. He was threatening to beat us up if we didn't pay the money back. He's fucking scary. But he hit a copper, so he's going down, right? So he can't get near us."

"Let's start from the beginning," Charlie said, wondering why Jack hadn't made the connection between Charlie's bruised face and Neville's victim. He thought Jack probably didn't notice much that didn't directly impinge on his own well-being, "What money do you have to pay back?"

"They've been gambling," Jack's mother said. "There was me thinking it was only drugs. God, they were so stupid. Lewis's dad caught them coming out of a betting shop in Rhyl. A *betting shop*. Pretending to be eighteen so they could play the machines."

"Mum, shut up," Jack said.

"It's true. That's what you said. He caught you in a betting shop and told you there was more fun to be had at a casino, and you fell for it because you're stupid, and you were probably stoned."

"Mum! Fucking shut up."

Charlie thought he knew how this ended—with Jack stomping out and the police not getting the information they needed.

"Let's all take a deep breath," he said. "Jack, is it true that you met Neville Evans near a betting shop in Rhyl?"

Jack nodded.

"And then what happened?" Charlie asked.

"He asked us if we liked to gamble, and I said 'sure.' He said casinos were more fun, and I said no one was going to let us in a casino. God, there are even age checks for online casinos." Charlie knew how ineffective such checks could be, but he nodded encouragingly anyway.

"So, he said his friend ran a casino just up the road, and he'd show us round, though we couldn't play, like, because of our age. It wasn't like he was a stranger or anything."

No, he was the father of the boy you've been excluded for bullying. Charlie said as much.

Both Will and Jack gave snorts of laughter.

"That was bullshit," Jack said. "We weren't like besties with Lewis, but the bullying was all for show. That dick Ellis fell for it. Lewis was a weirdo, but he was part of it."

"Part of what, Jack?" Charlie asked. He could see the Jenners looking sick. They knew what was coming. So did Jack's mother, but she had her usual furious expression.

"We went to the casino. It was totally cool, hidden upstairs above some shops, one of those old department stores, and this guy, Mr Evan's friend, the owner, like, he said of course we could have a bet, so we did."

"And you won?" Charlie knew the answer, because how else could the boys have been sucked into whatever the game was.

Jack nodded. "Yeah, mostly."

"You went back more than once, then."

More nods.

"And you spent your winnings on the things we found in your rooms?"

"What an idiot. Jesus wept, Jack," his mother said.

"Mrs Protheroe, please let Jack tell the story," Charlie asked as calmly as he could. He couldn't interview Jack without an appropriate adult, and she was all they had. Not for the first time, he wondered about Jack's father.

"I suppose you lost money sometimes, and I'm guessing that the owner of the casino said you didn't have to worry about it, you'd win it back next time."

Jack's mouth didn't fall open, but it might as well have done. Charlie looked over at Will. It looked as if his father at least had explained the way scams worked, and young people were drawn into debts they couldn't pay—except through crim- inality.

"That's what he said," Jack sounded indignant. "He fucking lied. He said we had to pay it all back, and that he'd never said we could win it back. 'That's not how it works, lads.' Wanker."

"Then he offered you a way to pay your debts? What did he want you to do?"

"It was nothing really. Just take some stuff to a bloke in a pub."

"Stuff?"

For the first time Jack looked embarrassed. Until then, he'd clearly felt they'd been justified in everything they'd done. Jack likely couldn't see anything wrong with going to a casino and betting. The owner had given them all the credit they wanted and had then reneged on his promise to let them win back their losses. The owner was at fault, not Jack.

It seemed as if Will had a better handle on the truth. He looked as if he'd been up all night, and he probably had. "The stuff was things Lewis Evans had nicked," Will said. "Credit cards and that. We took them to this bloke in The Yew Tree, he gave us some money and we gave it to Mr Evans. Coupla times a week. Lewis gave us the stuff at school, but we were supposed to hate each other so no one would guess. Then we walked through the college on our way home and gave Mr Evans the money." Will shrugged. "They said if we were caught with the nicked stuff we should say we'd found it in the street, and because we're kids, we'd be OK. But we were never caught."

This wasn't the time for a lecture about the age of criminal responsibility. Jack and Will were victims, for sure, but they weren't innocent, not by a long chalk.

"To sum up," Charlie said, "you were taken to an illegal casino, given unlimited credit to bet with, allowed to spend your winnings and then when your debt was high enough, recruited as couriers for stolen goods, under threat of what? A beating? From Neville Evans?"

Will nodded his head, and said, "He was in the SAS. Lewis told us. He broke Lewis's arm once."

Jack looked down at his feet. Charlie looked round the room. Only Eddy was relaxed, but he'd heard a few versions of the same story over the years. Mrs Jenner was wiping tears from her cheeks; Mr Jenner was clenching and un-clenching his fists and Mrs Protheroe was about to start berating her son.

Charlie got in first. "You dealt with Neville—Mr Evans. Who is the owner of the casino? What's his name?"

"Dunno," Jack said. "I heard him called Steff once or twice. Mostly they called him the boss."

"OK," Charlie said. "What do you know about the things Lewis Evans stole?"

"Nothing. I think he broke into rich people's houses. He used to call himself a cat burglar, as if he nicked cats. Tosser."

Charlie had to work hard not to catch Eddy's eye, or to imagine how patiently Patsy would have explained the meaning of cat burglar to Jack. He would save it up for their next whiteboard session. He needed to wrap this up before Jack's mother started again. They were all getting tired, and his head was aching.

"One last thing, and then we'll take a break," he said. "Where were you both the night before Lewis Evans was killed?"

"The casino. Not the one in Rhyl. A posh one near Manchester airport. The boss said he wanted us to help take people's coats and stuff and pick up glasses."

"He paid us in chips," Will said bleakly.

Charlie ignored that. "How did you get there and back?"

"Mr Evans took us, but we had to get a bus into Manchester and the train back in the morning. It took forever."

Charlie wrapped it up. What to do with the boys wasn't his decision, and he was glad of it. There were probably offences they could be charged with, but the information they'd given was worth more than convicting two teenagers of minor crimes. They'd painted a big, gilded frame around Neville Evans. Now all they had to do was catch him.

24

CAN'T PROVE ANYTHING: FRIDAY

Resolution for Whole Staff Meeting

1) THAT WE have No Confidence in the Principal of Llanfair College of Art, Professor Tomos Pennant.
    2) That we demand the immediate reinstatement of Inigo Vitruvious, Senior Painting Tutor.

AS HE DROVE TO WREXHAM, Charlie thought that they were on solid ground with Neville as their main suspect. It was horrible to think he had murdered his own adopted son, but the evidence was stacking up against him. In Charlie's experience, murder rarely made sense to anyone except the murderer. He had no doubt that when they caught up with Neville, he would have convinced himself that Lewis had brought it on himself, or there would be some other reason why Neville was not morally responsible. There was little to be gained from wondering about the motives of criminals. Instead, he thought about cars.

Charlie tended to buy the same car time after time. He liked his VW Golf, and every few years he would go to a VW dealer and trade in his old car for a newer version. He had never bought a brand-new car. He supposed that he could afford one, but why would he? Second-hand served him well. But there were people, and from his memory, several of them had been at the wedding at the Castle Hotel when Lewis Evans had been killed, who not only bought new cars, but must have paid £80,000 for them. Sometimes more. The car key he'd found in the mud had been cleaned up and revealed to be for a Range Rover Sport: £80,000 for the cheapest model—he'd looked it up.

Almost anything worth £80,000 was worth stealing, and if it was worth stealing, someone would steal it. The cars themselves were hard to steal, the keys less so. Will and Jack had talked about credit cards and "stuff" but not mentioned car keys specifically.

No Range Rover Sports were missing from the local area, but when he looked further afield, they were disappearing from garages and driveways all over the UK. Thousands were stolen every year, along with thousands of BMWs and Mercedes. Intelligence from the National Crime Agency suggested that the cars disappeared into unmarked shipping containers and onto the ferries to Eastern Europe and beyond. Given the numbers of cars going missing, it was clearly a very lucrative business for the thieves. Was he looking at organised car theft? And if he was, could he do anything about it? Was Lewis's death related to car-stealing?

In his mind's eye, Charlie visualised Lewis climbing into the bedroom windows of houses with an expensive car parked outside, stealing the keys and then passing them on to someone who would arrange the actual theft. Did the keys go to Huw Leader, or to Neville, or to someone else altogether? Was "Steff" Stefan Crane, and did he have anything to do with the burglaries? His name kept popping up. A coincidence?

It was like trying to solve a jigsaw without any idea what the picture was. Some pieces appeared to fit together, but then didn't fit with anything else. Or sudoku, a game he found endlessly frustrating, convinced that there was a trick to it that he simply didn't know. He *did* know who had killed Rico Pepperdine, or at least who had allowed him to die, and hopefully, this afternoon they would get a bit closer to nailing him.

CHIEF SUPERINTENDENT MAL KENT was waiting for Charlie in the reception area of the police headquarters in Wrexham. It took Charlie a few moments to realise that Kent was waiting for him, Charlie, because a chief superintendent didn't wait on a detective sergeant. But apparently this one did, at least today.

"Daniel wanted me to say hello," Kent told Charlie. "And Bethan, and all the rest of them. You're missed in Melin Tywyll. Though if they saw the state of your face, they might change their minds." In fact, Charlie thought his face wasn't too bad. The frozen peas had done a good job.

"I miss them too, sir," Charlie said, which was true, though not as true as it had been when he left.

"Don't say a word, but I'm hoping to persuade Daniel back to the police," Kent sai., "So we could be reuniting the old firm. But that's for another day."

Charlie wasn't sure how he felt about that, so he decided to worry about it later. He simply said, "Yes, sir," and followed Kent through the maze of corridors until they reached a suite of interview rooms. Kent opened a door. A computer monitor showed the (now silent) feed from a camera in the room next door, where David Yarrow sat with a man Charlie assumed was his solicitor. Charlie had last seen Yarrow in Tom's office, where he denied all knowledge of the money given as "donations" in exchange for places at the college. That David Yarrow had looked like a man in fear for his soul. This David Yarrow simply looked nervous and awkward.

"It's going to be you and me," Kent said. "If there's anything you want to ask, pass me a note. I've got a lot of information about who made the alleged donations, how much they were and when they were paid. What we need to know is what happened to the money after it arrived in the college accounts. I'm prepared to believe Kaylan Sully made this year's money disappear, but previous years would have been long gone before he arrived."

Charlie nodded.

"I found something out, sir," he said, and recounted what he'd heard from Tom the night before.

"This Ann. Do you believe her?"

"Enough to ask Yarrow about it," Charlie said. "It's circum-stantial, but it's good circumstantial if you see what I mean. Easy enough for him to explain if there is an explanation. From what I've seen of the college, it's such a gossip-shop that if there was a simple explanation, everyone would already know it."

"Right then," Kent said. He picked up a folder of papers from the table and gestured for Charlie to leave the room with him. As they left, Freya Ravensbourne and a man Charlie didn't know were waiting to come in.

"Forensic accountant," Kent said when the door closed behind them, but he didn't elaborate.

The interview room could not have been more different to the one Charlie was used to at Llanfair. It contained the same basic equipment, and the walls were the same pale blue, the window was high up, and the table had four hard chairs. There was the same voice recorder on the table top. But the video camera was concealed, and the room was light and bright. It didn't smell of mould, paint or old sweat. Unfortunately, it was too hot. Charlie felt moisture under his arms. David Yarrow and his solicitor had both removed their jackets, and Charlie longed to do the same. But Kent looked as cool as he had outside. Charlie followed his lead, and kept his jacket on, while wishing for the bag of frozen peas, this time to drape over the back of his neck.

Kent switched the voice recorder on and began the introductions. The solicitor was a middle-aged man called John Bernard, from a local firm. Charlie had met him and a couple of his colleagues before. They were good; maybe not the very best, though certainly competent. But no match for Mal Kent.

Kent delivered a masterclass in interview technique. It helped that Kent was, classically handsome, with decidedly beautiful brown eyes. Charlie had seen him and his fiancé, Daniel Owen, arguing at the tops of their voices, and then kissing to make up, but this was Kent the senior police officer, and he charmed David Yarrow within minutes. Without coming out and saying so, he convinced Yarrow that they were on the same side. Charlie wanted to take notes. As that wasn't an option, he committed what he saw and heard to memory.

"We know that Mr Vitruvious was behind this fraud," Kent said, leaning forward, and mirroring Yarrow's pose. "We *know* that you helped him by transferring the donated money to other accounts, but you didn't initiate the scam, so there's no expectation from this side of the table that you should be treated the same way as Vitruvious. And if you could *help* us..."

"Help you how?" Yarrow said. His voice squeaked, and he coughed to clear his throat. The room seemed to get even hotter, and Charlie smelled Yarrow's sweat.

"Did you know the college is being asked to return the money to the people who gave it?" Kent asked.

Yarrow nodded. "Yes."

"The college where you have worked for sixteen years?"

Another nod, another yes.

"No one works in a place for so long without caring about it," Kent said. "I think you care about the college. I don't think you want to see your colleagues lose their jobs, or the college merge with another. I think you'd like to go back to work and make the college a success again."

There is less than zero chance of that, Charlie thought, though it probably was what Yarrow wanted.

"I think," Kent continued, "that if you could put this right, you would."

"I would, I really would," Yarrow agreed.

Because you've been caught.

"Let's see how we can do that," Kent said, and, almost without anyone noticing, they were working together to catch Vitruvious.

"The bank accounts I paid the money into were just regular bank accounts," Yarrow said. "High street banks, no numbered accounts in Switzerland or the Cayman Islands."

"That would have made you suspicious," Kent said, and Yarrow nodded as if he would have refused to pay fraudulently obtained money into a numbered account.

"The accounts were in names like 'Llanfair Promotion.' I remember that one." Yarrow said. "They seemed legitimate." Charlie heard pleading in Yarrow's voice. "Could I have some water, do you think?" Yarrow asked, "it's so hot."

This time it was Kent who nodded. "I'm so sorry. The heating in this building is a disaster. DS Rees will get some water. Could you bring some for me please?" Mirroring a request for water, Charlie noted as he left the interview room. Ravensbourne opened the door to the room next door, the one with the video feed.

"Take a bottle of water and some cups from here," she said.

When he got back, Kent had removed his jacket, loosened his tie and was chatting with Yarrow and Bernard about how the building was either too hot or too cold. All friends together. He gave Charlie a brilliant smile, poured the water, took a sip and resumed in a voice as seductive as a caress..

"You were saying, Mr Yarrow, that the accounts you paid the money into were ordinary business bank accounts."

"I did check. Later. I started to worry. The accounts I paid the money into had been closed."

Kent nodded again. "How long after you paid the money over did you check?"

Yarrow swallowed. "A month," he said. Which had given Vitruvious plenty of time to move the money somewhere else, and somewhere else again until it disappeared altogether.

"Was that the year you bought your new house?" Kent asked in the same smooth velvet tone.

"You don't have to answer that," Bernard, the solicitor, intervened, obviously seeing the hole opening beneath his client's feet. Until that point there had been no suggestion that Yarrow had benefited from the fraud, but there it was, the cost of a new house when he had been homeless and broke. "No comment," Yarrow said, but his heart wasn't in it.

An hour later, they had a complete confession, including Yarrow's admission that he'd altered the college records so the payments didn't appear to have been received, and another admission that he'd been given enough money to use as a down payment on his house, and further top-ups until the mortgage was paid. Kent appeared genuinely understanding when Yarrow explained that once he'd moved the first tranche of money, Vitruvious essentially had the power to get him sacked and prosecuted for fraud. The self-serving nature of this hung in the air like a cobweb, hardly visible, but strong enough to tie a man up and send him to prison.

Charlie was in no doubt that Kent, or someone, would be talking about charging Yarrow with fraud, but Yarrow left seemingly convinced that by telling the truth, he was both vindicated and forgiven. That might work for a five-year-old accused of eating the last biscuit but it wasn't going to work for Yarrow.

Kent stood up and stretched when Yarrow and his solicitor left. "The problem is, Vitruvious can still deny it. We've got Yarrow, but those bank accounts have gone, along with the money. We can't prove anything."

25

ALL THE KEYS: FRIDAY

N otes from whole staff meeting made by Ms Ann
Hathersage
*Chair of academic trade union spoke in favour of the
resolution, citing the length of time it is taking to deal with IV's
suspension/disciplinary hearing/investigation. As a consequence, staff
in the painting department are overloaded. Chair of academic union
did not indicate support for IV—said she was neutral. Said issue was
overload for existing staff, also rumours of redundancies, further staff
cuts, threat of merger, making her worry about the future of LCA.
Cited lack of communication from senior management, esp Principal,
Governors.*

*Other staff members reiterated similar points, saying they were
worried about their job security.*

*Other staff members spoke in favour of part three of the resolu-
tion, saying that 'Dr' IV had been badly treated, slandered, etc. That
he attracted students to the college and without him, student
numbers were down for the forthcoming year, putting the future of
the college in jeopardy.*

*The principal spoke against the resolution. He said his hands
were tied re: IV as the matter was the subject of a police investigation*

into very serious offences and he had been advised (legal advice and HR) to await the outcome. He said there were no proposals to make redundancies, or to merge the college (he said he would resign first). He said Academic Board and Senior Management had been kept up to date with all possible options. The college was facing a serious financial loss because of a criminal fraud, which again he was prevented from discussing in any further detail as it too was the subject of a police investigation. In answer to a shouted question, he said that he believed the two cases may have a connection, but it was not up to him to speculate and it was in the hands of the police and the Crown Prosecution Service. There were further shouted inter-ventions.

The principal invited the staff to consider the reputational damage that LCA has already suffered, and the likelihood of further damage if this resolution was carried. He said that he would resign if the resolution was passed. He concluded by saying that he believed LCA had a future, that the next couple of years would be extremely difficult but that it was a unique institution with a superb staff team.

By a show of hands, the meeting agreed to vote on the resolution by secret ballot. The meeting was adjourned to allow for the produc-tion of ballot papers and the placement of ballot boxes in the library and other places. The head of HR was appointed by the meeting to conduct the ballot.

AFTER THE YARROW INTERVIEW, Charlie drove back from Wrexham on automatic pilot. Some part of his brain must have negotiated driving round roundabouts, stopping for traffic lights, speeding up, slowing down, but when he saw the police station car park he had no memory of the journey. All he could think about was Yarrow's confession, and the all-too-likely failure to make it stick to Vitruvious. Yes, Yarrow would be pros-ecuted, but it would take more to persuade the CPS to allow the police to charge Vitruvious unless he confessed, and that wasn't going to happen. And Tom would leave, humiliated by a man they both knew to be a thief and a murderer.

Patsy ran out to meet him as he opened the car door.

"Something's happened to Mags and Eddy," she said. "We need to get to the Castle Hotel." She opened the passenger door and got in. "Come on."

"What? Tell me," Charlie said, though he was closing his own door as he spoke. Patsy's agitation was palpable.

"They went to talk to Bosworth hours ago, and they didn't come back. They aren't answering their phones, and all I get when I ring the hotel is an answering machine."

"OK," Charlie said and reversed out of the car park, narrowly avoiding being crushed by a forestry lorry breaking the speed limit on its way out of town. He put his foot down, and they were at the hotel within minutes, parking next to the familiar police patrol car by the kitchen door at the back of the building.

"They're here," Patsy said, "so why aren't they answering their phones?"

"We'll ask at reception," Charlie said.

BUT THE DOOR to the reception hall was closed and locked. A neat, gold-painted notice informed visitors that the hotel was closed with no indication of when it might reopen. Charlie hammered on the door to no effect, while Patsy climbed up to the windows and peered in.

"No signs of life," she said. "Let's see if the kitchen door is open at the back."

It wasn't. Nor were any of the fire exits, or any ground floor windows that they could see. It didn't help that there were steps up to every door (and one set of steps leading down to a base-ment). Most of the ground floor windows were at least six feet from the ground. Charlie noticed that Patsy climbed up to look through the windows with ease, and dropped down again with equal ease, landing like a cat, without jarring every joint. He made a mental note to ask her for some tips.

"It's like the Marie Celeste," Patsy said. "Except that we know Mags and Eddy are here."

"People live here, too," Charlie said, thinking of Bosworth, and the rooms on the corridor above the kitchen where Landon had lived.

Patsy put her hand on his arm. "Shush, listen."

Charlie listened. From above his head he could hear the faint sound of a presenter extolling the virtues of a house. The words "kitchen diner" floated down until they were cut off by the sound of chainsaws in the forestry on the far side of the valley.

"It's a TV. Someone's left a TV on," Charlie said.

"Sarge, I'm not happy about any of this. Can we break in?"

Charlie wasn't happy either. Mags and Eddy were here somewhere. It was Friday afternoon, and the hotel should be getting ready for the weekend's events, not deserted but for a lone property programme.

Then they both heard it. The sound of a muffled cry, louder than the TV, though not much. There was quiet, and then another cry.

Charlie looked at the building. At first glance, the windows were Victorian leaded glass in hardwood frames. On closer inspection, they were modern double-glazed units disguised with fake wood, and fake lead. Fakes upon fakes, he thought, though that didn't help them to get in. He rattled the kitchen door, but it didn't move.

"The fire door by the bins was a bit rotten," Patsy suggested, and they jogged round to look. But it too held when they rattled it. Above it was a small window, the only one Charlie had seen that wasn't double glazed.

"We could break that," he said, pointing.

In response, Patsy grabbed a brick holding one of the bin lids in place and threw it straight through the window. Then she dragged an industrial size bin over to the door and vaulted onto it.

"Find me something to bash the rest of the glass out," she said. Charlie handed her a half brick and she quickly knocked the sharp edges from around the frame.

"Going in," she said, and before Charlie could tell her to be careful, because there was still broken glass, and a drop on the other side, she was gone. He heard a gentle thump and then the sound of the bar inside the fire door being pressed to open it. He hastily dragged the bin away so that he could get in.

"That was impressive," Charlie said as they crunched over the broken glass into a dark passageway lined with closed doors. Gentle humming suggested that at least one hid a cold store.

"Parkour moves," Patsy said.

"Kitchen should be at the end of here," Charlie said, and it was. They could hear the hum of fridges, and a dripping tap, but both the TV and the muffled cries were inaudible. All the stainless-steel surfaces were free of dirt and fingermarks, the ovens, grills, fryers and stove tops were cold, and the over-whelming smell was of disinfectant rather than food.

"This way." Charlie led Patsy along the corridor to the reception hall. Once out of the kitchen, they heard the muffled sounds again, coming from Bosworth's office, and they ran the few steps to the open door.

Bosworth lay on the floor, his red face showing above the silver duct tape binding his mouth. His hands were taped behind his back, and more silver tape bound his legs from ankles to knees like the beginnings of mummification. The duct tape didn't hide the bloody mess on the side of his head. It looked as if he'd been hit with a crowbar, but his open eyes and the increased groans indicated that he was aware and awake.

"Kitchen, scissors," Patsy gasped and ran off.

Charlie knelt down beside the agitated Bosworth. "We'll get you out of here," he said. "I'm going to call an ambulance, because that's a nasty wound on your head."

Bosworth's response was more frustrated noises from behind the gag. Charlie called for an ambulance and hoped Patsy found scissors quickly. A moment later she was back, without scissors, but with a wicked-looking knife. She quickly sliced through the tape binding Bosworth's hands and legs. Bosworth didn't wait for them to work out how to remove the tape on his face. He ripped at it himself, crying out in pain as the glue gripped his skin. As soon as his mouth was clear, he took a few ragged breaths.

"Thank you," he gasped. Between them, Charlie and Patsy helped Bosworth shuffle over to the wall so he could sit up. "Thank you," he said again, looking even more like a disinterred mummy, with strips of tape hanging from his face, and the arms and legs of his suit.

"What happened here, Mr Bosworth?" Charlie asked. "Who did this to you?"

"Where are Eddy and Mags?" Patsy interrupted.

Bosworth looked from one to the other of them, wincing as he turned his head. "Neville Evans came," he said. "He came to rob the safe. In my flat. The safe is in my flat. All Crane's money. Neville hit me, and when I woke up I was like this." Bosworth picked at a few of the stray bits of tape.

"Do you know where our colleagues are?" Charlie asked.

"Flat?" Bosworth whispered, his voice hoarse. Bosworth's eyes began to glaze over. "My head hurts. So cold," he said.

Charlie sent Patsy for all the blankets she could find in the linen stores along the corridor, and she came back with a king size duvet in a plastic bag. They ripped it open and wrapped it round Bosworth, who was now white and sweating. The adrenaline rush of his rescue seemed to be fading fast.

"How long ago did this happen?" Charlie asked, but Bosworth mumbled that he didn't know.

"The ambulance will be here soon," Charlie said, hoping it was true. "The flat is on the top floor," he said to Patsy. "Go through the kitchen and the stairs are at the far end. If you think Neville's in there, leg it back down here. But take your baton, pepper spray and radio. Just in case." She patted each of the items to reassure Charlie that she had them and ran off. "I'm going to open the front door for the ambulance, Mr Bosworth," Charlie told him.

"Locked." Bosworth said. "Neville took the key. All the keys."

Charlie looked at the wall behind Bosworth's desk. The key cabinet door hung open, showing only empty hooks.

"When did he come?" Charlie asked.

But Bosworth was fading, his eyes closing as Charlie watched.

Patsy ran into the room. "The door's locked," she said. "And it's a bloody great steel thing. We'd need an oxyacetylene torch to get through it. But someone's in there. Not just the telly. I hammered at the door, and I could hear things falling. And voices."

Charlie rang the ambulance service again. "Forty minutes," he was told. Twenty minutes which they could spend with Bosworth, or twenty minutes they could spend trying to get into his flat. Someone was in the flat, and if it was Neville with Mags and Eddy...

"Right," Charlie sai., "We need to elevate Bosworth's legs and go and see if we can get into that flat."

"I looked for ways in before. There's a window open. That's why we could hear the telly. I'll show you."

They eased Bosworth onto his back and put his legs on

some pillows Patsy brought from the stores, making him as comfortable as they could. He mumbled quietly, words making no sense. Charlie didn't want to leave him like this, but the image of Mags at the mercy of Neville Evans was occupying most of his bandwidth. He and Patsy jogged back outside, and she pulled him away from the bin store so they could see the rear facade.

"There," she said, pointing to an undeniably wide-open window two stories above the ground. The sound of the television, now playing commercials, drifted towards them.

"I'm sure that's the flat," Patsy said. "The telly, and it's in the right place above the kitchen. I don't know what was going on, but it sounded like someone moving furniture."

The next he knew, Patsy had run towards the rear wall of the hotel, jumped and had somehow levered herself onto the small canopy above the kitchen door.

"Patsy!" Charlie shouted and ran over. "What the fuck?"

"It's an easy climb," she said, "and I don't see another way, do you?"

He didn't. But nor did he want Patsy on her own with Neville Evans if he was up there.

"Tell me what to do," he said. "I'm coming with you." Because it was time to sort this out.

26

MAKE A DRINK, MAKE A PLAN: FRIDAY

From: Ori Wildwood, Librarian
To: Katy Kelly, Head Librarian

THIS BALLOT BOX behind the returns desk is giving me the creeps. Why did the ballot have to take so long? It's not like anyone is actually voting against Tom. Or are they? Everyone I meet says they've voted for him (against the no confidence). What if I'm wrong? What if all these people I thought were my friends are really voting for that dick Vitruvious to come back? The only reason the Governors didn't appoint Tom last time was that he didn't want the job. He didn't want it this time, but you know Tom, now he's got the job, he's trying to do it well. I'm going round snapping at everyone I suspect of being a secret Vitruvious supporter.

And they've put the other ballot box in Ann's office, so Tom has to walk past it twenty times a day. It's like they're torturing him.

Wanna have lunch and talk me down before I murder someone? Please?

CHARLIE COULDN'T INTERPRET the look Patsy gave him, but he didn't think it showed much confidence in his ability to climb up to a top floor window. Which was fair enough. He didn't have much confidence in his ability to climb up to a top floor window either. But she didn't waste any time.

"Drag a bin over to stand on, take your jacket off," she said. "Then jump up here."

That was the test, Charlie realised. If he could get onto the canopy, she'd let him come.

WITHOUT HIS JACKET, the bright day was chilly. The bin was stinky and potentially slippery, but it was better than trying to pull himself onto the canopy from the ground.

"Don't scramble, jump," Patsy said. "Put your hands on the top and run your feet up." He jumped, pressing his hands down hard on the top of the bin, and bringing his legs and feet up as if he were getting out of a swimming pool. The bin felt wobbly underneath him, so he looked up at Patsy rather than think about it. She looked relaxed; her body perfectly balanced. She pointed to the heavy cast iron drainpipe running down the side of the building. It fed into a large hopper a few feet above the canopy, and below that ran into a flimsy-looking plastic pipe down to the ground.

"We get over to that oversized hopper, climb up the pipe to the roof, then drop down to the open window," she said. "I'm going to test the pipe. If it'll hold me, you can follow." She casually reached over to the hopper, and swung herself across, holding on behind it, with her feet on toeholds Charlie could barely see. Then she did the getting-out-of-the-swimming-pool move again, and she was standing with a foot on either side of the hopper, her hands holding the pipe. She turned round to face him, leaning forwards, holding on with one hand on the pipe behind, and bouncing gently up and down. He felt a spike of panic in his chest, imagining the hopper crashing to the ground, bringing Patsy with it. He could barely bring himself to look.

"It seems solid enough. Get onto the canopy and I'll point out the footholds from there."

Charlie put his hands onto the canopy, concrete rough against his hands. There was nothing to run his feet against, so he had to jump. It took him a couple of tries to realise that he had to bring his feet to land beside his hands, but he managed it. His biceps strained, but he'd done enough pull ups at the gym to make it possible, though it made the bruise on his face begin to ache. Then he somehow had to stand up without anything to hold on to, and without knocking himself off his perch by banging his head on the wall in front.

"Breathe out, breathe in, and stand up," Patsy called quietly. He knew that. He did it, hearing his own breath and the scrape of his shoes as they centred underneath him.

"Right," she said. "Stand up straight. Do exactly what I say. You're going to lean over to the hopper so it takes your weight, then if you look down and to your left, there's a line of stones just proud of the others making a little ledge. Put your toes on the ledge and you're golden. Weight on your feet. Use your right hand to keep you steady. Once you're over here, it's easy after that. But hurry up."

Suddenly there was a crash from overhead, and the noise of the TV stopped abruptly. Charlie's body jerked. His centre of gravity shifted. He grasped the stone wall as if he could use it to hold on to, but there was nothing, only his own body. "Core muscles," he told himself, and the panic receded, and his heart rate slowed. Decision time. They could wait for help, or they could climb. The ache in his neck wasn't the only reminder of the damage Neville Evans could inflict, maybe was inflicting on Eddy and Mags. No real choice.

Charlie stood up straight, leaned over to the hopper and followed Patsy's instructions to the letter. One more pull up, and he was standing on the hopper, feeling it sag beneath his weight, as Patsy climbed onto the pipe.

"It's OK," she said, and began moving fast, limbs as co-ordinated as a spider. He looked at the pipe. The surface was marred with rust, but still smooth under his hands. Every few feet there was a joint, connected to the stone wall with thick bolts, that Patsy was using as if they were steps on a ladder, tucking her feet as far around the pipe as they would go. He breathed in, breathed out, and began to climb. The rust on the bolts was dark brown, thick and sharp, tearing his fingers. His feet barely fit onto the bolts below him, and when he stood, the pipe creaked. He felt one of the bolts give way, his foot slipping until the bolt held again, and tasted blood in his mouth. The effort of not screaming had made him bite the inside of his cheek. He moved up to the next joint, and the next, getting into the rhythm of it, not stopping to give any of the bolts time to fail. For a few moments it felt OK, as his muscles warmed up. Then Patsy dislodged a piece of mortar with a muffled curse, and it fell, catching his hand. His eyes followed it downwards, and he saw the canopy over the kitchen door far below, the car park with their cars, and then the whole of the river valley, sodden grass, bare trees and the sluggish brown water, and all he wanted was to look at the view from somewhere safe. Not here, with his knees beginning to shake and his hands sweating on two-hundred-year-old bolts. But Patsy was climbing again, and there was nothing to do but follow.

The rhythm didn't come back, and he smelled his own fear. He fixed his gaze upwards again and saw Patsy disappear over the "battlements" onto the roof. He got to the top and her head appeared next to his.

"Put your hand over here," she said, guiding him, and there was a rail, or a pipe, or something that was solid and reassuring he could use to pull himself to safety, while his feet scrabbled up the last few feet of wall.

"That was a truly horrible experience," he said, and Patsy grinned evilly. She beckoned him further along the roof, put a finger to her lips and pointed downwards. Just below them was the open window, and thank all the gods, a wide stone sill underneath it. No sound came from the flat.

Patsy pointed at herself, then at the window, and held up one finger. Then she pointed at him and held up two fingers. "Don't look down," she mouthed, and swung herself over the wall until her feet were on the windowsill, then she was gone. Charlie disconnected every part of his brain, except the bit that said *you've got this far*, and *if she can do it, so can I.*

He could hold on to the rail, as he lowered his feet out into space, easing himself lower, his clothes dragging on the stones, slowing his progress, until his toes reached the windowsill. A glance down showed the sill that had looked so wide and safe from the roof was narrow and crumbling at the edges. Patsy had let go of the railing with one hand, transferred her weight onto her feet, grabbed the open window and swung inside. On the ground, he could have done it easily. Up here, every cell in his body screamed that he would fall. A sob caught in the back of his throat, as the sweat on his hands made it harder to keep hold of the rail. He felt his feet begin to slip.

Patsy's calm voice said, "I am on the inside of the window, well anchored. Your feet are on the ledge, and the window is six inches below your hand. Bend your knees and it's done. Just one hand, then you're in. Trust me. Keep breathing and the shaking will stop. Look to your right. I'm right here."

But he didn't want to let go of the roof, with its lovely, secure railing, even as his hands wanted to slide off. Could he pull himself back up? Did he have enough strength left after the climb? What the fuck was he going to do?

"Look at me, sarge," Patsy said, but even moving his head risked unbalancing him. "Sarge," she said again, and, God, she sounded so close. He inched his head to the right, feeling the sweat on his hands, unable to breathe. There she was, just where she said, beside him, standing in the open window. On the inside, on a really wide and solid-looking window ledge.

"Breathe. Put your hand on the window," she whispered holding the window to show him where, and after a couple of very conscious breaths, he did. The window held. His feet didn't slip. His centre of gravity shifted, and he was inside. Shaking like a leaf, but inside.

"You did good for a first timer," Patsy murmured.

"First and last," he gasped back, as quietly as he could.

They were standing in a spacious double bedroom, with heavy mahogany furniture: bed, wardrobe, drawers and an easy chair. The walls were painted a pleasant pale green, and the carpet matched. Charlie and Patsy tiptoed to the door and listened. There was no noise. Charlie turned the round door-knob as slowly and quietly as he could. It opened onto a square hallway. Immediately opposite there was an old-fashioned bathroom. They could see in, because the door hung off its hinges, wood splintered. Charlie put a finger to his lips, then breathed out. Patsy did the same, because what they heard was Mags's voice calling, "Eddy, are you OK?"

Charlie put his hand out to prevent Patsy running forwards, and they walked silently towards the open door to their left. Charlie waited by the doorway where he couldn't be easily seen.

"Mags?" he called.

"Oh, God, Sarge, it's OK, there's no one here."

Patsy and Charlie ran in to the room.

"Thank God you came," Mags cried, apparently on the

verge of tears. She was tied to a dining chair with more of the silver duct tape. Eddy lay on the floor, half mummified, just as Bosworth had been. From his expression, he was very much alive. A large flat screen TV lay on the floor, along with several overturned chairs. Let into the wall near the door, a heavy iron safe stood open and empty.

"Scissors," said Patsy and disappeared. Charlie heard drawers opening and closing.

"Who did this?" Charlie asked. "Neville Evans?"

Mags nodded. "We were supposed to meet Bosworth here, in his flat, but Evans was waiting. He did some kind of choke thing to Eddy, and he collapsed. Then he came after me. Got between me and the door, so I locked myself in the bathroom." Her lips curled upwards. "Much good it did me. He broke the door down, threatened me with a hunting knife, tied me up, tied Eddy up, opened the safe, turned the TV on and left. It took him less than ten minutes. Oh, and he took our phones. Eddy came round and started knocking things over to try to get attention."

"He didn't gag you?"

"I cried." Mags said. "He worried I would choke. That's why he put the telly on, so no one would hear."

"What did he take from the safe?"

"I don't know what was in it," Mags said. "I saw him open it but then his body hid what he was doing."

Patsy came back with two pairs of clumsy-looking kitchen scissors. "Best I can do," she said. She started on Mags and Charlie on Eddy.

Which is when they heard the siren outside.

"Bosworth," Charlie said. "I'd better go and tell them where he is. Sorry, Eddy mate, be right back." Charlie had started to free Eddy, but the scissors were too blunt for him to have made much progress.

The flat door was across the hall, and it was locked.

"For fuck's sake!" Charlie shouted, to everyone and no one. "We're locked in." He sat on the nearest chair, pulled out his phone and started trying to get hold of the ambulance crew downstairs, ignoring the noises Eddy was making. When they were finally connected, he told them how to get into the building and where to find Bosworth. And then he called Ravensbourne.

Patsy released Mags who disappeared to the bathroom, demanding no one come out into the hall because she needed to pee *very badly indeed*. Patsy moved over to Eddy, releasing his hands and feet first, and then very carefully snipping at the tape over his mouth. Eddy pushed her out of the way and pulled it off in one awful rip, taking a layer of skin, and leaving tiny spots of blood over the lower half of his face.

"Jesus," he cried. "Jesus, fuck, that hurt."

The toilet flushed, the taps ran, and Mags came back. "If the door's locked, how did you get in?" she demanded. "And come to that, how are we going to get out?"

Charlie sighed. "We climbed up the outside of the building," he said. Patsy's face lit up. "It was not fun. As for getting out, Ravensbourne is calling the fire brigade. They'll either break the door down or use a ladder. I dunno. Patsy was brilliant, but I never, ever want to do anything so stupid again." He shivered. He would be reliving the moments hanging from the roof for a long time to come. "We'll have a drink, and then we'll make a plan."

27

CAN'T PUT IT RIGHT: FRIDAY

From: Graham Cheater, Vice Chancellor and Principal, St Paul's University College of Art and Design

To: Professor Tomos Pennant

Dear Tom

I'm so sorry to hear of your travails. It is hard enough to get a decent amount of funding here in London, so how you have managed in darkest Wales for so long I have no idea. I am full of admiration. Obviously, it can't last. The corporate state despises the small, the independent and the quirky. No wonder they are trying to subsume Llanfair into something safe and familiar. An 'art department'. Let them have it, my dear Tom, and let them have the vile Vitruvious too. He may find the water not so welcoming when his masters are in Bangor, or Aberystwyth.

I have official permission to offer you a personal chair in print-making plus a role (which they will design around you) in the Senior Management Team. I'll be retiring in a year or two, and you'd be a shoo-in for the job. You could do as much or as little

teaching as you like, and as you know, our facilities are world class.

No one here gives a monkey's about votes of no confidence.

I know this won't be the only offer you get; I'm just trying to get in first. You could have had your pick years ago, but for your perverse loyalty to little Llanfair. It's pretty, but you can do better.

Gray.

WOULD CHARLIE LIKE LONDON? Would he work for the Metropolitan Police? Tom couldn't visualise Charlie in a big city, but then he couldn't visualise himself there either. Orianna would be fine, she'd grown up in London. Everyone else, not so much. That was assuming they wanted to leave Llanfair, where the girls were settled at school. They might threaten to leave the college in solidarity, but would they? He thought about the apartment in New York that he'd left a few months before. He had unfinished business there, a fellowship on hold because Llanfair had called him back. Someone else would be in the apartment now, but it would be free again in the Spring ...

RESCUE TOOK over an hour and involved an oxyacetylene torch to open the door to Bosworth's flat. The fire brigade left a trail of broken doors showing the route in and out of the building. While they waited for rescue, Charlie nurtured the seedling of a plan, but he doubted he could make it grow. It depended on too many assumptions and things outside his control, not least getting it past Ravensbourne.

Once out of the hotel, he sent Mags and Patsy home, and took a protesting Eddy to the hospital. "You were unconscious. You're getting looked at. End of story," Charlie told him. "Just be grateful I didn't make you wait for an ambulance."

Eddy complained about Charlie's slow driving all the way, so Charlie had no compunction in dumping him with the A & E triage nurse and going to find Bosworth. Bosworth was in a cubicle, 'waiting for a bed.' His head had been bandaged and some kind of solvent had removed most of the remnants of tape and glue from his face. He didn't look well, but he was propped up, and seemed quite prepared to talk to Charlie.

"Back at the hotel," Charlie said, "you told me Neville was going to steal the money from the safe, and that it was Crane's money."

Bosworth nodded. "It's Crane's hotel. He owns it."

"It's a front, too," Charlie said. "I think guests who arrived in expensive cars often had them stolen when they got home. I think you knew that. I think Landon Emery knew it too, and Lewis Evans certainly knew it because he was the one stealing the keys. I'm guessing Lewis brought them to you or to Landon to get copies. Stolen cars could make more money in a week than that hotel could make in a year."

Bosworth nodded. "Crane liked having the hotel. Just like he liked being the big noise in that casino in Manchester. He makes more from the back-room poker games in Rhyl and Prestatyn than he does at the Ringway club, but the Ringway Club has status. Back-room clubs in has-been seaside resorts are for losers. Or that's how he thinks."

"The Castle Hotel is for status, too?" Charlie asked. "How much money was in the safe?"

"Tens of thousands. It goes into our bar tills, and to the Ringway, but there's always too much. Gambling is a cash business, or this sort of gambling is, anyway."

"Neville will have enough to get away then?"

"Plenty."

"Mr Bosworth," Charlie asked, "why are you telling me this now?"

"I'm telling you because it doesn't matter." Bosworth said. "I don't want to go to jail, and perhaps you can help with that. The hotel will close, probably. It doesn't make enough money without the car thefts, so Crane will sell it. Crane won't go to jail, his sort never do. And Neville has gone. That's the main thing."

Charlie thought that if he knew more, Bosworth would be making sense.

"Neville was what? Crane's enforcer?"

"That's one word for it. He's killed a lot of people, DS Rees. But his own son? I know he owed money. We all owe money. No one would work for someone like Stefan Crane if they had a choice. But I think Neville liked hurting people."

Bosworth had been unconscious and left tied up for hours. He must be feeling terrible, even though Charlie was sure he'd have been given painkillers. He looked defeated. His statement that 'it doesn't matter' set alarm bells ringing. He was telling Charlie things that were going to put him on the wrong side of a serious villain, and he didn't appear to care.

"What are you planning to do when you leave here?" Charlie asked.

Bosworth gave a tiny smile. "Believe it or not, I'm a good hotel manager. I'm also an experienced croupier. I run the private poker games at the hotel, and sometimes at one of the casinos. I'm going to try to get a job somewhere warm and sunny, and a long way from Stefan Crane, and I'm going to keep going to Gamblers Anonymous. It's been six months, the hardest six months of my life, but worth it. It's an addiction, and don't let anyone tell you otherwise."

Charlie didn't doubt it. He'd experienced addiction from close quarters; knew how it wrecked lives, and how hard it was to overcome.

"I believe you," he said. "Six months is good going."

"Huw made me go the first time, Huw Leader ..."

"So you helped him disappear?"

Bosworth nodded. "He's a...friend." Bosworth blushed. Charlie had the thought that he was hearing a lot of things Bosworth hadn't told anyone else outside Gamblers Anonymous, and possibly not even there. "We had planned to get away soon, after the next poker night at the hotel, but to be honest, Neville killing that boy brought it all forward. Crane traps people and then Neville terrorises them."

"You were part of it," Charlie said gently, because maybe he and Leader were having second thoughts, but they hadn't been innocent bystanders.

"I know. I would put it right if I could, I swear I would."

"Say that again," Charlie asked. Bosworth looked puzzled.

"I said I'd put it right if I could," he said.

In Charlie's mind the cogs whirred and began to click into place, like picking a lock, feeling the tiny levers move until the door swung open.

"When is the next hotel poker night?"

"Sunday evening. It's always the second Sunday of the month."

"I don't think you can put this right, Mr Bosworth," Charlie said. "But if you are willing, there is something you can do that might very well put some of it right and would reduce the likelihood of receiving a long jail sentence by a large percentage." Unless it doesn't work, he thought, in which case the police would mop up the smaller fry, and Bosworth would be caught in the net.

EDDY WAS WAITING FOR CHARLIE, having managed to persuade the doctors in record time that he wasn't concussed.

"Perhaps we could go home at a faster than glacial pace?" he asked.

Eddy was a trained police driver and acknowledged petrol head. Charlie wasn't interested in shredding his nerves for the sake of shaving five minutes off the journey time. "My driving is fine. Live with it," Charlie said.

Eddy just smiled and got into the car. "I heard your bloke's in trouble," he said once they were out of the hospital grounds and on the road back to Llanfair.

"What?" Charlie's attention shifted from the road to Eddy's words. He felt the car drift towards the kerb and re-focussed.

"That banner, then the Courier and Post having a dig at him, then this vote of no confidence. What happens if he loses?"

"He won't. Anyway, what's it to you?"

Eddy settled back into his seat, a seat he had to push as far back as it would go.

"Just wondered if he'd be leaving Llanfair, that's all. Leaving you all on your own."

Charlie felt a tide of anger rising through his body. It was none of Eddy's business, and he had a bad feeling he knew what was coming next. He liked Eddy, but he was also Eddy's boss. With a small team, working together constantly, the boundaries were easily blurred. Eddy had tried to blur them more than once.

"I kind of think that falls under the category of none of your business," Charlie said, trying not to let the anger show in his voice. He consciously relaxed his hands on the steering wheel.

Eddy shrugged. "Wouldn't want you to get lonely, that's all."

"I won't be." As he spoke, Charlie felt something settle inside him, and the anger drained away. He knew with complete certainty that if Tom left, he, Charlie, would go with him. No matter how much he liked Llanfair and his colleagues, (which was a lot) he was at home with Tom, in love with Tom. He could let Eddy's words slide off him because he was going home to Tom, and he was going to tell Tom the truth about his feelings.

"We've got a lot to do," he said, and told Eddy what Bosworth had said and how they might proceed.

28

NEW PLAN: SATURDAY

F rom the North Wales Courier and Post

CHAIR OF LLANFAIR Governors admits suspended tutor has 'a lot of support'

Embattled Llanfair College of Art is balloting all its staff on a motion of no confidence in the Principal, Professor Tomos Pennant. Professor Pennant is said to be behind a campaign to oust popular painting tutor, Inigo Vitruvious. Dr Vitruvious has appeared regularly on television and talk radio discussing the role of art in the modern world. He told this newspaper that he is the victim of a witch hunt because of his radical views.

Our reporter asked the chairman of the governing body which oversees the running of the college for his reaction. He said that he had every confidence in Professor Pennant, but that Dr Vitruvious had a lot of support around the college.

The results of the ballot will be revealed on Monday.

Professor Pennant was not available for comment.

. . .

TOM TRIED, and failed, to remember being asked for a comment by the Courier and Post. He imagined the comments he'd like to make, comments that would include words like *two-faced, murderer* and *thief*. If I'm still here next week, he thought, that bastard Carroll is out of here. My predecessor boasted that he chose his own governors, and if he could do it so can I. Was there a connection between Vitruvious and the Chair of the Governors or was Carroll simply looking for an easy life, one where he didn't have to take sides? Tom's pencil moved, apparently of its own accord, over the back of an envelope. When he looked, there was the Chair's face on the front of an egg balanced precariously on top of a wall. Tom drew a disembodied hand behind the egg, and in his imagination, gave the egg a hard push.

CHARLIE ARRIVED at the prison before eight. He would wait as long as it took, but he didn't think Kaylan would refuse to see him. Most of the drive had been in the dark, and as he got closer to the conurbations of Manchester and Liverpool, the traffic began to build, roads crowded with cars and trucks, though where they were all going on a Saturday morning he had no idea. It didn't matter. He had arrived and given his name and business to the prison officers, along with his phone. He'd bought two magazines for petrol-heads, and he settled down to find out as much as he could about the kinds of cars people wanted to steal.

The call came an hour later, and Charlie was escorted to an interview room where Kaylan was waiting. *Here goes.* The day before he had watched Mal Kent persuade David Yarrow that they shared a common cause. Now Charlie planned to do the same with Kaylan. He wasn't going to react; it was time to take the lead.

Charlie smiled at Kaylan. He told himself that Kaylan was frightened, that he wasn't even of legal drinking age in his home country, and that someone he admired had let him down. That was what mattered today.

"I'm not going to say I was passing," Charlie said, "but I do have a meeting not too far away and I thought I'd come."

"Sure you did," Kaylan replied.

"I've been thinking about Vitruvious, and I wanted to run some things past you. That's part of it. I was reading online about those Supermax prisons in the States, and that's part of it too. But I have to say that I don't think they'd send you to one of those."

"No?" Kaylan said. "I've hacked into more computers than you've ever seen, Mr Policeman. My dad basically hates me because he's had to turn all his stuff over to the feds, so he's never going to pay for a lawyer to defend me. I can't pay for a lawyer because I can't get at my money without a computer. I'm fucked if they send me back."

"I don't see any plans to send you back though," Charlie said. "You're going to jail for shooting me, and probably for a while. You kidnapped two people and implied you stole a lot of money from Vitruvious. He probably deserved it."

"Not a Vitruvious fan?"

"The man's a toad. Except that's disrespectful to toads."

Kaylan started laughing. Charlie thought it was probably the first laughter this room had heard for a while.

"You said one true thing, Mr Policeman, fucking Vitruvious deserves everything he gets."

He looked more relaxed than Charlie had ever seen him, leaning back in the hard metal chair, hands folded on the table in front of him. Remand prisoners wore their own clothes, and Kaylan wore grey sweatpants and a hoodie with a sports logo.

Not that different to what he'd be wearing once convicted. The blond hair was short, and his skin looked puffy and unhealthy.

"We agree about Vitruvious if nothing else," Charlie said. "The thing is, he's going to get away with it. All of it. Stealing money, long before you arrived. Rico's death. The big conscience-of-the-arts act."

Kaylan sat up and leaned forward, staring straight into Charlie's eyes.

"What do you really want, Mr Policeman? You don't like me. I shot you, and I'd have killed you if I had to. You aren't my friend. So why are you here?"

Charlie wanted to lean away. Being close to Kaylan made the hairs stand up on the back of his neck. Instead, he mirrored Kaylan's pose and stared right back.

"No. I'm not your friend. But Vitruvious ruined your life, and he's about to ruin mine. I came here to see if between us we could ruin his instead."

A little of the tension left Kaylan's face. He looked away and moved back. Charlie did the same, feeling the sweat break out under his arms and roll down his ribs. The ribs that Kaylan's bullet had burned raw.

"What's in it for me?" Kaylan asked.

"Revenge." Charlie said, because he couldn't make a no-deportation deal. That would be a matter for the politicians. "Cards on the table, that's all I've got. I can tell my bosses that you co-operated, and that will make the judge a bit happier when it comes to sentencing. There might be other stuff I can do, but it's small beer compared to getting your own back on Vitruvious."

"I'm not telling you what happened to Rico." Kaylan said.

Charlie shook his head. "You don't need to. I already know. I saw the drawings. But Vitruvious says they aren't his. They aren't signed, and even if he admits he made them, he can say they were from his imagination. He lies, and he does it without shame." Charlie studied Kaylan's pose to mirror it. Thoughtful, head slightly to one side, mouth relaxed. Was it going to work?

"How long had he been stealing money from students?" Kaylan asked.

"We don't know. A few years."

"I asked him if he was so concerned about poverty, how come he drove a vintage Jag? He said he'd won it playing cards. That's when I decided to take his money. Well, that's when I decided to have a look, because I stopped believing what he said." Kaylan smiled. "I lie too."

Charlie smiled back, feeling more sweat wetting his shirt. "I know you do," he said. "You're as shameless as he is."

"You, too, probably."

Charlie shook his head. "Not today. I told you the truth. I want Vitruvious convicted of fraud and murder. I think you do too. I get that you aren't going to put your hands up to Rico's death, but if you can help put Vitruvious away without incriminating yourself, I'm guessing you'd do it." .

"His phone. He took hundreds of pictures on his phone. Latest model, brand new. He never let go of it, even for a second, but the passcode is 164324. I remember numbers. He does play cards too. For money. I wondered whether he stole that money to pay gambling debts, but ..." Kaylan shrugged. "By that point I didn't care. Let me know if you get him."

This time it was Kaylan who stood up first and asked to be let out. Charlie shuddered in pure relief, the end of the adrenaline that had kept him going leaving his body limp and exhausted.

CHARLIE'S IDEAS turned themselves from a series of disconnected thoughts into a plan that might just work. If he could sell it to Ravensbourne, and ideally to Mal Kent. Protocol dictated that he spoke to his immediate boss first.

"This could be a big deal, boss. Do you want to ask the Chief Super? Because we'll need a warrant and there isn't long."

"Don't trust me to get it done, huh, Charlie?"

"Of course I do." He did. Ravensbourne could get warrants faster than anyone Charlie had ever worked with. "But it looks like Vitruvious will be there. And anything to do with Stefan Crane is Serious and Organised Crime, boss. Gold Command stuff."

"Tell me, and I'll decide."

He told her, and she told him to come to Wrexham, so he could explain it to Kent. That meant she would be calling Kent, on a Saturday. He would definitely be paying a price for this one. Especially if it didn't work.

"IT'S AN ILLEGAL GAMBLING CLUB," Kent said. He didn't say "Why have you called me out at the weekend to discuss a raid that a rookie with six months experience could have organised?" But it was there in his voice.

"Stefan Crane himself is likely to be one of the participants, sir, and so is Vitruvious. The Gambling Act allows us to seize evidence including electronic devices. That means we could seize both their phones, and Kaylan Sully says Vitruvious took photographs of Rico Pepperdine's death on his phone."

"We couldn't use it in evidence," Ravensbourne said. "You know that."

"We could if we got a warrant to say we could," Charlie said. "Roll it all up in one raid. Illegal gambling, and Rico."

What Charlie didn't say was that if they couldn't get Vitruvious's phone, or if Kaylan had lied, then at least Vitruvious would have been caught in an illegal gambling club, associated with a major league criminal, and maybe that would be enough to keep him out of Tom's hair.

"You think this Rupert Bosworth will help us?"

Charlie nodded. "It's part of his twelve-step programme to make amends where he can and I think he's genuinely remorseful. Lewis's death was the last straw. He's afraid that if he'd told us everything he knew when Lewis was killed, Landon would still be alive. I'm not sure he would. I think Crane and Neville were cleaning house, ready to move on."

"Which begs the question," Ravensbourne said, "of why Bosworth is still alive. Why didn't Neville kill him?"

"If I'm right, boss, he's alive because he knows where Huw Leader is." A thorough house-clean would include Leader as well as Bosworth. Then Kent asked the question to which Charlie had no answer. Or possibly an answer that would derail the plan.

"Is Neville still working for Crane? Or has he stolen Crane's money and gone rogue?"

Charlie had a good idea where the money had gone from the safe, but he couldn't be sure yet, and anyway, it didn't answer the question. It was time for a distraction. Charlie looked between his two bosses. Ravensbourne had forgotten to brush her hair again, and she had her usual baggy black trousers on, today coupled with a black sweater that may once have been OK but was now a mass of bobbles with a few bits of white from being washed with a tissue. Kent was also in all black, jeans and a sweater rather than his usual suit because it was the weekend. His hair was just so, his shoes polished, and he smelled of an expensive cologne. The overall effect was of someone who had just stepped out of a ribbon-tied box, where he had been carefully and lovingly wrapped in tissue paper to prevent any creases. But the two of them had the same eyes. Eyes that said *I want to know, and when I find out, someone's going to jail.*

"I don't know about Neville and Crane," Charlie said, "but I have an idea about how we can find some of the missing money

—or rather we can find out where it went. I doubt it's still there."

Kent and Ravensbourne both got the look again.

"Vitruvious's father was a refugee. I thought it would be interesting to find out where from," Charlie said. "East Germany, as was, is where. Which means that since reunification, he's entitled to be a German citizen, and consequently so is Vitruvious. If he took up his German citizenship, he would have German identity documents, and he could use them to open a bank account, possibly in his father's name. Yarrow said the donation money was paid into a British bank and disappeared from there. I'm thinking Vitruvious has a financial profile with his UK identity, all innocent and above board, and another one in his German identity, from whence he pays himself large sums in cash, from alleged gambling wins. Worth a look, don't you think?"

It took Charlie another hour to persuade Ravensbourne and Kent that his plan would work. In fairness, he wasn't a hundred percent convinced it would work himself. There was something Golden Age Crime Novel about getting all the suspects together in one room and seeing what happened. In this case, a poker game, and they had less than twenty-four hours to set it up.

PATSY'S BOYFRIEND WAS UNEXPECTED. For a start he was called Unwin, which he was quick to explain was his surname. "I was at school in the year of the Josh," he said. "I think there were four others in my class alone. All the Joshes used their surnames, even Josh Brocklehurst. Unwin just seems like my name now." He was as dark as Patsy was fair, and they were about the same height and build, which Charlie thought he would probably describe as 'compact.' Unwin badly needed some fashion advice, starting with the pointy shoes and the check trousers that were more suited to the golf course than the police. But the point was that he didn't look like a police officer. Charlie realised that he and Eddy were giving Unwin the evil eye, and the don't-mess-with-our-mate vibe. When had it started mattering to him who his colleagues dated?

Unwin said he'd been practising poker since the day before. "I knew the rules, kinda," he said. "But I don't want to look like a jerk. Until I'm supposed to, anyway. I even had a go at one of those online casinos. Lost some money, but it was a good lesson in how to play." He slid an arm around Patsy's waist and kissed her cheek. "Never thought I'd be an undercover cop," he said.

"You're not," Eddy growled. "Don't get overexcited."

29

HOT POKER GAME: SUNDAY

Minutes of Extraordinary General Meeting, Llanfair College of Art Student Union

The SU President explained that the meeting had been called under section 26a of the constitution, which states that if twenty members in good standing request a meeting, one must be held. A meeting may only be held to discuss a single motion, which must be attached to the request. The motion to be discussed was to demand the reinstatement of the Senior Painting Tutor by the college authorities.

The motion was proposed by Patch Conway who said that Dr Vitruvious had been badly treated because he was a true radical in a swamp of conservatism.

Harry Parry opposed the motion, pointing out the college's hands were tied while the police investigation continued. She said that they would all feel very stupid if they voted to support someone who was later convicted of a serious offence. In this case, the college was right to be conservative.

The debate continued. On several occasions, the chair of the meeting reminded members that personal attacks were not permitted.

A vote was taken.

For the motion: 25
Against the motion: 119
The motion was therefore defeated.

Ann told Tom about the Student Union general meeting.

"The students aren't supporting Vitruvious," she said. "And I don't think the staff are, either."

The ballot box stood on a side table in Ann's office. It would be collected the next day, and the votes counted, and they could all get on with making plans for their futures. Tom had several good offers, but he wanted to talk to Charlie before deciding anything.

"I've been working on my resignation letter," Tom said, ignoring the information about the Student Union vote. "I can't decide whether to tell the truth, and risk being sued for libel, or just go with the usual good wishes for the future."

"You're going to win," Ann said.

Bosworth had set the poker table up in the library. Charlie and Patsy had visited to see the lay of the land. It felt strange to be back in the hotel, knowing it was probably going to close its doors after tonight, possibly forever. Bosworth had said Crane would sell it as a going concern, that there were bookings for weddings, anniversaries and 'corporate events,' but Charlie wondered if anyone honest would take it on once they'd seen the books, with their unexplained cash deposits and bar takings for nights the hotel was closed.

"There are honest-to-god crossed swords over the fireplace," Patsy said. "I thought they were fake."

"Everything else is fake," Charlie said. "I'm prepared to believe they are really made from steel, but I refuse to believe

they have ever been used for actual sword fighting." Luckily the
swords were high up on the wall, above a genuine marble fire
surround. The marble was real, but in every way that mattered,
the stone was as fake as the wood panelling—expensive mate-
rials used to make a rich man's folly. In the fireplace was a log
burner, fire laid and ready to light. A basket of logs stood next
to a set of fire irons and a pair of heavily studded red leather
chairs, one on each side. The doors had those swivelling brass
poles with tapestry curtains hanging from them—the kind that
swung open with the doors. The windows had heavily lined
drapes, with every kind of swag and furbelow.

"Polyester," Patsy said, rubbing a bit of tapestry between her
fingers. "Might look like the real thing but it's probably made in
a Chinese factory and shipped in by the container-load."

There were books in the library, almost a whole wall of
them. Some, Charlie thought, had been bought by the yard;
leather-bound volumes no one was ever going to read. The
lower shelves were filled with popular fiction, not exactly up to
date, but titles and authors he recognised. In keeping with the
rest of the hotel, the books were dusted, and the wood
panelling on the walls glowed with polish. Whatever else
Bosworth was, he was a good hotel manager, just like he said.
The red leather Chesterfield sofas which had previously been
arranged in conversational groupings were now pushed back
against the walls to make room for the poker table. There
would also be a table for what Bosworth called 'nibbles,' and
another for drinks.

The table itself was a purpose-made octagonal one, with a
green felt top. Each place held a small tray for a drink and the
player's poker chips. Hanging low over the table there was a
green glass shaded lamp, now fitted with a minute microphone.
It, and the security cameras, could be monitored from the
police van, already discreetly parked out of sight in the trees to
the side of the hotel.

"It's very professional," Patsy said.

Bosworth reddened as he had done when they first met him. "It's a high stakes game," he said. "The gentleman's club look is part of the attraction."

"People would rather lose their money in a Victorian neo-Gothic castle with polyester curtains than in an online casino?" she asked.

"Some people," Bosworth replied, and Charlie wondered how he felt about setting this up when he was fighting his own addiction. Bosworth must have expected the question or picked up on Charlie's thought.

"Horses," he said. "That's what I like to bet on. I trained as a croupier a long time ago, and I know the house always wins. Horses are different. I couldn't go racing, or even watch a race on TV. Not any more, not ever again. This I can deal with." But there had been a longing in his voice when he said the word racing, and Charlie had a powerful vision of a red-faced Bosworth in the stands at some racecourse, yelling for the horse carrying his money.

THE GAME WAS SCHEDULED to begin at eight. Bosworth had switched the lights on around the main entrance, and the door stood open invitingly. There would be no more than seven poker players, so there was room for them to park their cars at the front. One of the security cameras showed the entrance, another the reception hall. First to arrive was Vitruvious in his vintage Jaguar, the chrome detailing shining in the lights. He was dressed down as usual, what Tom called his "man of the people" look, in low-waisted jeans and a sweatshirt featuring a cracked and faded Union Jack. His Converse trainers were streaked with paint. Last time Charlie had seen Vitruvious, he'd been tied to a chair, shouting about the injustice of his treatment at the hands of Kaylan and the police. Later that day,

Charlie and Tom found the drawings of Rico's death. Charlie felt a visceral revulsion so strong that he was surprised Vitruvious didn't turn round. If there was any sign Vitruvious regretted Rico's death, it wasn't visible on his face. Next into view was Mr Mags, aka Dylan, bringing Unwin. Mags hadn't wanted her husband there, arguing that his connection to the police was easy to find. But he was the only one who could provide an introduction for Unwin, and if no one had bothered to find out Dylan was married to a police officer last time, why would they now?

Another Jaguar rolled up, this time a new one. The kind of car that Crane would arrange to have stolen and shipped overseas. Charlie watched a tall, rather paunchy man get out, lock the car and climb the steps to the reception hall. Once inside, he greeted Vitruvious warmly, and shook hands with Unwin. That was four. Was that it? Would Stefan Crane turn up? Charlie was holding his breath. The raid would still happen without Crane, but he'd sold the plan to Kent on the promise of Crane's presence.

He breathed again when Crane arrived, looking as if he'd come from work in a suit and tie. A man Charlie didn't recognise, also in a suit and tie, got out of Crane's car and followed him into the hotel. One of the security cameras in the reception hall had been angled to show as much of the inside of the library as possible. What they couldn't see, they would pick up from the microphone in the lantern hanging over the poker table. For now, the men were chatting in the reception hall, while Bosworth hovered in the door to the library. At an unseen signal, everyone moved towards the poker table, becoming vague blobs on the camera feed, although the listeners in the police van could hear as clearly as if they were in the room. Charlie heard each of the participants buy piles of poker chips, several hundred pounds' worth in each case. Bosworth announced that they would be starting in five minutes, invited everyone to help themselves to a drink and take a seat. Once everyone was seated, Bosworth announced something to do with blinds, which Charlie found incomprehensible, and judging from the puzzled faces around them, so did most of his colleagues.

"You can tell we aren't gamblers," Eddy said. "A lottery ticket is as exciting as it gets for me." Charlie nodded. He couldn't even remember buying a lottery ticket. He judged that play was about to begin, when a car drew up outside the hotel and a figure got out.

"Oh, shit," Charlie said, as Neville Evans jogged up the steps into the hotel and into the library.

"Sorry I'm late. Deal me in, Rupert." They saw the blob that was Neville take the final seat at the poker table.

"That answers the question about whether Neville is still working for Crane," Charlie said.

"Not necessarily," Kent held his hand up as if stopping traffic. "I'm interested to see how this plays out. I don't want anyone to move until our diversion."

The poker game was quiet, the only sounds the bets, requests for cards, then the small sounds of victory or defeat. From listening, it was impossible to tell who was winning and who losing. Charlie recognised Dylan's Welsh accent, and Vitruvious's loud arrogance. Evans's voice should have been familiar, too, but for once he didn't sound angry. The police officers kept checking the time on their phones, waiting for the noise inside the library to change.

"They're raising the stakes now," Kent said. "Get ready."

Charlie felt the tension rise in the van, and he knew that it would be rising amongst the uniformed officers waiting in the dark of the hotel kitchen. They would move on Kent's command.

"Hey, that's great, second time's the charm," Charlie heard Unwin say as clear as a bell, and then a few minutes later, "I thought I was no good at this," and a few mumbled congratulations. But the table was still mostly quiet. Bosworth was dealing winning hands to Unwin, the rookie player, and then,

"Hands on the table!" came a cry, followed by "I wasn't doing anything," from Unwin, amid rising protests around the table, until someone made the first accusation of cheating. Voices rose, and Unwin announced he was going home, which Charlie understood to be very bad form, and the noise got even louder, Bosworth ineffectively trying to calm everything down.

"Go!" Kent spoke into his radio. The chaos inside the library provided enough cover for the police to get to the door before anyone noticed.

"Police! Nobody move!" Charlie shouted, and the uniformed officers spread around the room, trapping the players by the table.

"I have reasonable suspicion that this gathering..." Kent began, but Neville didn't wait for him to finish. He lifted his side of the table and pushed it over, then whirled round and punched the uniformed officer behind him in the stomach, knocking him off his feet. As he hit the floor, Neville jumped over him and was free of the circle. He flung the doors of the log burning stove open, and without any effort to protect his hands reached in and threw burning wood towards the police.

The poker players reared back as the table fell, a flinching as burning wood rained across the room.

Charlie and Patsy ran towards Vitruvious and without giving him time to blink slipped the handcuffs on. He struggled and yelled, attracting attention away from Neville. "Come with us, Mr Vitruvious," Charlie said calmly, hoping his colleagues would be able to control Neville. Vitruvious shouted louder, but Charlie and Patsy held his arms and marched him backwards out of the library and into the reception hall.

"We have a warrant to seize any electronic devices, including mobile phones," Charlie said. Patsy pulled Vitruvious's phone from his back pocket and handed it to Charlie who had the evidence bag ready.

"You have no right!" Vitruvious shrieked.

Which is when the first set of curtains went up with a whoosh of orange flame.

30

DISLOCATION: SUNDAY

DEAR BRYSON

*P**lease accept this letter as my resignation from the post of
Principal of Llanfair College of Art. As I am sure you know,
I did my first degree in London, before moving to Wales for
my graduate studies. On completion of my PhD, I accepted a junior
lecturer's post, and I have worked here ever since. You, by contrast,
have been a member of the Board of Governors for less than two
years. You all but begged me to accept the principal's job, because I
was the only person who could not have been embroiled in the cover-
up of assaults on our students. Did you know that I was offered the
job before Sir John Singer was appointed? Foolish me thought I could
better serve the college by continuing to work on my printmaking,
and to teach...*

Nope, Tom thought. This idiot does not need my life story.
He started again. Then he deleted everything he'd written. Get
a grip, Tomos. He was being pathetic, and he didn't like himself
for it. Charlie had his face all over social media for hooking up
with the wrong guy, and Charlie had stuck it out. He opened
the sketch book on his desk to the drawing he'd made of
Charlie in bed and his heart ached. He didn't want to lose the
vote, but either way, he'd survive.

CHARLIE SHOVED the phone into his inside jacket pocket and ran back into the library. "Get him out," he shouted over his shoulder to Patsy. He heard her say "Move it, dickhead."

In the library, the flames had hold of the curtains, and tendrils of black smoke were curling up from the carpet. The door from the library to the reception hall was still just clear, the nearest flames a yard away, but the blaze had begun to spread, and suddenly the tapestry by the door burst into flame, blocking the exit.

"Ballroom," shouted Charlie, feeling the heat of the flames behind him, pushing the poker players in front of him towards the far end. Uniformed officers joined in, but to get to the ballroom door, they had to get past the smouldering carpet.

"Move!" Charlie shouted, but they didn't. "Fucking move!" he shouted again, and then he understood. On the floor between the overturned table and the ballroom door, three men were fighting, and one of them had a knife. Eddy had taken a cut to his face and was dripping blood, but he kicked at Neville as he writhed and slashed. Mal Kent hung on to Neville's knife arm, though it was like trying to hold the wind. Two of the uniformed officers moved in, gingerly, batons drawn. They were as likely to hit Eddy or Kent as Neville. The poker players watched like the mongoose hypnotised by the snake, until a third uniformed officer did what should have been obvious and kicked Neville in the face. It was enough. Not to stop him, but to give them all time to act.

One kicked the knife from Neville's hand, the others piled on to him, one struggling with a pair of handcuffs as Neville continued to thrash beneath them. Charlie turned back to the poker players in time to see Stefan Crane run through the door to the reception hall, his jacket over his head.

"Stop him!" Charlie yelled, feeling the pungent smoke in

the back of his throat, making him retch. He couldn't leave the remaining poker players until he had them safely in the ball-room and out of immediate danger. Patsy cried out from the reception hall and Charlie was pushed aside by Unwin running over the burning carpet a bottle in one hand, straight through the flames.

At last, the door to the ballroom was open, and they were through: Bosworth, Dylan and the two poker players Charlie didn't know, plus three uniformed officers, followed by Kent and Eddy, dragging Neville behind them, still fighting to get free. He landed kicks on anyone who got too close until Kent grabbed a baton and hit Neville so hard on the knee that everyone in the room heard the bone crack.

"Fuck you!" screamed Neville, but he stopped struggling.

THE WINDOWS in the ballroom were set high up in the walls, but they opened, and there were tables and chairs to climb on. Neville Evans couldn't climb, but between them, he was manoeuvred out, though without much in the way of gentle-ness or sympathy. By the time they were all away from the burning library, the fire brigade had arrived, and not long after that, the fire was out. Charlie went to look for Patsy, and found her and Unwin, arms around each other, talking to Ravensbourne.

"I couldn't stop Crane," Patsy said.

"She tried," Unwin said. "But he was too quick." Unwin's shirt had scorch marks. His jacket lay on the floor, burned and blackened, half concealed by a fire blanket. The bottle Unwin had grabbed stood next to it. Charlie wondered who Unwin had intended to hit with it.

"We didn't get his phone," Patsy said.

Ravensbourne shrugged. "If we'd got it, it wouldn't have told us much. But we've got enough evidence to put him at an illegal poker game. He'll get a fine, and every time he applies for a license it'll be that much harder. At the very least he will have to shut his other illegal clubs. We might not be taking him down, but we will be causing him a lot of grief."

Patsy didn't look mollified. "It's a war of attrition," Ravensbourne said. "He's lost Bosworth, Huw Leader, Jack Protheroe and Will Jenner. Most importantly he's lost Neville Evans. The car stealing will have to go on hold until he can set it up again. He'll have to settle for the legal casino."

"One thing though." Patsy looked back towards the charred library doorway. "Those curtains couldn't have been polyester. Polyester doesn't burn like that."

CHARLIE FINGERED THE PHONE, safe in its labelled evidence bag. He should leave it to the techs, but he needed to know if the photographs were there, and he needed to know now. There was no question that this was Vitruvious's phone. The chain of evidence was strong enough to lift the Titanic from the seabed. He could try the passcode. He slipped the phone out of the bag and put the numbers in, and the phone opened. The background wallpaper screen was one of Vitruvious's own paintings of a small boat tossed about in a heavy sea. Of course it was.

Moment of truth.

Charlie touched the photographs app, and thousands of tiny pictures filled the screen. He scrolled rapidly, looking for Kaylan and Rico.

He smelled cigarette smoke, and expensive cologne, and knew that Ravensbourne and Kent were as impatient as he was. They had Yarrow's confession, and the forensic accountants would look for the German bank accounts, but Charlie had promised Kaylan revenge, and he'd promised Tom, well, everything. Kent had sworn his life away for the warrant, and the hotel had almost gone up in flames. Neville was behind bars, at the cost of some injuries, and Bosworth had risked letting Crane see whose side he was on. All for this. A gamble that Vitruvious would have kept the photographs he'd taken of a dying man, when they would have been easy and much safer to delete. He scrolled frantically, peering at the screen, until he felt a blow on his arm.

"Charlie, stop," Ravensbourne said. He looked up. "Stop scrolling. They are there. Go back a bit." Charlie went back and slowed down, then blew the picture up. Kaylan and Rico looked out at him. The picture had a date, the first day the students had gone missing.

"Thank God," he said, and felt faint with relief. "It's enough, it's got to be enough this time."

31

RESULTS AND RESOLUTIONS: MONDAY

R esolutions for Whole Staff Meeting
Result of secret ballot

1) THAT WE have No Confidence in the Principal of Llanfair College of Art.
   Agree 4
   Disagree 76
   Spoiled paper 2
   The resolution falls.

3) THAT WE demand the immediate reinstatement of Inigo Vitruvious, Senior Painting Tutor.
   Agree 4
   Disagree 76
   Spoiled paper 2
   The resolution falls.

. . .

MESSAGE FROM PROF Tom Pennant to all staff

I AM GENUINELY MOVED by the ballot result. Thank you. The year ahead looks as if it will be a difficult one for the college, but I am confident that we will survive as an institution: unique, independent and with our excellent reputation intact. That's down to the staff who work here.

TOM SENT THE EMAIL. He wanted to tell the whole story: about Rico's death, and how Vitruvious had stolen money from students' families, and had it stolen from him in return by Kaylan Sully. But he thought the gossip network that was Llanfair College of Art would tell all, and if it didn't, the newspapers would when it came to trial. He also wanted to talk to Charlie, to tell him the result of the ballot and to ask him something important. But his phone went to voicemail. He tried to compose a text, but some things could wait until they were together.

In the meantime, he had needed to prepare for his date with a sketchbook and a minibus full of students.

CLEARING up after the raid on the hotel went on all night and all the next day. Charlie kept going on coffee and sugar. Ravensbourne seemed to have limitless energy, provided she went out for regular cigarette breaks. Kent drove Eddy to the hospital to have his wound stitched, and to, as he put it, "Make sure Neville Evans survives his knee surgery so I can arrest him for murder." He rang Ravensbourne later to say that Neville was intact, his knee only dislocated.

"They put it back, which I understand is very painful." Kent said.

Ravensbourne told Charlie that Kent didn't seem at all upset at the thought of Neville Evans in agony. "But you do know that we'll struggle to get the CPS to agree two murder charges without a confession or some forensic evidence?"

Charlie nodded, but he was on too much of a high to worry. It had taken them months to get the evidence against Vitruvious, but they'd got it. They could do it again. Vitruvious himself had been released on police bail, having handed over both his passports. A uniformed police officer sat in a car outside his house.

The rest of the night they spent in front of the whiteboard, making a plan of attack for the morning. Charlie tried to send Mags home and failed. At seven, Dylan and Unwin appeared with bacon sandwiches, neither of them looking as if they had slept. Both had given their statements the night before, and both were now on their way to work.

CHARLIE'S first interview was with Huw Leader, arrested at his flat before dawn.

"I saw the murder," Leader said. "Not the knife going in, but I saw Neville and Lewis and then Lewis was lying in the water and Neville had disappeared."

"You're going to ask me why I didn't call the police," Leader said. Charlie thought he had a good idea why Leader didn't call the police. He was a petty criminal who did jobs for a major-league villain. And he was probably even more terrified of Neville than he was of Crane.

"Rupert and I wanted to get away. Away from Steff, away from this miserable place, somewhere we'd just be two guys working in a hotel or a bar." He sighed. "I know it doesn't work like that.

But you might not have believed me anyway, and anyway, Steff would have had us both killed." He said the last sentence as if it were a given. They would have been killed because that was what happened when you worked for Stefan Crane.

It was hard not to think about the arrests they'd made at the poker night—Vitruvious and Neville Evans. Two murderers, with enough evidence to convince even the Crown Prosecution Service. Would they be under arrest if Huw Leader had made that call? Would Landon Emery still be alive? They couldn't know, and that was the devil of it, Charlie thought. If someone had made a different choice...

"That rigmarole with the car at the quarry," Charlie asked. "Was that for us or Crane's benefit?"

"Both?" Leader answered. "I'll be honest, I didn't think it would fool anyone for long, just for long enough for us to get away."

"So, where were you hiding?" Charlie asked.

Leader blushed and looked down at his hands. "In one of the hotel rooms. Right up at the top in one of the towers. There are a couple of rooms no one ever uses. The windows leak. Rupert locked all the doors to the stairs, and the lift. Not that the lift goes up to the very top anyway."

Charlie leaned forward in his chair. "But we could get access to the room to verify your story," he said. Leader looked uncomfortable.

"I suppose so," he said. "Though there's nothing there now. I went back to my flat. Rupert's staying with me."

"Where have you left the money you took from the safe?" Charlie asked. "Did you leave it in the hotel, or take it home?"

THE DENIALS WERE AT BEST unconvincing. Charlie led the subject round to Neville and his family: how Gina and Lewis's two brothers were facing homelessness. He didn't know how much money there had been in the safe, but Bosworth had implied that it had been a lot, hopefully enough to get the Evanses out of the mess Neville had left them in. There were no records of how much money was in the safe, and in his opinion, Gina and the boys needed a break. He couldn't come out and tell Bosworth and Leader to hand the money over, in exchange for letting the two of them walk away, but he could drop some heavy hints. He'd know soon enough whether they had picked them up.

STEFAN CRANE HAD, in the jargon, "lawyered up." His solicitor was not local, not even Welsh from his accent, which was a generic educated northern voice. He was a young-looking thirty, handsome, Asian, in a suit that fitted him to perfection, and Charlie noted, shoes with pointed toes. The other thing of note was that he was very sharp. Crane had chosen well, but then he could afford to.

With advice from his solicitor, Crane answered all Charlie's questions while managing to impart no information that they didn't already have.

Yes, he was aware that the Gambling Act 2005 did not permit for-profit card games of the kind that the police had raided at the Castle Hotel.

Yes, he owned the Castle Hotel.

No, he was not aware that the poker game had been for profit.

Yes, he had been at the Castle Hotel for his daughter's wedding when Lewis Evans had been killed. He could not remember where he had been at the time of the murder.

No, he had not been at the Castle Hotel when Landon Emery had been killed.

Yes, he had employed Will Jenner and Jack Protheroe at the Ringway Casino.

Yes, he was aware of the law about underage gambling.

Yes, he was aware that both Jack and Will were attracted to gambling.

Yes, he had employed Neville Evans as a debt collector.

No, he was not aware Evans used violence.

And so it went on. Co-operative non-co-operation as Charlie thought of it. He made notes throughout the interview and told Crane that they would be meeting again.

"Argh," he said to Mags when they let Crane go. "We need a lever to get him talking."

"Or at least to get him to react, even if it's to go No Comment," Mags said. And she was right. Crane was too calm. He and his solicitor were running rings round them.

In the event, it didn't matter. With Kent's approval, Manchester Police swooped in and picked up the case against Crane.

"They've got the resources," Kent said. "And even if they get as far as a charge, it's going to take years. We'll keep our eyes open for illegal casinos on the coast, but he'll probably keep his nose clean for a while."

A war of attrition, as Ravensbourne had said the night before.

IN THE AFTERNOON, Charlie and Ravensbourne drove out to Vitruvious's house. Charlie was running on fumes. Fumes from fires stoked months before, when he and Tom looked at the drawings Vitruvious made of a man dying. Ravensbourne had seen the drawings too, and the photographs from Vitruvious's phone.

"Inigo Vitruvious," she intoned, when he came to the door of his house, "I am arresting you on suspicion of the murder of Rico Pepperdine. You do not have to say anything..." He didn't wait for her to finish the caution before he was pulling the door closed behind him, and holding his hands out in front of him, wrists together.

"Do your worst," he goaded them. "Snap your cuffs around the voice of the oppressed."

Ravensbourne laughed. "I don't think so, Mr Vitruvious. I dare say the voice of the oppressed will have a good lawyer waiting for him at the police station. Let's not make this any more melodramatic than it needs to be."

Vitruvious kept up a constant oration about the evils of the police state in which he claimed he lived, so that Charlie was ready to drive into the nearest tree rather than endure any more of it. Thankfully, they pulled into the police station car park before he had killed them all for the sake of relief. As predicted, a man in an expensive suit was lounging by the reception desk being pointedly ignored by Mags.

"Ah, Inigo," the man said. "Perhaps these good people will allow us some privacy for a chat?"

Charlie felt Ravensbourne's hand on his arm, for once a touch rather than a blow. "PC Jellicoe, perhaps you will show these gentlemen to the interview room, and wait until DS Rees and I are needed? DS Rees will bring you a chair."

Charlie took a deep breath and sighed it out. "Of course," he said. He collected a chair from the break room and set it down next to the wall by the interview room.

"You OK?" Mags asked.

"I will be," he answered.

PATSY HAD BEEN out to stock up the fridge, so Charlie had his sugar fix, while Ravensbourne went out to the car park for some nicotine. He had only managed a few quick bites before Mags was back to say Vitruvious and his solicitor were ready.

"They can wait," he said. He finished his doughnut and began another. Then he stood up, still chewing, and headed for the back door, not wanting to send a pregnant woman to talk to Ravensbourne. She was, as he had expected, puffing like a steam train. He leaned against the wall and waited.

"He'll plead to manslaughter," she said. "It's what I'd do. Anyone seeing those pictures will send him away for life with a minimum term of fifty years. His only chance is a guilty plea."

"And the Crown Prosecution Service will go for it," Charlie said, because of course they would. A guaranteed conviction rather than a long and expensive trial that was likely to end the same way, or worse, with an acquittal. Without Kaylan's testimony, and possibly even with it, there was no way to prove Vitruvious had intended to kill Rico. It was as good as they were going to get. Ravensbourne stubbed her cigarette out with her boot, and they turned back into the building to hear how the voice of the oppressed explained his sketches and photographs of a dying man.

"Tragic accident?" Charlie offered.

"Terrible error of judgment," Ravensbourne countered.

THEY LISTENED in stony-faced silence as Vitruvious's solicitor offered the manslaughter plea.

Ravensbourne nodded sharply. "Bail will not be granted at this time," she said. "Please wait here, Mr Vitruvious while we arrange transport."

Then she led Charlie from the interview room with a grip on his arm like a steel clamp.

"He's going to spend tonight in the cells," she said. "He'll stay there until his sentencing hearing if I have anything to do with it." She paused. "I'm going home, and so should you. Call the Pepperdines before you go." She gave him her signature pat on the arm, another bruise to add to his collection.

"Will do, boss," he said. Then he was going to tell Tom the news.

32

AFTERMATH: MONDAY

From: Bryson Carroll
    To: Tomos Pennant

Dear Tom

Please accept this as my resignation from the Board of Governors of Llanfair College of Art. I have very much enjoyed working with you and your colleagues and wish the College every success for the future.

With best wishes
Bryson Carroll

Tom's yell of "Yes!" brought Ann running into his office. He turned the screen towards her.

"Tosser," she grinned. "I'll work on a list of names. HR has sent the adverts for a new Director of Finance, and a painting tutor. You have to sign them off. Now get your stuff and get on the minibus. We'll be round for dinner."

THE PEPPERDINES HADN'T BEEN as angry at Vitruvious's manslaughter plea as Charlie expected, just sad.

"We'll come for the sentencing," they promised. Charlie sat on his own for a while after that trying, and failing, to tell himself that getting some kind of justice was enough. Vitruvious would spend a long time in jail even if he wasn't branded forever as the murderer he was. Then he went back to Dilys's for a shower and a change of clothes and texted Tom to say he was on his way over, stopping at the supermarket for a bottle of wine.

Tom opened his front door looking exactly like a man who'd spent the day in a howling gale. His cheeks were reddened, almost abraded. There was a battered sketchbook sticking out of a sand-streaked backpack by the door.

Charlie put the wine on the floor next to it and wrapped his arms around Tom. "We got him," he said.

Tom kissed the top of Charlie's head. "Thank God, and thank you," he said. "I hope he rots in jail."

Charlie heard a door opening, and he stepped back from Tom's embrace, flushing. Behind Tom, two identical faces with dark hair and huge wide eyes looked at him with shy smiles. His heart melted, and he smiled back, equally shy. Tom turned and drew Charlie back towards him.

"There are some people I want you to meet. Charlie, this is Amelie, and this is Ziggy. Ziggy is the one in black. Amelie is taller. A to Z, this is Charlie."

"Hi," Charlie said. "I'm sorry I missed lunch last week."

"We know, you had a *murder*," Ziggy said, sounding as excited as Orianna earlier in the week.

It was going to be fine.

Much later, when Orianna, Ann and the girls had left, Tom pulled Charlie towards him on the sofa. "There's something I want to ask you," he said. "Would you move in here? Or if you didn't want to move in here, we could get somewhere else. Together I mean. If you don't think it's too soon? You can't stay at Dilys's forever, and I know there's nothing to rent, but even if there was, I'd still be asking..."

Charlie grinned and put his hand over Tom's mouth. "Stop gabbling. Yes. I would love to move in with you. I love you, Tomos Dylan Pennant."

THREE MONTHS LATER

CHARLIE DROVE to Liverpool for a final visit to Kaylan Sully before he was deported back to the USA. Kaylan was escorted into the bleak interview room, looking as arrogant as Charlie had ever seen.

"No Supermax prison then?" Charlie asked and Kaylan smirked.

"What can I say? I'm the best hacker they're going to get."

"I think the FBI know exactly how good you are Kaylan, and they know what you've done. We, that is Clwyd Police and the British Government, have asked them to ensure the College of Art gets the money you stole from Vitruvious. You offered it to us before, and we need it."

"We'll see," Kaylan said. He was on a high, getting out of prison to work for the FBI. The UK Government was glad to be rid of him. Charlie hoped the Americans knew what they were doing.

"Vitruvious is going to be sentenced this week," Charlie said. "He won't be getting as long as he deserves, but he's getting longer than you. You shot me, Kaylan, and you owe me. I got you revenge on Vitruvious, and you owe me for that, too."

He got up and knocked on the door to be let out. Time would tell whether Kaylan would return the money.

"Wait," Kaylan said. "What did Vitruvious say about me?"

"Nothing. He said nothing. He pleaded guilty, so none of it will come out. But the FBI have seen the pictures. They know what you did, you and him. They know you had a gun. They know all about you."

"Whatever," Kaylan shrugged, and this time Charlie left. He had an appointment to meet baby Amy Elizabeth Jellicoe.

Vitruvious's sentencing hearing was coming up, and Rico's parents had arrived. Lewis Evans and Landon Emery were still waiting for justice, and for funerals. Neville Evans had been charged and Gina had begun divorce proceedings. Such grapevine as Charlie had access to suggested that Crane was putting pressure on Neville to follow Vitruvious's lead and plead guilty. It was more pressure than the police could provide since Huw Leader and Rupert Bosworth had disappeared. Enough money to pay off all the Evanses debts and put them back into credit had appeared in Gina's bank accounts in several instalments, none large enough to trigger the bank's alarm systems. The money appeared to have come from Neville. Gina had asked Brian Telford about it, and he'd told her to spend the money and say nothing. Then he'd told Charlie, who had just smiled.

FROM THE NORTH WALES **Courier and Post**
Townspeople in Llanfair woke up yesterday morning to a banner with the words "Happy Winter Solstice" fluttering from the roof of Llanfair College of Art.

Neither Clwyd Police nor the college authorities had any comment to make.

For Sale: Castle Hotel, Llanfair, Clwyd
An outstanding example of a Victorian folly built from local wood and stone.

I HOPE you have enjoyed Charlie's latest book. If you have, I'd be delighted if you could leave a review on Amazon or Goodreads.

Charlie will be back soon. You can pre-order Murder in Shades of Red now.

It was supposed to be a holiday. In New York City. A chance for Tom to do some drawing, and for Charlie to see the sights.

The streets of the city seem safe and clean. Everyone is friendly, and the donuts are to die for.

Charlie and Tom have an unexpected encounter with the past in a piano bar, but it's OK. They've got the Atlantic Ocean between them and the troubles of the last year. It's all behind them.

Until they get asked for help in an unexplained death.

What could possibly go wrong?

ACKNOWLEDGMENTS

I promised myself that I would write a straightforward mystery with room for Charlie and Tom to get together. Ha! The book turned into the usual festival of despair (and a bit of elation). With a bit of help from my friends, it came together. So...thanks are due to:

G, *traceur,* who lit the spark for this story. I hope I have managed to impart some of the magic we discussed.

Lou for endless encouragement and nitting. Maybe we can get some of those trips made now it's finished.

Glo, who more than anyone else, has given me the space and time to write, by doing the impossible with the Wayward Dog.

Bill and Austin for more encouragement and your calm assurance that I am now a proper writer (as are both of you).

JL Merrow. You are the Freya Ravensbourne of my writing, though not in appearance obviously. Praise on one hand, followed by four hours hard re-writing. It's a much better book as a result. She said.

Layla Ndn PA. Thanks!

Pixelstudio for the great covers.

The real A to Z (and Aubrey) who gave me the excuse for two amazing weeks holiday. You can read all about it in the next book...

SF for keeping me sane.

To my many friends on social media. Social media gets a bad rep, but I have found lots of support and encouragement (as well as kitten pictures).

Above all, thanks to you, dear reader.

ABOUT THE AUTHOR

Ripley Hayes lives in West Wales, in a small town surrounded by green hills and ancient woodlands. She didn't take up writing fiction until she retired from a long career as a university lecturer and housing researcher. Since then, she has done little else, to the despair of her friends and dog. Her books are the kinds of books she likes to read: mysteries with wickedness but not too much blood, and romance with real people who make mistakes, all set in interesting places.

When she's not writing, Ripley likes to read, travel, knit, and eat chocolate, ideally all at once.

Ripley has a website, and a newsletter.

You can also contact her on Facebook at Ripley & Co.

ALSO BY RIPLEY HAYES

Daniel Owen Books

1: Undermined

2: Dark Water

3: Leavings

4: A Man

5: Too Many Fires

6: An Allotment of Time

7. A Teachable Moment

8. Interwoven (forthcoming)

DS Charlie Rees

Murder in Shades of Yellow (standalone novella)

1. Murder in Shades of Blue and Green

2. Murder in Shades of Wood and Stone

3. Murder in Shades of Red (forthcoming)

Peter Tudor and Lorne Stewart Cosy Mysteries

1: No Accident in Abergwyn

2: No Friends in Abergwyn

3. Murder Without Magic

Teema Crowe

Badly Served

Paul Qayf

Secret State: Enemy

Printed in Great Britain
by Amazon

39153790R00149